# JOHN A. MEYER

# CASEY
## Strikes Again!

**'NUFF TO MAKE A CAT LAUGH BOOKS!**

Cover Photo © 2016 http://www.istockphoto.com/portfolio/AskinTulayOver.  All rights reserved - used with permission.

'NUFF TO MAKE A CAT LAUGH BOOKS!

ISBN:  978-0-578-17326-9

PRINTED IN THE UNITED STATES OF AMERICA

**Humorous satire stories told by Casey, a cat who reads minds and solves crimes travelling all over the world.**

# Acknowledgments

Dedicated to my father, John Meyer, who perished in World War II as an aircraft fighter pilot, my dear Mother Florence who loved me so very much, my Stepfather Joseph Nespor, and my dearest brothers and sister, and especially my Grandfather Foley who collected the letters I sent him filled with my stories every week, stacks of them covering his fireplace mantel. His love, laughter, and encouragement upon receiving them continue to give me inspiration today.

To my dear Grandma Meyer who would throw balled up socks to me, playing catch at two years of age, inspiring me to become an athlete. They all would have loved knowing this book was written and would have been so proud of all their Irish/German offspring accomplishing so much.

# Casey Comes to Bat

*I* was in hiding. John had me laughing so much I had to go away. For some reason he was trying to learn a new language, and it was not going well. He was trying to learn Chinese. With my mind reading abilities, I took the liberty of taking a peek inside the Irish mind, and there was too much confusion. His Irish heritage was getting in the way of learning Chinese. He could not pronounce a single word. Well, maybe one or two, and that made me laugh even more. Someone had told him Ohio meant good morning, and so far that is about all he can say. Too much! I had to go on the roof by the chimney overlooking the entire city of San Francisco and talk to my two buddies, Seagull Joe and Uncle Al. We puffed on some of our special Castro Cancer Killing Cha Cha Cigars, and slowly but surely I quit laughing. I hate it when I get the cat hiccups. I am halfway through with a hiccup, and then I let out a tiny meow, and it is just a mess. Too much laughing can kill a cat. Bad as having too much curiosity I heard in some cat circles.

Meanwhile, Uncle Al's protégées came along for our wizened meeting conversation. I could hear a few of them laughing quite loudly on the other side of the roof. I don't know if it was the cigars or Seagull Joe saying how he and some of his flying friends bombed the mayor's car after a dubious decision was made by city hall. Someone brought up the subject of too many seagulls on the wharf. The Seagulls did not take kindly, and it was bombs away. The mayor got the message, and all was forgiven. The young protégées

1

were laughing like crazy none the less. I told them to settle down or put on a seat belt. The last time they were laughing like this one almost fell off the roof, and only by landing in the roof gutter was he saved. He is now called Guttercat. That too makes me laugh, so I decided to go back home. We cats never ever let humans see us laughing. Smiling is okay, maybe once in awhile. It is one of our top secrets we keep confidential. It was almost time for our daily walk on the embarcadero.

John was up and at 'em at about 5 am. I knew why. His Chinese lessons were not taking hold, and he thought he needed some Irish hot toddy to get his mind moving. Well, that insured me a brisk walk as we went over to his favorite restaurant that just so happened to open at 6 a.m. We were there at 6:03 a.m. three minutes late. When the bartender saw us come in, with me being in my usual position, standing up in the backpack with my paws on each of John's shoulders looking here and there with my statuesque Siamese head, the bartender and John nodded at each other, and pronto, a hot toddy was served. John had to settle down. The toddy would help, and I could not stand to laugh much more. John took the toddy as we walked around the place looking at whatever there was to see. Someone had played 'Ghost Riders in the Sky' with Frankie Lane singing, and I could tell John was for sure on a two toddy morning. This was his favorite song; give him three toddies, and he sings along. Cat batting ensues, and he gets the drift, or starts to laugh and sings louder. 'Nuff to make a cat laugh, some more.

While we were walking around and through the establishment, I noticed four men at the very back of the place having an enthusiastic conversation. By counting the empty glasses on the table I knew why. Each had three empty toddy glasses in front and were nursing a fourth. Coincidentally enough, they were Chinese. They were speaking in Chinese quite loudly, and it was very interesting. Since I speak Chinese, as well as every other language in the world, I could not help but hear what they were saying. I only hoped that John would not try to listen in, but I knew all was safe. He only knew one word and even that was not Chinese. It was Japanese. All was under control. John was on toddy number one, and things were secure so far. It's the third toddy when he plays the juke box and sings along with Robert Mitchum's only song, 'Thunder Road'. Love it myself. The conversation of the three toddy men, working on four toddy men, and maybe even more was very disturbing. Bells and hackles and hair were standing up and going off all over in my body. They were going to block the entire San Francisco Bay by placing container cargo ships under the Golden Gate Bridge. If their demands were not met, being one hundred billion dollars, they would plop a container into the bay once every hour. Since there would be four container ships blocking egress and ingress, to and from the bay, this would take on a catastrophe of uncountable measures. Let's just say lots, much worse than John and six toddies, very grim indeed.)

The cargo ships would be pirated at sea by a very clever plan. On the very top of the cargo ships would be a container holding twenty men on a suicide mission if need be. Their armament was very impressive. Machine guns, Glock hand guns, and devastating bazookas able to shoot down helicopters and maybe even lob a few loads into the heart of The City. Once upon the open sea they would take over the giant ships, set up their blockade under the Golden Gate Bridge, state their demands, and begin the process. Foolproof! Yes, but in the very word foolproof was a word that would spell the end of their evil sick plot. Ho hum, dear reader, you have figured out the word by now I am sure. Fool. They were such to think they could get away with a crime on the high seas with me and my watchful minions throughout the world. With their always vigilant paws and feathers, it is impossible to slip anything by them. (I'm not so sure about Uncle Al's protégés, however. They need seasoning, especially Guttercat. He may need one more session of boot camp. They call it cat camp but more on that later.)

I told John of this plot. He has connections and most of them are ok. This time he contacted the Navy Seals. Immediate action took place and this is what the Seals did. They boarded all four ships, welded the containers shut holding the suicide commandos, and sailed the containers into the sea. The evil men were on a suicide mission, and so they got their wish. Besides, the Seals don't take prisoners. The Bay was saved. Brouhaha did not take place except for the Seals and John and I.

We all met at a fashionable Coronado Restaurant just across the water from San Diego, and relived and talked flamboyantly about what we had done. Someone suggested playing cards, and it was an instant go ahead. We took the moveable feast to a convenient back room after three toddies and began to play. John does not know how to play cards, but guess who does. Since I cannot only read minds, I was also able to see all their cards as I did my cat thing. I simply walked around the room, supposedly innocently enough, and took it all in. Groans, sighs, and yes, dear reader, the Seals were vociferously vocal upon occasion. After five toddies and four beers each, they shut the restaurant down, and let everyone there all join in on the fun. They were amazed at John's luck. He backed it all with blarney, and not to forget, he was the one, ahem, who had told the Seals of the dastardly plot. It was great fun, and the drinks, humor, camaraderie, fellowship, and bonhomie overflowed all there. Fantastico! John won about ten thousand dollars. He offered to treat the entire restaurant to all the food and drink they wanted. Of course, his offer was gallantly refused. Just the presence of the Seals, John, and the great mission they accomplished was more than enough to give food and drink to all. (To this day that restaurant is known as "The Restaurant" and its business quadrupled after the grand get together.)

While going back home John put all the money "he" had won in the backpack where I was standing with my paws on his shoulders while overlooking all. He communicated to me how wonderful I was, and he swore he would never drink more than two toddies at once ever again.

I said, "How about singing along with Frankie Lane as he sings 'Ghost Riders in the Sky'?"

"Of course," John said. "But I thought you liked to hear me sing that song? Sometimes I even heard a meow or two and felt you cat batting me while keeping time? I said I was only kidding, and since you gave me ten thousand dollars, you can have three toddies."

We winked at each other and began to laugh. He put me in the backpack, and we hurried down to his favorite restaurant. The bartender and John nodded at each other, only this time, they nodded twice. Two toddies appeared. One glass had my name on it. Along with my name was the inscription, 'To Casey from the Seals'. There was also a note. It said, "Great card game, Casey. You are sure John's good luck charm. Wink!" Hmmm...you don't think?

# Tiger

*G* rrrr! That's how my relations were all the time, and maybe more correctly, I should say ancestors. Now, I am a completely cultured cat who can read, mind meld, and make certain "suggestions" to anything that has a mind. "Including ants?" you say. "Yes, including ants." I took a peek into one of their minds for a millisecond or two, and it was very boring. Move this, move that, turn around, go back, follow, and repeat, so very industrious those ants. Once thousands of them band together, they can get a lot done. We all know about the ones that we see in movies eating people and such. They can get ornery. Stay away from them is my advice. Don't feed them coffee grounds or else they will never stop. I repeat. Stay away!

Yes, in some respects we are a lot like dogs. We cats are now human's best friends. Dogs may claim first place but we don't care. For sure both of our ancestors were very "heavy" actors. I now live in San Francisco with a human, and we get along great. We communicate as needed, and he, John, takes me with him for rides and walks. In the morning he puts me in his backpack, and away we go right through the fog, sun, wind, drizzle, or some old hippies left over from the summer of love. Still trying to get it right I guess. When I am not doing that, I also have friends on top of one of the "power points" on the planet. The power points are located throughout the planet, and they are very beneficial for thinking. We meet at the power point quite frequently. It actually happens to be a chimney located high above San Francisco over the house in which I live. My two main friends are Seagull Joe and my Uncle Al. Uncle Al also brings along some of his protégés from time to time. They are young and without parents. We give them a helping paw from time to time.

Tonight we gathered around the chimney with the proteges off to the side doing what young cats do-horse around, er...should I say cat around? Sometimes, we use them for errands and small jobs trying to break them in. Believe me… they need breaking in. Lots of well intentioned spirit but at times it goes sideways. Ahhh...the ignorant bliss of youth. Tonight, I was going to tell them about their ancestors. If they could stay awake long enough, they might learn something. Oh well, here goes.

Their forebearers were giant tigers up to 800 pounds. That is lots of pussy. They were very fast and strong, killed and ate just about anything they could get their jaws on. After eons, because of changes on the planet, they adapted to their surroundings, and voila…here we are. Oversimplification but much more, and I would lose the "class." Some of their kind still exist and can be found here at the zoo. Those of you who are interested can take a trip to the zoo via the Seagull Joe taxi service and take a look. A few raised their paws and a plan was made. We would meet at the zoo tomorrow at high noon. Sardine snacks would also be provided. Some meows were heard, and they cat batted the air for a second or two.

We met at the zoo as planned the next day only to find people running out the gates and getting in their cars fast! I took a look into their frightened minds and found out why. One of my ancestors got out. Uh oh! I told John to stay in the car, and I would go and take a look. To be safe, I told him to leave the window open about half way. Who knows what my nasty relation might be up to? (We've all heard about crazy relatives, but this is a topper. This one will eat you.) I looked up in a tall tree, and there were Seagull Joe and company, safe but shaking. I ran up the tree as well and looked around. Sure enough there was "my relation" standing by a hot dog vendor's cart eating all the hot dogs for free. He was growling and knocking things over, and I looked into his mind. He was angry and hungry, and he did not like being locked up. He had eaten some very hot mustard, and now it was burning his mouth something terrible. I mind melded with him and told him what his options were. He looked up into the tree at me and his gaze was something to behold. It was fierce and fearsome, but not to worry. I guided him back to where he was living. He jumped back over the wall where he had been and calmed down a bit. At least he was alive, burning tongue and all with plenty of water to drink.

Police and animal care types arrived only to find Tommy, the tiger, back in his surroundings. He told me he wasn't happy with all this, but what else could he do? It was either be a rug or stay here. I said maybe we can do something. The next day we consulted the animal care people. We said convincingly it would be better to let him and most of those animals penned up to be put back more in their natural surroundings. They were miserable there, and it actually amounted to animal cruelty. That night, up by the chimney, we discussed what had happened. The youngsters were now paying attention. The very real possibilities of being eaten for lunch had woken them up. The moral of the happening is this. 'Let mad relation lie' or something like that. They won't make you laugh.

# Cat Happiness

*H*appiness… that is the secret of us cats. We are happy. Most people do not know it. Since I am the rarest of rare and with all my mental abilities, I am able to figure it out. When people see cats doing what cats do, there is always a small wonderment in their minds. What is that cat up to? Just being a cat, I must tell you. At times, I need a stimulant and that is why I like to be around John, most of the time. But, sometimes I do have to keep a cat eye on that guy like today, for example. He is swimming again, and he wants me to come along. "Meow" to you, you old fox. I know you just want to get me in the jacuzzi, so you don't have to wipe me down with a wet towel once in a while. Although some cats love to swim, I am not crazy about it. Maybe I will go and jump in to make him happy, and then he might take me for a long car ride listening to one of my favorite songs that goes "flash, bam, alakazam, over an orange colored sky." I call Nat, the singer, "cat" King Cole...such a great song. It was on the radio as I was lying on the dash of the car, and I immediately became invigorated. John started singing the tune as I was cat batting the air. We were ready for the big stage, at least inside the car. (little cat laugh) Music makes John and me. Ahhhh, bliss!

# Remember When You Were Born?

*A*t three days of age, a coat was laid down next to the cubicle where my mother and eleven siblings were meowing, crying, stumbling around, and trying to get a "feel" for things. I already knew it all. I had figured out the cosmos, quantum physics, and now I had to get out. I was, in addition to what I mentioned, also able to read and mind meld. I know, I know, seems so unbelievable, but it is the truth. Now, I needed to get out. I crawled, meowing and purring into the coat's pocket. Voila! The final piece to the puzzle was found, for that day at least. The coat belonged to a man named John. (Good title for a book, "A Man Named John." As you can see, I can write, as well, and like most writers, I am always looking around for good things to write about. Any ideas?) Where was I? He walked around the pound, and then came back, and luckily did not forget his jacket. He took it and walked out to his car, put it on and took it off when he got there. About a mile down the road, (So many good book titles), he put his hand in his pocket and checked for his phone. He found me instead, all furry, smiling, meowing, cat batting, and wanting lots, but not sure of what lots was. But, I did know how to "communicate." I spoke to John and told him not to be confused. This was not a Budweiser flashback. It was the real deal, and I was talking to him. John said, "Ok, now what? I always wanted some pussy to talk to me, and now it has happened." That was my first cat laugh. It was, yes, 'nuff to make a cat laugh. Not all that much, but it was a start. It was because I had chosen him. John could make me laugh. Now all was complete. Not to worry. What he said and did to make me laugh would improve, would not be hard to do. But for being three days old, having a cat laugh was very important to me. Cats are after all very serious. I needed laughter to make me perfect. Maybe somewhat humble, and at least know what it felt like kind of. I mind melded with him instantly. (Yes, just like Dr. Spock, but I did not have to touch him to do it.) I told him my entire story, and John said, "What's in it for me?" It was a better joke and we both laughed. I said, "I know we will at the very least have a tremendous time. More than likely, you will profit financially, and maybe get a better car." (Almost the first joke I told.)

John said, "I think I understand. Just guide me along, and let's see what we shall see."

I said, "I probably need to see a vet, and for now I need some milk."

John immediately went to the store. He just placed me back in his pocket and waited for "suggestion" on what to get. I loved it, a real live shopping cart that does what I tell it. After shopping we went to his place and he put me, the food, and a blanket in his chest of drawers. I was the top cat indeed. I was only three days old, but the information to my mind was increasing at exponential speed, and I needed to sleep. Sleep I did. John later told me I meowed a bit, purred, and cat batted the air with reckless abandon. Something I still do. John liked it and said someday he should take me to Hollywood. Maybe, he could make some money off a cute cat like me. I meowed and cat batted him a bit.

I said, "We can do much more than Hollywood."

John said, "Hmmm, you have an attitude as well. I'll be able to make even more money. Can you smile and walk on a two by four?" 'Nuff to make a cat laugh at three days old anyhow.

The next day we went to a sports store, and he bought a back-pack for me. That way I could keep whatever I needed in there and ride and sleep until I matured. So funny… John telling me about maturing. How many mature people would take in a three day old cat, listen to them in a mind meld, put them in their best drawer, buy him a backpack, and then intimate to them they needed to mature. Loved it, this was going along just fine.

Meanwhile, the entire knowledge of whatever was in this world and other worlds was transferred into my mind. It all seemed so natural for me. I understood it all perfectly. I needed to sleep a lot during this time, and when I would awake, I would discover what more I had learned. It's impossible to tell it all to you. For example, in addition to mind reading, mind melding, and "mind suggestions," I could understand every language ever spoken here and everywhere in the cosmos and beyond. To make it completely understandable for you, there was not one thing I did not know or knew how to do. But it was nice that John knew how to drive a car. I was too small to drive at that time, and it made John pay attention to traffic. He had "responsibility" now, and had the weight of the world on his shoulders. Really! I told him all the things as I have told you, and John was impressed and very happy. But no matter, he continued to treat me exactly as a cat. He would look at be quizzically at times and say things like, "Do you even know about football?" He would then wink at me, and we would laugh. He was definitely the cat's meow as well. I needed laughter because there is nothing more se-rious than a cat. Laughter is very unusual to us. Hence the saying, 'nuff to make a cat laugh, so true and even cosmic. (Ok to smile, dear reader.)

As time went on, I naturally became much bigger. My heritage was complete pure bred silverpoint Siamese. It means that I will grow very big for a cat to about twenty pounds. My fur will be a creamy white undercoat with dark chocolate silver gray markings on my ears, face, legs and tail and back. My eyes will blue, and be different colors at different times, and of course, I will be very strong and athletic. The rest of my abilities that were given to me must have been partly because I am so big. My statuesque head and beautiful eyes once seen arrest your attention and gaze immediately. But, I can camouflage myself if I choose. With a shake of my head and a cute purr, I can look exactly as many of my minions of cousins do, or as a little kitten.

One day as we were getting ready to go for a walk. We found it impossible to fit me into the backpack. My tail and one of my paws were hanging out. John looked at me with mock seriousness and said, "Are you sure you told me the whole story about your birth? If you get much bigger, you are going to be in the small tiger category." We went and got a bigger back pack. Cat pack John called it. I could stand up in it and look all over. My paws were on either of his shoulders, and my head was on a swivel, taking in all the sights as we go. My weight, "only 20 pounds", gave John more exercise when we went for a walk. It was great, and I highly recommend for everybody to get a cat like me and walk around. We are lots of fun, but you will find that my compadres don't laugh as much as I do. Crazy pussycat, I know you are saying. (Don't let a feminist hear you saying that.) Uh oh, I think I am picking up on some of John's humor, especially what I just meowed. Don't want to wake up what is left of Gloria Steinem's hairy followers. Talk about cats not laughing or having a sense of humor!

Walking, well for me it is riding, around the San Francisco waterfront is as good as the world can be. There is the brisk sea breeze blowing gently all around us, the sun peeking through the fog, and the skyscrapers, and of course the fantastic smell. One restaurant after another having its distinct smell of whatever type of fish is its specialty. Mix in some pizza, pasta, sweet rolls, and a cigar, here and there, and it doesn't get any better. Momma Mia! The area I am describing is Little Italy. Now I want to go to Rome, Venice, Florenzia, and you pick a place. Hope my nose would not explode with all the great smells and sights one must experience there. Meanwhile, my schnoze is very happy here. Taxi service isn't too bad either.

One morning while on our almost brisk walk, the bigger I get, the less brisk the walk, we stopped in one of John's favorite restaurants. Since it was a bit chilly and since I was packed full of chocolate cake from a birthday party, John's walk was even slower. He needed a hot toddy, coffee and whiskey with a touch of crème on top. It is a great place. At six in the morning, the bar is buzzing with conversation, an occasional juke box song, and there is electricity in the air, drone level deluxe. The good and the not so good come here quite frequently. It has been here for about a century, and it is very much a part of The City. My aura and being are always aware of whatever vibrations are going on around me. Even more so than my schnoze that is used mainly for food and... where was I? Oh, yes. I sensed immediately upon entering, there was a jolt to my senses that needed my immediate attention. Three men were standing around the juke box. (They were playing 'Moon River', and I communicated to John to lighten up and put 50 cents in the juke box. Change that smarmy stuff to something that has some hop.) While he was changing the "vibes," I listened in on their talk. They were speaking in their native tongue, so they felt completely secure. One even looked at me disparagingly and blew a puff of smoke my way. (Since I was feeling very aggressive that morning, I gave him a mind suggestion that he had to go immediately and take a swim in the bay. He went as I directed him, clothes and all. By that time, I had all the information I needed.) They were speaking about a diabolical plot to spray all of Columbus Street before the Columbus Day parade. It is one of the major streets in the city and runs from the bay to the heart of the financial district, right at the foot of the Transamerica building, for a couple of miles long. The spray would be deadly to anyone who walked on it. Not only killing the people who walked on the spray, but also anyone or where they came in contact with for the next day. The killing spray had a delayed killing time of twenty four hours. Terrorism at its worst! Not only murdering the inhabitants, but also destroying the moral of humans throughout the world. People would think how can one be safe anywhere? I immediately "communicated" to John what those murderous creeps were up to doing now. (Including the one moron now treading water in the bay... ('Nuff to make a cat laugh) and he went into action right away.)

As it so happened, one of the extremely good people of the city were in the place while we were there having a toddy as well. We moved over to where he was standing contemplating another day. I gave him a slight "suggestion," and he turned our way saying, "Don't I know you from somewhere, and how are you doing?" with total bonhomie. John said, "Yes, we have met a time or two in here, and worked on some projects. This morning I have something very important to tell you. May I get us another toddy and let me explain it to you. It will only take about half a toddy." The gentleman, whose name was Thomas O'Malley agreed instantly, and we told him what dastardly plan was afoot. (It just so happened that Thomas was the Chief in charge of the San Francisco terrorist elimination team. They are serious about terrorists in The City.) Before the smarmy song 'Moon River' was over, the two stooges by the juke box were walked surreptiously out the door by the terrorist team. They are always ready to go in an instant. After all, this is war. The three men were taken to investigation cells, including the wet man in the bay. With not too subtle investigation tactics, all their conniving was known in a jiffy. I knew what it was as well, but thought it best they find out for themselves. All in all, sixty three terrorists were arrested and vetted completely. I helped as well as I could. My suggestive abilities sped things along, and it was a major coup, not only here, but all over the world. It was said that the man paddling in the bay greatly helped with the investigation. Terrorists can't swim and hate water. 'Nuff to make a cat laugh!

John and I were very pleased with ourselves. The Chief became our steadfast friend and toddies were always free to us when we came in. After seeing me while I was at my usual position in the backpack, paws on either shoulder, and "casually" looking here and there, the Chief decided that I was a good luck charm. My picture was taken and put on the front page of the San Francisco Chronicle. I was referred to as the Good Luck Cat. Little did they know, and that's just how I wanted to keep it.

# Mafia Cat

Meow! I have to let you know every now and then that I am the great, great, great, great, great, great grandson of a Siberian snow tiger. Sure glad I got out of that branch of the family. They don't live long, and neither does anything around them. Cats are on the loose, really loose. When you go to the zoo, please take a look at the big kitty cats. Oh so sweet you think, oh so pretty, oh such big teeth. Yikes! Never had a pedicure as well, not to worry, their nails have little chance to grow very long what with all their feeding habits. They are in the habit of eating everything all the time. Need I remind you of the great cat trainers in Las Vegas whose act was halved by one of their little darlin's? No, thank you! I have been to the zoo with John and have taken a peek inside their minds, and I told John we are going to leave. Now, the one tiger (poor sweet little kitty) knew that for a millionth of a second I was in his mind and realized we might be related. He spotted John and I immediately and let go with a growl from Siberia. Believe me their instinct doesn't stop at the zoo gate. He did some rapid cat math and realized he would be about one foot short of jumping across the moat and over the twenty foot concrete wall. *Nuts*, he thought. His five hundred pound body sure needed us for breakfast but the thought of falling back in the moat discouraged him. I wanted out. Great, great, great, great, great, great grandfather or whatever I don't care. So, yes, I am a cat, very sophisticated and the most intelligent thing on this planet. To interest me, and you, ahem, I like to visit the greatest people and things of all time. Let's see...getting back to where I began before I had a scary flashback to having my twenty-fifth cousin or whatever wanting to eat me and John for breakfast, let me introduce who the great people are that we are going to visit.

Starting with beauty, always beauty, we will start with me. No... only cat kidding...now, where was I? Oh yes, the beauty comes in with the women-Marilyn, Lana, Elizabeth, and mix in Maria, Lois and, of course, Ava. For humor, charisma, power, music, and creativity here comes Sinatra, JFK, John Wayne, and whoever else happens to stop and visit Frank. I am there, too, getting chinchucked with Chinese smiles and properly placed meows, a wagging tail and maybe a purr for Marilyn. JFK likes to glance at me sideways and try to read what is in my mind. I know he does. I am much more complex than the Russians or Cubans. Frank wants me to somehow help him win and cards and is convinced I work for the Mafia. I say to Frank, "*Fly yourself to the Moon.*" We were all in the kitchen. Big John got the Jameson Irish Whiskey bottle mixed up with the pancake syrup bottle, and he said, "Har, Har," and topped off his coffee with just the right amount. He had his spurs on for some reason and Frank said to him, "God damn it John, do you wear those things to bed? And I don't know what kind of tobacco you are using but it..." Then, Frank saw me, "Well, look who's here. Come here, kitty, kitty kitty."

I walked close by on the huge oaken kitchen table, meowed and gave him a high four paw. Everybody guffawed and Frank continued, "Well Prez, did you bring that cat with you or what? Every time you show up so does the cat. Then, you win at cards. I am going to tell that cat right now. No more caviar until I win a game!"

Disinterested, I meowed and turned around and walked over to where Marilyn was sitting having a cup of John Wayne's coffee. As I walked, I waved and flicked my tail at Frank as Marilyn picked me up. She said, "Oh Frank, this poor kitty (wink wink) needs more love. You can't treat him like rock and roll. If you would give him caviar now, your luck might change." She continued on with the kitty, kitty, mommy, mommy stuff, and I hopped back on the kitchen counter and knocked Big John's hat on the floor.

"Har, Har," JW said, "guess I better get a new hat. That must be a sign that I all my luck is used up. Rats! Do they have any trail busting shops in this town? Better be good ones. That's why I can't get my spurs off. The last one glued them plum on. I went back the next day and put some glue on that California cowboy. Looked like Dean Martin trying to get away from Jerry Lewis when I left the store. Har, Har, what a pussy! By golly, lookee there, that cat is making me talk about pussy this early in the morning."

JFK said, "Pass the JW coffee and then we can go and get ole John some new boots. Those spurs will give his poker hand away and then he will have an excuse for losing like Castro. Which reminds me Francis… (Only JFK could call him Francis) where are those special cigars that ended up on your doorstep so mysteriously one day? A good toke, er' smoke, would go just right with this coffee."

Frank said, "They're on the way. Hope they don't bother Casey. (They got my name from my collar.) I want to keep him happy. Maybe if I sang a few lines… I wonder what song he likes. Aha, I've got it "Witchcraft!" Frank was elated and drinking special coffee with his best friends in the world, smoking contraband cigars, and now the most famous voice in the world was up singing a few bars of witchcraft. I loved it. One of the servers had given me my special cup, and I meowed appropriately, and for a second, at that very moment I'm sure I saw a bright light surround us. Marilyn must have seen it also because she squealed.

"Well put," JFK said.

Big John gave it one "Har!"

Frank sang a couple more bars. Me, I'm just a cat, but I said a few meows to sing along as I watched a bug busy crawling across a bougainvillea bush.

Time to shop! We all got into the Rolls and off we went to get some spurs or a deck of cards or more pancake syrup. I got in the back window and stretched out. Frank opened up a cabinet and pulled out a few bottles of Dom Pérignon. Don't want to get all thirsty before you start shopping. Glasses were passed around and more giggling from Marilyn ensued. Two more girls appeared as if from nowhere and were all smiles and thirst and giggles as well. One of the girls said, "Can I pick up that pretty kitty? He almost looks like a shawl I have, so furry and shiny and warm. I'd like to take him home with me." A quick fraction of a second glance from JFK, charming, yet there was something in that smile that said, *not a good idea and...* The champagne continued to flow.

About a mile out of town Frank said, "There is a ranch out here I want you to see. It's on top of a mountain and we should be able to see LA today. We can play some cards when we get up there as well. That way the Mafia Cat won't have time to tip off his buddies and make me lose." (Frank is always being Frank.) Soon we were on top of Mount San Jacinto taking in the beautiful view with Castro's silly cigars, JW's syrup coffee, JFK's scintillating presence, Marilyn, Frank, and me... the Mafia Cat.

"Howzabout my spurs and boots and hat, and where in the hell is this goddamn place anyhow?" JW said, "Why, you bunch of pussy-footers, har har, damn cat talk, are just going to make it worse on yourselves. Outdoors is what I know best."

"Oh Johnny," Marilyn said, "When you talk like that you give me the shivers." She then picked me up and held me close as if to settle the shivers down.

I smiled at everything as if to say, *see there, I really know what I am doing after all.* This was a limo-sized Rolls Royce and it had a built in card table. We all sat down, er' I laid down in the back window area, and the cards were dealt. Simply beautiful view for hundreds of miles all around and if I could get Frank to sing one more song it would be perfect, but not this time. This was time to play cards and they meant business. If only those damn spurs would quit jingling. They played and they played. I slept and slept. Soon all but the chauffeur and I were blasted and laughing and talking and you know who was squealing. The morning sun illuminated the rolling card game on the top of the mountain and a good time was being had by all.

The Prez said, "I've never had a better time," (always a politician) "but my beeper indicates something is going on somewhere and it needs my immediate attention. How about one for game for double or nothing and if I win everybody has to wear a pair of those stinky JW's jingling cowboy boots for a week even in the shower."

JW started to "Har, Har!" so loud, that he blew out some smoke from somewhere, ahem, and no one could see for a while. When the dust had settled, the cards were dealt and guess who won?

"Goddamn Mafia Cat!" Frank said while grinning and chin-chucking me. The girls were giggling nervously, big John was cussing, and a big helicopter just landed outside the Rolls. About twenty marines came out in full body armor ready gear.

The Prez saluted us, winked at me, and said, "When I come here again, I want to see somebody wearing those boots. Call it the Puss and Boots Show!" Was a pretty good line for the most powerful man in the world. 'Nuff to make a cat laugh, anyhow!

# Jock on the Dock

*A*liens are everywhere. Cats don't care. Boy, will they have a surprise when they meet us, not to mention me. I have had a few dealings with them, and they have their own rule book. I didn't bother to show them the cat rule book because they were so confident their rule book was as good as it got. Not to worry, my furry minions and me will save humanity if need be. In fact, you can bet on it.

In today's paper's headlines read "Aliens causing drought all over the planet." Another headline, "Earthquakes begin after saucer-like objects seen around Fresno, California." Another one, "I was abducted by aliens and it was too shameful to tell." It goes on and on. Is the human race scared of those tiny, gray, goofy looking guys who drag young women up in the sky into their spaceships to do who knows what? It reminds me of dopey college kids riding around trying to get a date. If they had an abductor ray like the little gray men do, they would probably use it as well. All they have is a pickup truck and a six pack…nice to see where we are headed. Trade in one's pickup for a flying saucer with a people sucking up ray, make easy payments and never use any gas, just fly all over and be as strange as you want. Yee Haw! Aliens can be a nuisance and the classic Orson Wells reading about the Martians on national radio pretty much shows how paranoid people really are. And, by the by, wasn't Orson just great? If you remember the movie "The Third Man," I can't forget one of my brethren stealing a scene by walking up to Orson when he was hiding in a doorway. Sigh, we cats are so great. I can't help it.

It was time for a drive. So, into the Bentley and off to drive around the City of San Francisco before the rays of the sun splayed across the bay, Alcatraz, the Golden Gate Bridge, and continued on to Hawaii. I loved it. I sat on the dash and waved at whomever as we went by. From the stares we received one might have thought we were the aliens. Well John maybe, but not me. We had to stop in for some coffee and caviar at our favorite morning restaurant. Everybody was bright-eyed and cheery as we walked in at about six o'clock. Well, they were bright-eyed at least, and some were working on a morning cheer. Mostly off duty policemen who had just pulled a straight eight. We were familiar with a few and had helped them out from time to time. One waved at us and motioned for us to come over to his table.

"Glad you guys showed up," he said. It was Chief Inspector O'Malley. "We had a crazy night last night, and I have to tell you what happened. Aliens all over the place down on some of the piers, I swear. Their saucer hovered right over the water, and they jumped out and chased people all over trying to catch them and put them in their ship. Really, and this is only my first hot toddy."

I took a quick glimpse into the inspector's mind, and it was all true, exactly as he described it. He was scared. It would take at least three toddies to calm him down this morning. There was indeed trouble afoot, and he surely needed our help to solve this.

After he gave us all the details, we left and took a drive over to where all the action had occurred. We got out and walked around and my keen cat senses were immediately alerted. I smelled and saw a strange object laid off to the side. *Aha! Now I have you*, I meowed to myself. It looked like the kind of cap an alien would wear, or maybe a shoe, jock strap, or who cares. But it was, for sure alien. I did some quick cat forensics on it, and it told me the whole story. There were some strange aliens around here. Whatever it was smelled like a giant hot toddy, like a two gallon one. Phwew! At least they would not be hard to catch.

As if often the case, there was a major movie being shot in Frisco, an Arnold Swartzenegger movie. Arnie was doing what we all like to see, looking at people with that stern face, grrrrrrr. Then saying something like, "I vill squeeze you like a pretzel right now. Tell me vhat I vhant or ya, ya… and da, da,… and blah, blah…" Going to be a great movie, I could tell. Arnie would then drive a motorcycle off the pier onto a cruise ship, crash through the captain's quarters, take over the ship and save the day, smile while looking into the camera and say, "I vill be baack!" Schnoockims or whatever, I mean a cat, any cat, could write that stuff, and where was I?

Since the headquarters for the movie had been set up on the adjoining pier, "we" decided to go over and see what we could see. How lucky? There was Arnie, just completing his morning jog and probably getting ready to go for a swim to Alcatraz and back.

John pulled the Bentley up alongside Arnie and said, "Let me see your ID punk."

Arnold laughed that great laugh that he has and said, "I vill squeeze you like a pineapple!" Guess the pretzel joke needed freshening up. We laughed, and I meowed. They shook hands, and Arnie thought it was someone he knew. I mean, this was a Bentley after all. John invited Arnie for a ride so he could explain to him what had just happened on the adjoining pier. Arnie jumped in. I jumped up on the dash, and it was back to Chief O'Malley's headquarters, Gino and Carlo's, the morning restaurant and speakeasy back in the day.

I had to make Big Boy feel at home, so I "suggested" to him that he had met us somewhere before and that this was a crucial time in the crime scene, and since he was right next to it, he might be of some help, just like in the movies. What? Arnold has a great sense of humor, excellent judgment as well, ahem, and he took to me immediately and listed to what we and O'Malley told him. By now, the place was hummin'. San Fran is sophisticated, but here was Big Boy, the former governor and an icon in the movie world. He insisted upon hot toddies for all, and it was done. Everyone calmed down, someone played a Sinatra song on the juke box, and we laid out the details, especially what I had found laying off to the side on the dock. Heavens, it was a jock strap. Arnold started to laugh, and so did everybody else.

He said, "Ve vill just have to go back to the movie set, get everyone to take their clothes off, and see whom it vill fit. Could be anybody." Arnold winked,' er maybe I should say vinked. In fact, Arnold said, "Maybe we should start right now in this bar by having everybody take their clothes off and see if it fits. I vill go first." Don't need a laugh track when Arnold is around. He's a tremendous comedian as well.

We were even getting a clearer picture of what actually happened. It was an alien with a jock on, medium size. Uh oh! Right then, I had the case solved, as in Casey, but let's play it out. These are humans and not used to cat efficiency. More toddies were consumed, and Arnold paid for it all, left a tip, and said to buy a new juke box. When we went out the door, he jumped up on a chair, holding me, as I coyly meowed and said, "I vill be back!"

We got in the car with clapping and cheering and sounds of approval surrounding us. We were all smoking cigars by now, and the jock was secure in a plastic bag, medium evidence. We drove around the wharf, smoked up the Bentley, (and with that funky evidence, it needed it) told lies and drank another hot toddy that suddenly appeared from Arnold's jacket. He saw John's glance at where the toddies came from and said, "The cat made me do it! Ha! Ha! Ha!" Arnold is great!

Back at the movie set, Arnold took over. He gathered the entire crew on the dock and said there was going to be an extremely delicate shot to be made. Before it was to be made, everyone would have to take off their clothes to be absolutely sure it would fit in with all the high tech movie mumbo jumbo that had to be done to make the take. All disrobed with pleasure. Hey, this is Hollywood at work. There were about a hundred people counting the entire crew, even the cooks. It was easy. Just find the person the jock would fit, and you would have your alien. The women had to be naked as well. No discrimination this morning, and besides what with all the new laws, one never knows who is what or… John and O'Malley particularly enjoyed this part of the investigation. Sitting in a Bentley looking over one hundred naked people trying to figure out which one had worn the jock on the dock was police investigation at its finest. The men in blue want to take a look at you. But surely, I digress again, intentionally of course.

In no time at all, it was evident who the culprit was. Can't say but it wasn't Big Boy. It was someone we know who likes to be "up front" about things. He was confronted with the situation, confessed, and since no actual damage had been done, made proper reparation. He paid everybody off, donated a dock, and guess what they named it, and it actually gave the movie more publicity than it ever dreamed it would get. In fact, they had to rename the title of the movie from, "Big Boy Socks the Dorks on the Dock" to an even schmaltzier title of …I just can't say it. But you know there is the word "jock" in it. Hey, this is Hollywood. 'Nuff to make a cat laugh!

# A Night with Elvis

Hollywood is almost right next to us, one hundred miles away. I "pointed" that out to John, and he soon thought it would be a good idea to take in a show there. Pretty much any one would do, so we picked the first one we noticed in the paper. Yeaaaaa! Hollywood here we come! I slept while John drove. I felt great when we got there, and John was pooped. He mumbled something about how he was going to take a "power nap." "Sure," I thought, "Ha!" There, he made me laugh again. This "power nap" could be as much as eight hours. I made sure the doors were locked, and I went to take a look around. The play was about to begin in a half hour and that was plenty of time to "check out" the area. I immediately met one of my furry friends, and he told me what was going on around here. He said the Elvis Presley impersonator show was coming up next. This was a safe neighborhood, and he could get me right now if I wanted. "Fantastic," I said, and we went right in. The Elvis impersonator was getting big time ready for the show by getting stoned and drinking Santa Rosa's original. I, yi, yi! This could be a short show. "Elvis" looked down and saw me sitting in one of the chairs.

He said, "How yuh doin' kittee?"

"Pretty good," I thought, "He has the voice down okay, but can he stand up?"

Elvis continued to talk to me. He said, "You 'mind me of my kittykat bek home. I loved that cat, but had to leave her with my

Momma (sigh) 'cause I travel suh much. So you want water or some Santa Rosa's Original? Ha ha ha ha!"

"Very good," I thought, "He sounds like he has some wit left before Santa Rosa hits the spot. He may have to keep the Santa Rosa coming, so it will have problem hitting the spot. Dangerous tradeoff but necessary because the show must go on." Somebody knocked on the door and said "Showtime, five minutes!"

"Let's go!" Elvis said as he picked me up and out on the stage we went.

The curtain had not opened yet, so he yelled out, "Hey motor-boy, bring me a chug a chugga, a great beg mugga, and two bar chairs with a wooden stand in the middle. I'm doing this show sitting down. Burp, and this cat will help suh much. I can feel. Anyhow, I sure am feelin' sumpin'. By god, I feel good, just like back home when...and where was I?"

The stage hand came out with the "props" and a mike, and it was three minutes to curtain time. Elvis was never late, and never missed a date. (Just a natural poet as well. Wink)

Elvis tested the mike. "Booba boooba do, I only want to love you...hold me close and do what you do."

People started to scream and wow! The whole place was on Santa Rosa's original. It seems the lounges in the very middle of the theatre were having, you guessed it, a Santa Rosa the Hoseuh night. Free and they all were on the same plane with Elvis, yup, musical plane, mental plane, or even an airplane. Come on Santa Rosa! Showtime! The curtain pulled back, and there we were-Elvis and I and good ole' Santy. Santy was everywhere. Elvis introduced me, saw my name on my necklace and said, "I want yuh to meet a very good friend of mine, Casey!" All were silent and listened.

When Elvis talked, people listened, and when he sang, they were entranced. He went on, told them of the beautiful cat he had back home, and how I reminded him of that wonderful cat. He told them how terrible he felt when he had to leave. He said this life isn't what it's made out to be by them writers and such.

Elvis then said, "This show is devoted to my new friend, Casey! And let the show begin!" The stage lights then shifted behind Elvis, and there were his fantastic backup singers and band. He started out with, 'Love me Tender' which was kind of corny I thought, but the audience loved it. He continued to sing without stopping or talking for one hour. The audience was fantastic, and every nuance and note was perfect they thought. Good ole' Santy was doing what he does. He was at the Last Supper and way before that. He gave people oomph when they needed it.

I hardly napped and loved it. At the very end of the show, when the lights moved around the stage and the credits were given, I slipped away back to the car where John was still sleeping. I jumped in the back seat and took a nap as well.

About an hour later, John awoke and said, "Missed the show. Time to go back, I guess." Then, he looked at me with a smile on his face and said, "How was the show Casey? Before I fell asleep, I saw you go backstage. You're something else!" 'Nuff to make a cat laugh!

# China and Atlantis in One Day

*A*ll my alert vibes were tingling. Something not right was happening, and it was very close to me. Even my mind reading, melding, and suggestive powers could not give me the answer. I had to find out. First of all, John and I were going to Marin to eat pizza with wheat crust. I mean first things first, right? We just walked out the door with me riding in John's backpack, and we noticed our good friend and neighbor, Jim the 120 lb Labrador scrutinizing the street. His front paws were tamping the ground, and he was making sounds of barking, whimpering, and snuffling all at once. He was very disturbed. We went over immediately, and I asked what happened. He told me he had been watching the two little girls of the family play in the yard. One had lost her toy and he went over in the front bushes to find it. When he returned twenty seconds later, the children were gone.

I said, "How long ago?"

Jim said, "About two minutes ago?"

"Did you see who took them?" I asked.

Jim said, "After I saw they were missing, I looked up and saw a blue BMW sedan take off at a fast pace. I had no idea. I feel horrible."

I told John, and he immediately called the kidnapping hotline. I got a hold of Seagull Joe and Uncle Al. The seagulls would cover all of the bay area by air, and my brethren would cover the ground. Within five minutes, fifteen blue sedan BMW's were pulled over with no results. Number 16 rang the bell. It was found in a red zone by a fire hydrant in China Town only a mile or so from where we were. It was a stolen car and had children's toys in the back seat. Immediately, the area around was completely searched by swat teams and police. The two little girls were found in the basement under a five story rooming house. They were heavily sedated and about to be transferred into one of the labyrinth of tunnels going under the city. We were just in time. They were returned to their parents with a police psychiatrist. When the children were able, they might be able to give some info on the kidnapping.

Meanwhile, Jim the Labrador was feeling very badly. He told me he had guarded them with his life if need be for two years. In twenty seconds, while turning his back to look for a toy, they were taken from under his very snout. I told him if he would have been with the girls, he would have been killed, and maybe a stray bullet would have hit one of the children. No one would have known what happened. Now you all are safe and sound. You actually did a good thing when looking for the toy when you did. Jim looked at me and tried to smile, but he only let out a faint whine. John then asked the family if we could take Jim for a ride. The fresh air and I, of course, might help him feel better. We all got in the car, and put Jim in the front seat. He was so sad and making woofing sounds.

John, looked over at Jim and said, "First one who smiles has to buy the pizza." Jim came around a little, barked softly, and looked at me in the back seat.

I said, "Don't worry, Jim, I already laughed, so you don't have to buy." Jim smiled, gave it a big bark, and we were on our way.

In getting to Marin, we had to cross the Golden Gate Bridge. After what had happened, I needed to take my usual cat nap. The back seat was a perfect place. My eyes were just closing as I saw the towers of the bridge, and I felt the front wheels hit a bump in the road. I was waiting for the rear wheels to bump but no bump. I looked up, and we were flying off the bridge heading west toward Hawaii.

John said, "Let's go north up the coast, and take in all that beautiful scenery. I'll keep the car at about 2000 feet elevation, so we can get a good look." We kept flying up along the coast, and it was fantastic. It put Jim in a good mood, but I was beginning to wonder how this car was flying. For now, let's just keep going.

We were almost to Canada, and I had never seen that coast line. Shortly, we were on the Alaska Canada border line. We all looked out the window. (Can you imagine what someone would have thought if they would have seen us flying a car with a cat, a dog, and John looking out the window?) Then we saw what we thought was a phenomenon. There it was, amidst all the crashing waves, a calm area about one mile square. What was it? I said, "Let's go down and take a look." In we went. At this point in the journey, you have to hope the car can go under water as well. Why not? We rolled the windows up good and tight. What we saw was eye boggling. We all made appropriate exclamatory noises and said, "Forget the pizza, this is phenomenal." It was a mile square granite underwater city abandoned, of course. It had regular streets, buildings, homes, and looked like what we all heard it to be. We went down, drove on the streets, and looked around. So fascinating! (We may have even seen a pizza place.) It was time to go home. Jim was back to normal, thanked us, and we did a rare paw high four. All of a sudden, I heard a bump and what..?

I opened my eyes and saw we were just entering the garage. John said, "About time you woke up. You were all over the back seat and looking out the window with your eyes closed. Then, you jumped down on the floorboard, and it looked like you were swimming." I noticed that I was now on the floor board, and it suddenly all made sense. Another dream and it cost me a pizza. They had saved some for me. John and Jim don't like anchovies.

Whatta' day! Kidnappers foiled, Atlantis found, flying and sub-marine car, all in one and more. Now, we were going to track down the kidnappers until their entire organization all over the world would be stopped. We had plenty of evidence and a place to start. Kidnapping was evil incarnate. The punishment would fit the crime. 'Nuff to make a cat get serious. But, that's another story.

# Kidnappers Maybe

*I*t was a scintillating San Francisco night as all of the crew was sitting on top of our huge three story house where I lived by the chimney. This particular place was where one of the "power points" on the Earth was. It just so happened I lived here. Ahem. In addition to having mind reading, melding, and tremendous power of suggesting abilities, I have also been given the powers of all knowledge that was ever known or will be. I am also a cat. Probably the latter is the most important. (Cat Smile) I am able to handle all this power succinctly and with grace just like a cat does in whatever he does.

We were all assembled by the chimney, Seagull Joe, Uncle Al, his protégés, and our newest member, Wrigley. Wrigley was a hefty 120 pound lab who lived next door and was the guard of two precious little girls. They were asleep with their family now. But, he was always on constant vigil. His house was next door, and if need be, he could jump from my house to his. (He would probably crash through the roof as much as he weighs, and would scare away whatever was there. No matter though, he would surely get the job done. You betcha!

Not too long ago a kidnapping had taken place next door and the two girls were missing for about fifteen minutes. They were found in China Town in the basement of a five story apartment building. Underneath the basement was a labyrinth of tunnels that went all over San Francisco. If they would have been taken into the tunnels, it would have been very difficult to retrieve them. We were drawing up a plan to get rid of the evil incarnate organization that kidnaps people from all over the world. First of all, it was decided for all of us to go to where the little girls had been found and do some detective work. Then, we had to get some disguises. We could not go as we were because in many of these places in China Town where we were going, we were on the menu.

Uncle Al, who is very clever, knew of an excellent disguise shop in the Mission area of San Francisco. I told John, my great human friend whom I lived with, what we were going to do. He said, "Let's go," and we jumped, well… Al did, into the car. This was a great place for disguises. It had everything for everybody. (Really… everybody!) As soon as we had all walked, jumped, and partially flew in, John told the owner what we needed. All of us, except John, he could go as he was, were to be dressed up like a Chinese person. "No probwem," the owner said in his Chinese accent. He went on to say, "Why just last week, two pigs and three, of I don't know what else, came in and wanted to go to Paris, France. I dressed them up like Frenchmen, and no one was the wiser. He even threw in some passports. Hush, hush plwease, about the passports, but I aim to plwease all my customers." In no time at all, we looked exactly like four Chinese persons all dressed up for a night out. The owner used to be the top makeup man in Hollywood. Lately the actors in Hollywood didn't need any type of makeup or get ups. They all looked exactly like the parts they were going to play. (I will let the reader discern how that was.) There was no more work for him, but this was much more fun he said. Besides, all those parties in the "stars" trailers were getting a bit much. "Ah, for the good old days of Gable, Monroe, Mitchum, and Lancaster, who were powerful actors and great to work with," he said.

Up to China Town we went to begin our investigation that would be the beginning of the end for a great evil. We started in the building where we had found the girls. On the floor above the basement was a restaurant. We went right in, sat down, and ordered. Since I can speak any language in the world, we had no problem ordering. There was nary a suspicious eye in the place. All the customers had their faces squarely placed over their plates shoveling food in with the waiters were scurrying all around the place. Good, we would scurry too. Wrigley went downstairs to where the girls were found and found the tunnels immediately. I mind read the owner who was standing over an abacus passing out lengthy food checks. After reading his mind, I could not wait to see his face when he saw our food bill. Uncle Al and Seagull Joe really tore into some octopus and frog. Wrigley had never seen such food and got a huge bowl of noodles wolfing it down. However, I was too busy and excited to eat, my mind was filled with thoughts from everywhere.

The owner was the mastermind of the organization. Their plan was that they would take the kidnapped people or animals or whatever to the basement. Then, transfer them out to the tunnels, onto to a waiting plane, and off they would go. It would have been a foolproof plan had it not been for me and my minions of feathered and furry friends. In addition to reading the top kidnapper's mind, I found that the entire five story building was used for this ongoing evil. They worked 24 hours a day, (24/7 is so pretentious... harrumph) and would kidnap anything they were told to do. Yes, there were many more levels to this crime than one top creep. They were all over the world is every culture and country.

Our plan was this. Wrigley would go below and secure the tunnel. No one would get in or out. His sensitive snout could still detect the scent of the little kidnapped girls. Wrigley was very vigilant. I pity anyone who came across him tonight. Seagull Joe and Uncle Al went to the top floor and jammed the trap door to the roof denying access in or out. And yes, dear reader, there was a helicopter on the roof made to look like an original Chinese toilet. (Where they went after this would be an original prison toilet in San Quentin. No more silks and satins and scented wipe-olas. It would be the cold powerful stream of a fire hose used by a very large guard to insure prison sanitation after "business" was done. While the "sanitation process" was carried out, all watched and got ready for their turn. Making for lots of constipation in prison I heard, anything to avoid that.) The remedy for all of this could only be done by us. This kidnapping evil was very powerful in all levels of government everywhere. Warrants could not be obtained. But, we had coordinated with the San Fran special crime unit to be outside and around the five story building at exactly 8:23 am. People would be streaming out by the numbers, and they were all to be placed in waiting "paddy" wagons. The time arrived, and it all happened at once. From the fifth floor on down came many people dressed and undressed in every kind of condition imaginable and then some. Those who did not jump out the windows or literally knocked holes in the walls to escape fell into the police wagons below. Some had tried to go into the basement and that made Wrigley happy. He put a wompus chomp on them they would never forget. San Quentin looked good after that experience. They commandeered seventy eight people in all.

It was reported the very next day in the paper that a seagull flew out followed by two cats riding a large dog. Just goes to show how low those creeps would go, kidnapping animals as well. This would only mean every building in the area would have to be searched by animal cruelty squads. Later on, everyone would be questioned, and that should prove tremendously interesting. John and I would attend, and my powers of mind suggestion would be used, if necessary. They will be. All is now calm in China Town. I've gotten word that certain foods have been removed from many menus recently. The Chinese animal gods, it was also heard, had used a huge dog, cats, and birds to strike back at those who had misused animals. 'Nuff to make a cat laugh! We were on the roof by the chimney when I read the article to everybody. We had a good laugh making a lot of racket.

# Casey Goes to Dreamland

Yes, cats dream a lot. Big time! That's why we only sleep for a short time, and then wake up and try to trip you. Kidding! I had a dream yesterday that was a dream deluxe. Maybe too many cat treats. Whatever, it was a "big fat" dream, and I liked it a lot. Only problem was I could not get out of it, and it had me worried. With my great mind and power, I have to be careful with everything, especially dreaming as I have discovered.

Here's what happened. I was taking a short nap at the half time of a football game. The dream began innocently enough, and then, I found myself flying all over the planet earth. You name it. I went there-New York, Paris, Moscow, London, Mexico City, and on and on. I was just flying all over the place. It was fun, but I kind of wondered if I was really where I was flying to, or was I at home. I tried to wake up, but couldn't. I waved all my extremities around but nothing happened. I thought I heard John laughing, but how could he know? Well, I would sure tell him later. I would say, "When you see me flopping all over the floor, and I am asleep, come over and calm me down. I mean, that's what I do to you when you are sleeping and start singing and growling in your sleep." (The growling reminds me of my ancestors, the big tigers. They were quite a sight. One growl and that was enough. Leave.) I think John was just having a blarney dream.

So there I was, flying all over the planet, and it was getting tiresome. Really! I thought, "Hmmm, maybe I can fly into outer space as well." I gave it a try and bingo! Right on the moon for starters and then I kept going. I flew way beyond this solar system and made Star Trek look like a trip on a small one engine plane. Where I went, it was entirely different. There were all kinds of things that were different. One planet was full of my brethren. They were doing what I was doing, when I was awake already, and they seemed happy. I just kept going. I wanted to see how far all "this" went. Much of it was entirely empty. I went completely beyond the stars you see at night, and I was getting hungry. So strange how I knew I was at home, and I also knew I was zillions of miles away at the same time, and that I was also hungry. I knew it was not logical, as Spock would say, but I just decided to land and see if they had any food. It was a small planet as planets go. It almost looked like earth, and for some reason, I wanted to laugh, but now I did not want to wake up. I saw a bunch of old pickup trucks around a diner out in the middle nowhere. I went down to see what I could see. Before I went in, I gave a quick mind read to the people that were in there, and they had never seen a cat in their lives. It was a planet with just all cowboys and old pickup trucks. For some reason, I thought I should stand up as I went in the door, and so I did. When I stretch out, I was about four feet tall. These cowboys were about six feet tall and lots of them looked oddly like John. Hmmm...I found some boots and a hat in the back of one of the old pickup trucks, put them on, and in I went. Name of the place was Lucy's.

I went in and hardly anybody paid attention. I just looked like a beat up old cowboy that hadn't shaved in quite a while. Since most of them looked like John and were telling blarney to each other, I felt right at home. I guess it was Lucy that sidled on over to where

I was sitting on a counter stool and asked me, "What'll you have, stranger?"

They understood cat talk here. I told her, "I want the special of the day and a beer."

She just continued chewing on her gum, scribbled something down and said, "Sure, and by the way, today is karaoke day, and you can sing if you want. You look like a singer to me."

I said, "Thanks think I will." But first, I had to go to the can. I had some serious laughing to do.

When I returned, the little stage over in the corner was all set up, and my food had not arrived yet. The beer was there, and I took a slug, and went over to the stage. With my hat and boots and walking on my hind feet, I got on the stage and let out a few Marty Robbins songs. I saw a few guys who looked like John, only uglier, get up and go to the bathroom. I figured they were laughing their brains out in there as well. Finally, my chow came, and she gave me a sweet smile I was getting to like it here. I was beginning to think I might stay. If only I could drive a pickup. More beers and blarney flowed between me and the cowboys, and I thought I would sing one more song, 'Ghost Riders in the Sky' by Frankie Lane. I cranked up that microphone and let 'er rip! Boy was I good! Hollering and yelling and stamping our feet proceeded. (These boots I had on were great for stomping the floor. Heck yeah!)

Suddenly, someone who looked like John, picked me up and said, "Hey, cowcat, how are you feelin?" I blinked, looked around, and realized I was in the John's kitchen. I had moved a chair over to the kitchen counter, pulled some food out of the fridge, turned up the radio real loud, started meowing way off key, and did this all when I was "sleeping". We had a good laugh and just in time, as the second half was about to begin. John looked over at me and said, "That was a pretty good show you gave. Putting that napkin on your head and wearing my galoshes was a good touch. I also see you have the keys to the car tucked under your chin. Don't worry. We'll go for a ride as soon as the game is over, and maybe sooner, if you put another napkin on your head!" 'Nuff to make a "cowcat" laugh!

# The Farce Meets the Force

*I*n the dead of night two men got out of a car that had been parked down the street for about two hours. Each was carrying some type of a suitcase and was walking with purpose. They turned into an alley for about a minute, then returned, got in the car, and drove away. They had been working under surveillance for ten days with good reason. They were part of what nowadays is called a cell, usually associated with people who sneak around and kill people in the worst ways. This horrible activity was taking place in my hometown San Francisco, California. These two creeps were hoping to blow up the Transamerica Building. It was built like a pyramid. They could identify with that type of structure, but this pyramid was used to store money, not dead bodies. In their demented minds, it had to be destroyed because it was defiling their belief. Actually, just about any excuse would do for them. They were loaded to the gills on souped up drugs and never felt better, but that was about to end.

Another car being watched became active, its lights turned on as it went down the same alley the two men had just came out from except it was going very fast and heading for the bay. One minute later the car flew zooming off Pier 39 like a gunshot and disappeared beneath the water. Fifteen seconds later a helluva lot of water and noise shot up into the air, and the good guys watching on smiled. The creeps in the first car had been pulled over, and were put under arrest being questioned. In the middle of all the shouting some chant, the arrested men's bodies blew apart taking some of the city's finest with them. Good help is hard to find.

John and I had been taking our usual walk a bit earlier that day since John could not sleep. I was not about to let him go out without me. Besides I was hungry and the all night deli on Columbus Street had my favorite chow, beef jerky. They were crazy about me in that place. I brought in business for them, and they knew it. As I stood in John's backpack purveying the store, John went to buy the beef jerky, two donuts, and off we went. By the time we got to the door I would always let out a fat meow and start eating the jerky. I got more looks and laughs than the Kardashians. Go figure, me a cat. But hey, I am one handsome looking cat, that's for sure. We no more than got out the store's door when a squad car pulled up motioning for us to hurry and get in. Inspector O'Malley, the big cheese of the San Francisco Police Department, needed our help urgently. We had helped him before on unusual cases and this one was a dandy. He told us what had just happened and said, "This has got to stop right away and in any way possible." He went on to say there were about fifty of these madmen loose in the city somewhere, and so far the police had dodged one gigantic disaster but more were certainly on the way. John said, "How much does this pay? The last job got Casey all dusty, and I had to have him bathed and perfumed. (I don't know why he said perfumed.) It also ruined my shoes, and all we got was dinner at Gino and Carlo's. This time I want lots more than that." (Isn't John just one great negotiator?)

They took us home, and the plan was set out. I contacted my "associates" immediately, Seagull Joe and Uncle Al. The other third member could not be woken up, that would be Wrigley, the pleasant, pondering, slightly overweight Lab who helped with this and that. He was very good at showing people how big he was, taking their attention from us, and when he barked things fell off the shelf. After all, we are not dealing with theoretical physicists. Sometimes, just one big woof gets things going. The plan consisted of my crime stopping buddies and their minions covering every inch of ground within a fifty mile radius of San Francisco.

Nothing went unnoticed. They worked for sardines and actually just about any type of fish that was in season. They were fussy about their fish. They wanted fresh fish, and they wanted it now. I just gave the sardine combination to Uncle Al and let them have at it. Their feeding noises were fantastic to hear. Hundreds of cat meows and seagull cries going on at once were so much better than any concert they have nowadays. (I know somewhere Sinatra is listening and laughing. Francis was never a big fan of those types of bands. He said they named themselves properly however, Grateful Dead says it all. Frank said that not me. Me and mine will back him with every meow we have.) Two hours later, there was a knock, 'er woof, at the door. Loyal Wrigley had helped out the furry minions on the ground, and they had discovered about fifty men in a tunnel. (Good old Wrigley was so anxious to help after sleeping through the first half of the plan that he was quite anxious to make amends.) Wrigley jumped right in the middle of the terrorists, lucky for him they were just fifty bad, smelly, ugly, sweaty creeps, as he threw them around like hamburgers. Very impressive as the cat patrol sat back and watched Wrigley at work. All they had to do was pick up the pieces and cuff 'em. It will always be remembered as the night Wrigley got woken from a nap, got mad, and caught the people who got him up. They deemed it "Gotcha Night."

As Wrigley told me what happened, from the dog's mouth actually, he was jumping all around the room and giving great woofs and smiling and showed us all by demonstrating with a couch how he did it. Ring up one shot couch after that. He said he personally questioned the leader and that was that. The paddy wagons came and what was left of the frightened fifty was packed up. One of the terrorists managed to make a phone call while hanging from his heels at the top of the tunnel, but we had intercepted every word and it was beyond scary. The terrorist told the leader of the world terrorist group, Dibbid Dahbid, that a terrible furry force had descended upon them like acid rain.

Here is an excerpt from the terrorist's description of what it was like being in the tunnel with The Force. "Oh, yi, yi, oh wonderful Dibbid Dahbid, who leads us into battle by staying in the Waldorf Astoria drinking Dom Pérignon 4 to throw off the Western world's idea that you could not possibly be the great tootie of all tooties. This is my dying words before The Force will come back to polish me off. Yes, the terrible Force is even polishing off the bombers. It is not enough that we say Oh, yi yi and giva uppa---like you told us to do--it only makes the Force worse. Oh, yi, yi, here it comes for me. Not, yet, I may have another fifteen seconds. It is polishing off what it already polished off. Such terror, evil… Oh, yi yi, now here it comes and it is going to stuff a bomba in my booba. Such a mucha pain. One more thing-boy that hurts-I guess I should have read the fine print when I signed up, but why is my wife with you? She is ten years of age but won't that number four booze make her completely corruptible and unable to properly suicide bomb? I, yi, yi... I have to go I guess. Could you put my wife on for a little while before The Force jams the bomba in my booba. It is a clumsy force and is jamming the bombs incorrectly. Stupid Americans! Hey…there is interference here, but it sounds like a small girl's voice."

"Hi honey, howzitgoin'? These Americans will soon be ours. I am drinking all I can to be properly westernized. I am also learning pole climbing---naked with cooking oil all over my body? So evil but why waste the cooking oil? They will stop at nothing, but... uh, oh... gotta go. Here comes Dibbid Dahbid and he is showing all how really evil westerners are. He is naked now, wearing sinful cowboy boots and a giant hat. Well, almost naked. I also thought you would want to know this before the bomba blows your boomba to seventy nine virgins in the sky. (Now I am almost getting jealous...grrrrrrrrrr) He is also wearing some fake glasses with a big schnozzle and he says this is the best disguise ever, so cruel but we must serve his desires. Bye... bye... bbb...”

There was a loud explosion and that was it but it was still very valuable intel work. I heard John laughing quite loudly in the kitchen, and he brought out a box of puppy biscuits for you know who. Guess we know who to wake up from now on when there is a tough job going down. Oh boy and I thought my ancestors, the Siberian snow tigers, had a temper?

# The Devil & Me

*I*t is three thirty in the morning and my good buddy John is going for a walk at this hour. I better help him. It's foggy this morning and my cat alertness warnings are up. My whiskers are feeling frisky and I think there is something more than fog in the air. Although I am the most brilliant entity in the world, my alert awareness can be felt by any of my cat brethren.

Fog and San Francisco, reminds me of a poem. (Yes, there is poetry in me as there is in every cat and... where was I?) Carl Sandberg's poem *Fog* goes like this. "It sits looking over harbor and city on silent haunches and then moves on." The poem describes the physical presence of the morning perfectly. But I still had frisky whiskers telling me all was not right and something evil was afoot as well. It is the devil I suspect. He is everywhere, and this morning I knew I must be with John to protect him.

John and I began our walk in the usual way. I was standing in the backpack with my paws on John's shoulders. My head swiveled around looking making sure all was in order. Ahem. We were soon on the embarcadero strolling by the bay when I heard muffled noises and saw fleeting shadows. Aha! That is one of the signs of the devil for sure. He comes and goes in sound and sight taking on many forms in every way, but he cannot fool me simply because I am smarter, and that is very good for John. We crossed to the other side of the street as I made a "suggestion" to John. I felt much safer immediately, but I could still hear the sounds and see the shadows. It became clearer now as the morning light was approaching. There was a mother and her daughter wrapped in a blanket sitting on a bench trying to keep warm. Not particularly alarming but there was more here than meets the meow. Further on we came across somewhat similar situations. What could this be? John said, "Looks like the bums are out early today." He cannot see or hear nearly as well as I can so... As we continued our walk more of the same people continued to appear. "Hmmm," John went on, "there appears to be women with children here. Maybe I should give them a few bucks, or buy them some cookies anyhow." We bought some cookies from a nearby deli and when we passed another couple we gave them a bag. As we progressed down the embarcadero, we noticed many other women with small children. What was going on here? We soon came to the shelter for homeless women but nobody could be seen through the large windows. We decided to go inside and see if anything odd was going on. Two nuns immediately greeted us, and we told them (well John did) what we saw on our walk. They appeared to be very confused and told us what had just happened.

Sister Mary Elizabeth said, "It was at the last stroke of midnight that a very dapperly dressed gentleman entered our shelter. We walked to greet him as we have just greeted you. He smiled most graciously as he looked into our eyes, and we immediately directed all the women and the children to go with him. He was going to take them all on a midnight cruise. He said he would feed and clothe them all in exchange for being extras in his upcoming movie. He showed us his "credentials," and there were four waiting limos to take them to the cruise ships. He said they all would return in about three hours. That's the last we saw him or the girls, women, and children.

John said, "We have just found what I believe are the women and children who were in your shelter while we were on our walk. I think you were tricked into some kind of a nefarious scheme, and I believe some type of hypnosis was involved."

Sister Margaret said, "Surely, it does seem so and thank you for telling us. We were so worried about what had become of them. We will go out right now and bring them back. What a devil of a thing to do! Do you suppose?"

"Yes, I do suppose" John said, "It is the work of evil." Soon the women and their children were back in the shelter. John ordered two cases of cookies and milk and that seemed to be the antidote for the devilish trick.

The shelter was not far from "our" hot toddy place so we went there. It was crowded at six in the morning and the talk of the town was about a boat that had been commandeered on the bay where a number of mothers and daughters were held prisoners for a couple of hours. The Coast Guard had saved the day and rescued them, bringing them back to shore. We took in the atmosphere of the restaurant and the hot toddy and tried to figure out what happened that was actually a large kidnapping caper.

Again, my hackles were on alert! (Indeed a very busy day for my hackles.) There was someone in the restaurant selling pictures of mothers and their daughters. Aha! Cat hackles are never wrong. We approached the table where the pictures were being sold. Since this was a type of international restaurant, it took on more liberties than others normally would especially at six in the morning. The hot toddies were doing a very good business what with the kidnapping caper affair and such news of the day to discuss. As we got close to the person who was selling the pictures, I knew immediately that it was Scratch, that old devil, getting everyone in trouble in any way imaginable. This time he was also buying the clientele unlimited hot toddies. Not only were the people getting "loose", they were incriminating themselves in child porn, public drunkenness, and probably causing a few car accidents after they sashayed out of the place all hot toddied up. He was hard at work making degenerates for his causes.

I said to John, " *'nuff of that*!" With friendly persuasion and suggestions John and I, ahem, spoke to the owner and explained what was going on. We had a plan. Five of the most robust, toddied up big men grabbed the devil, took off all his clothes, poured toddies over his entire presence, and handcuffed him. (It seems that two of the young men were just getting off work from, you guessed it, night police patrol.) A black and white pulled up, and Scratch was gently kicked into the back seat, naked and stinky, then taken down to the least desirable jail places among the general populace. Ouch! Of course, Scratch escaped in a few hours as soon as he asked for a bucket and mop, but he did make a "clean" kind of getaway. So difficult to keep him locked up for long, he is a very tricky fellow.

The devil, although a ruthless, diabolically, horrific killer in every way, likes to think he is classy. (*There is no accounting for taste*.) When whomever he hangs around with finds out what has happened, there will be "hell to pay." But, it won't do to laugh at the devil. What more can be done to him and his cohorts? They are already in hell. For now, a huge battle was won. As long San Francisco has my hackles, they will be safe. Meow!

# Casey Brings Down the Curtain

$E$ ven the most brilliant cat in the whole world that knows it all from all that is to be and what was must take a nap. After all, I am still a cat, you know. I am living with my best friend John, who is relaxing on the sofa with a beer "busy" watching the National Basketball Championships, the NBA. Good time for a nap. Just before I drifted off into cat world there was a commercial tune on the radio. The tune was, 'Night and Day', lyrics by Cole Porter and now sung, on the TV, by Sinatra. My subconscious took this all in as I nodded away on my back slowly waving my paws back and forth, and I found myself in Sinatra's home.

As usual Frank was with his friends. His friends this afternoon were The President of the United States, that's right, JFK, Marilyn Monroe, Peter Lawford, and my best buddy, John Wayne. John Wayne was quick to say, well, quick for John Wayne, "Well, Mr. President, it looks like all this being President of the United States isn't too tough a job. Haw, Har, Har! So far all you have had to deal with is Russia, Cuba, Mexico, and the Vatican. No problem there, so far as I can see. 'Cept for the Vatican. Ha Har Haw!"

Marilyn said, "Gee whiz, big boy, what in the world is the Vootican? Sounds like something really dumb?"

Frank said, "Goddamnit Marilyn, ease off on those…whatever

you are drinking, and pay attention! What we have here is the most powerful man in the world, the best actor in the world, the best singer in the world, and...whose cat is that?"

I was sitting on the kitchen counter in all my beautiful countenance, all twenty pounds of me, looking so handsome with my sparkling cat eyes at the beginning of a great party. Of course, I had to meow. So "Meow," and I put in a few cat tail waves to hyphen the meows, completely charming.

Kennedy said, "Why Frank, you old dago you, that is the indoor/outdoor cat that always seems to show up when Marilyn and I get here. Come here, kitty kitty," he said to me.

I gracefully leaped onto JFK's waiting arms and purred upon landing. JFK laughed with his Boston accent and said, "Oh, boy, what a load of pussy!" Big John laughed and told Marilyn, "Get me another bracer."

"Boof you cowboy, help yourself!" Marilyn said loudly and giggled.

"Make it four," Frank told her, "And hurry up, or you'll have to sing the President another song!"

Marilyn flicked up her dress defiantly, showed all her bottom, sans panties, and all gasped.

Big John, said, "Make 'em all doubles."

The kitchen klatch carried on for a short while, and Peter Lawford spoke up, "Time to eat. Where are we going with five of the best known people on the planet?"

Marilyn said, "Make it six, don't forget about my little kitty witty."

"Ok, already and that's enough. Go put some underpants on, so we won't give the Prez a bad look, and let's hit the trail. See JW, I can talk cowboy as good as you can. Har, Har, Har! And laugh just like you too." Sinatra quipped.

JFK was laughing so hard he almost fell over, but with my cat strength and lightning quickness, I put one paw on his belt and another on Marilyn and leveraged his chair back down. All were taken aback for a second, and Big John said "Reminds me of the time at the dusty corral where we..." And then, four lemon martinis found their mark.

I meowed loudly and JFK said, "Don't scare the cat. If you had done that around the Russians, by now we would all have been shot. I was thinking about taking you four with me on my next "detente tour." Then again, the way the Russians drink, that might have been just the ticket. So many things a President has to think about."

Big John said, "Watch this," as he called to me, "Come here kitty kat, come on, come on." I jumped instantly from JFK's lap over JW's head, and landed on Marilyn's lap with John Wayne's hair in one of my paws.

"By god," John Wayne said, "That cat is sumpin' else. Good thing there ain't no Chinamen around. Haw! Haw! Har!"

"Sure," Frank said, "And, you would probably try to shoot them. Goddamnit, we gotta' clean up our acts. This is the President of the United States. The most powerful man in the world. Here here, and huzza huzza. Let's salute!"

They saluted, laughed and smiled, and Marilyn sang the President's favorite song, and mine too, 'Night and day'. Oh boy, we almost evaporated and flew away, but we had to eat and that we did.

It was the best restaurant east of Los Angeles to New York City, Giovanni's, which was owned by Frank, of course. We had it all. They had a special place for me, and I was served first. Had I not just saved the President from who knows what? Caviar, of course, with some of what Marilyn thought I would really like. (She claimed me as hers. I think it had something to do with the synonym of cat and whatever. Wink.) I sat on her lap demurely, and put my paws on the table only for a bit of food and a cat sip of what she thought I would really like. Peter Lawford, the organizer, said, "Since the stage is empty, might someone want to grace it with their presence, and sing a song or tell a story or two. Ok JW, looks like you are ready."

Big John was, and he ambled up, and clinked his spurs, (He had come from a set earlier and left his "stuff" on.) and sashayed onto the small stage in the middle of the restaurant. Big John said, "I am sure glad to be here with people that make me happier than a good bean dinner and coyotes yelping out on the trail. That big kitty cat reminds me of a lynx that once had me cornered in a box canyon somewhere on a Hollywood set. He jumped me, and let me show you where he scratched me plenty. Ha! Haw! Ho! ... Next!" Not to worry. Big John ambled off the stage to loud applause and a great drone level and kept the scratches to himself. Whatta' man!

Lawford said, "Are you ready, Marilyn?" and "Meow!" was she ever.

JW ambled and she walked, well, kind of like a big, sexy, slinky tiger. I could hardly believe my eyes. You don't think? She sang two beautiful songs a capella and who cared? So wonderful, charming, warm, and Frank described it best, but I can't repeat it here. Silence was her reward. The ultimate show of awe, and it was like the audience was paralyzed. I walked on the stage and rubbed up against her legs, she picked me up, and none will ever forget that moment.

I continued to purr and meow, as she picked me up and even waved my paws in perfect geometric circles. I blinked instantly as I started to pull on her dress. As I kept tugging on Marilyn's dress, one of my claws got caught in it. When she put me down, the claw remained there, and whoops, down came the top of her dress. No silence now. The applause was shattering. Marilyn smiled and waved, tugged her dress back up, and sat down. I went and sat on the President's lap. Maybe I needed some back up. At the moment, this was the best place in the world to be.

The President said, "You're the best pussycat I have ever seen. You are smarter than all of my cabinet and Vice President combined, even Kissinger, maybe me as well. Something tells me there is a power about you that is not what you seem to be, and perhaps you're not just a cat, surely. Meanwhile, don't get your claws clipped." He then chinchucked me, and I gave him my mysterious Chinese cat smile. He said, "Hope big JW didn't see the cat smile, or he might try and shoot me."

It was Frank's turn. He sang three songs. Three of his greatest and since they are all great, it doesn't matter which ones. By now, I was on Marilyn's lap again, and all was forgiven. Maybe she liked me even more. Ooh, la la! Frank as usual brought the house down, and they should have bronzed the place, except for the cook. The calamari was like rubber. I saw Frank make a cutting motion to his throat to one of his buddies, and then pointed to the kitchen. Uh oh.

Marilyn was getting tired, and again my claws caught onto her dress. All of a sudden, I felt someone tugging on me, and I thought it was Big JW tugging on me, and then I heard, "What are you doing, Casey? You almost pulled the drapes down while you were sleeping. Lucky my team won or I would not have noticed. Not only that, but you were slapping your paws together. You also jumped over the coffee table with yours eyes closed, grabbed a flower, and landed on the couch. You then took a drink out of the flower vase, and let out a big meow. We have to get a patent on your ability to sleep while leaping over stuff with a single bound. You're the greatest!" 'Nuff to make a cat laugh and blush!

# Casey Strikes Again & Hits a Homer!

*T*here is a dog show in progress at the Pac Bell Park. Wow! Just what I want to see! Since one of the members of our club is a honed down 150 pound Lab, I have taken a different outlook at dogs. They eat more than I thought they did and some I have found smoke pipes. (Wrigley, I hope you are listening.) Wrigley is also very thoughtful. At times all that thinking leads to sleep, then one of two things usually happens, either sleep or smoke, except for this time. We were having our usual get together at midnight on top of our three story building sitting on the roof overlooking San Francisco and the beautiful bay. Suddenly Wrigley woofed a small woof but we could tell it was of import.

Seagull Joe, the air taxi specialist, said, "By God Wrigley, glad you put that pipe down and joined the party. What's on your mind?"

Wrigley said, "I guess you all know about the largest dog convention in the world being held at the Pac Bell Park?" We nodded, and Uncle Al meowed. Wrigley blew some smoke in his face, and we all felt as ease. He went on to say, "There is a gigantic monetary purse being paid to the top dog, (*I have never heard him be so clever.*) almost a billion dollar reward in fact. It is a lot like cattle breeding. The winner gets all that money and then is sent out for breeding. Since animals are now being recognized throughout the world as being as much a part of the planet as other things, they are attracting what they have never had before-plenty of trouble."

"Gee whiz," Uncle Al said, "does that include stinking up the environment with smoke and stuff?" (The humor was getting some-what cutting.)

"With all that money they get don't you think they could just eat about twenty hamburgers and call it good?" Wrigley said with a loud woof. He smiled, well it looked like a smile I guess, and said, "Don't forget we saved the Swiss Alps walking around with the little whiskey barrels under our chins. We saved lots of people and during WWII my grand-dog Wilbur told me lots of stories of heroic dog deeds done during the doom days of depression and desolation."

Seagull Joe could not leave that alliteration alone and responded while picking his beak with a herringbone, "Oh, yeah, well howz-about seagulls save some centuries in Sumatra soon after surviving several shots seen sufficient blah blah blah?"

"Enough already," I said, "Ok, Wrigley, will you please tell us what is going on at the Pac Bell Park? Quickly before Uncle Al hurts himself laughing without breathing while lying on his back and waving all his furry feet to and fro." (I get one try anyhow.)

Wrigley began, not without tapping out his pipe, filling it to the brim, making a small woof, lighting a match while striking in on Uncle Al's whiskers, (so there) two puffs to make sure, and in a sonorous tone told us what was happening. Who was doing this dia-bolical plot and how? That's where I would come in, the brains of this outfit. (Don't laugh now or I will tell Wrigley.) "When billions of dollars are involved in a project that is just beginning, there are many loopholes that the criminal minds can exploit. For example, they could make sure who will win the contest, or make sure who

will not win the contest. Then there is the bookie element, the bribery business, and if I told you any more, they might arrest me. (Just
kidding...I'm too smart for a bunch of those kinds of dogs.) There
are three showings leading up to the selection of top dog of all the
dogs in the world. Simple enough, whoever gets the best showings
will win, and billions of dollars are given to the winner."

'Nuff to make a cat jealous... almost. After two showings, when
everyone thought a particular dog was going to win, some of the
judges had simply called in sick. There was talk of financial bail-
outs, and some dogs had suddenly come down ill. Methinks something smells in Denmark. The first thing we had to do was to go to
the Pac Bell Park to see what was going on and do some selective
looking around, and make some suggestions, if need be, into the
minds of certain people which might prove invaluable.

John had been listening, and said, "Jump in the car and let's
take a look. We know dogs are awake most of the time, so any time
is perfect, right Wrigley?" To which, Wrigley just caught the pipe
falling from his mouth and stifled what almost looked like a yawn.

Off we went. There were people walking around the park, and I
immediately found out what would help us. There were some suspicious looking characters hanging out on a street corner wearing
trench coats with the collars pulled up as in the days of Bogart and
Bacall. I took a quick glance peek into their minds, and it found a
very strong lead as to what was going on. Even more unusual was
that they were wolves, yes, the real kind with tremendous disguises I must say. Only their small shoes were the dead giveaway. They
were all clean shaven, wearing glasses, smoking cigars, wearing
leather gloves, with Bogart hats, of course. Their minds revealed
who the winner would be and who was behind the diabolical dog
dilemma.

Wrigley started telling us about it. Today at 2 p.m. the winner of all the dogs in the world would be chosen. I had to make sure it all was done properly, and the first thing I did was to bring back the so called "sick" judges. They confessed and told a judge that they had received life ending threats to them and their families. What could else they do? John contacted the police commissioner of the San Francisco force and told him what was going on. Aha! The top financier of the show was contacted and "realized" the error of his ways. The punishment would be much less if they would fully confess to which they agreed. The financier of the nefarious plot was Dog Chow. The bigger the dog that won the competition the more money they would make, so they obviously wanted an Irish Wolfhound to win. Figures...hence the wolves on the street corner, probably watching all the dogs go by. Uh, where was I? Oh yes, they would make sure that a certain type of dog did not make it to the competition such as a twelve ounce French Poodle. (Some of the Irish don't like the French very much anyhow.) Simply, their dog would win and Dog Chow would get a big pay off. Irish Wolfhounds weigh about 150 pounds. (Watch out Wrigley.) Easy math says that a 150 pound dog and a twelve ounce dog have different eating habits.

The show began on time. Hundreds of beautiful dogs from all over the world, and yes, there was the twelve ounce French Poodle, the 150 pound Wolfhound, and by golly, there was a good looking Labrador doing his huffing and puffing with the judges. (He looked kind of heavy to me.) The crowd was abuzz. Everyone was so excited with anticipation. The dogs were at their best behavior, running along so grandly and smoothly, and then standing just so while they were inspected by the judge. Even I must say so, being a cat and such, that it was a good show, tut tut, old boy and all that. After much deliberation, judges going here and there, much hand waving, sighs and cries throughout, it was decided by 2 p.m. that they had selected a winner. It was the magnificent 150 pound Labrador.

I had noticed one of the judges to be dressed not unlike the wolves at the corner last night. He too had on a big Humphrey Bogart hat and had an all around funky way about him. I also noticed wisps of smoke coming out from under the hat only noticeable to me. Ahem, do you think? Naaaah! 'Nuff to make a cat laugh!

# Tiny Bubbles, Catsinos, Yellow Slickers...What?

"Cats Gone Wild" was the headliner on the San Francisco Chronicle this Sunday morn. The article went on to explain that suddenly thousands of cats were seen all over San Francisco where before they were hardly noticeable. In the Sports Page section one cat was seen walking on top of the scoreboard in center field stopping for awhile and licking itself clean. Later a hot dog wrapper was found where he had been. Somebody said the dog in hot dog was what the cat was making fun of, like I kicked the dog out of him, he dogged it, and doggone it, and... I refused to read anymore of that drivel. The main message was there were cats where cats had not been seen before becoming bossy, meowing and waving their paws in circles and doing circular cat dances for whatever the onlooker's bill of fare might be. They were getting more fussy and demanding day by day as were their numbers. So far they had caused no actual trouble but they were pushing what cats push...everything. A great number of cats had gone to the trolley car tunnel, got into the car with such density that the doors could not be opened until the cats were bribed with food. By that time the commute was a mess and some cats seemed to be smiling and giving the chinchuck to the trolley authorities. Harrumph! And, that isn't all as the story continued.

In the famed Transamerica Building thousands of cats were running from floor to floor, up and down, and in and out, and setting off
alarms. To keep themselves fed, they rifled the vending machines of
food and some were found sleeping on the president's desk belching
and would not listen to any type of bribery. The SPCA specifically
said they must be treated with decency and delicacy. They explained
how cats had come a long way since the days of being on a Chinese
menu. It was only a short fifty years ago when cat was a featured
delight in China Town. Most people who ate my furry friends said
they tasted like chicken. But the sadness continues.

On Ocean Beach, for a four mile stretch from the Cliff House
going south to the end was lined with who knows how many cats. It
was what a person would think a cat world would be like. Most were
sunning themselves and lots of them apparently had families too.
Some were in the water acting like seaweed and catching a number of fish that way. The fishermen thought this was a good idea
and bargained with some of them to come aboard and help them
fish. But there were still too many cats for anybody to understand.
They even took over the volley ball places, using their own nets and
rules, and the beachcombers and volleyball jocks were put out. A
few challenged the cats to some games and were quickly dispatched.
The winner stays. They said the cats were too sly and did things
they had never seen before. One group of cats simply had a cat riding the volley ball at all times. If the beach bums, 'er 'combers, or
jocks tried to hit the ball, they were hissed at. Some were whapped
in the head by the tail and lots of cat batting went on as well. The
cats were making a mockery of the rules. Hundreds of cats would
gather around a game and make all kinds of cat noises, and it was
impossible to play like that the beach boys said. They were eating
fish and throwing the bones under the feet of the players. One group
even had cat cheerleaders doing what looked like very naughty cat

dances. There was talk of gambling. Some small cats would roll out and cat bat around for awhile.

The most disturbing thing was what appeared to be gambling going on. A hundred cats or so would dig up a couple tons of sand and build what looked like a gambling casino. Somehow they had rigged up a type of lighting system that blinked on and off. It attracted lots of attention and soon a steady stream of people was seen going into the cat casino. They had to crawl as the cat engineers were not used to such big gamblers. It was said that already, at the end of the beach, they were building a casino on the rocks that was big enough for anybody. Some fishermen were seen to anchor their boats and go in. Laughter from inside ensued, and they left later very happy indeed. One fisherman was only "wearing" sandals upon leaving saying he had a lot of fun, and mentioned you had to be real quick at dice. The cats ran around in a circle on the craps table, served cat drinks, and got the players dizzy, fun but hard to win. Cats were swinging back and forth on trapezes hanging from the ceiling wearing very scanty cat clothes. "Helluva show," one fisherman said, "easy parking too. I'm coming back after I sell more fish. They got all the money I had at Dead Fish Poker, very complicated, and they said they didn't have change for ten dollar bills." "Damn good business men, 'er cats, if you ask me," another said. Those gambling at the casinos ran, walked, crawled, meowed, or purred all the time. How could anybody resist? The cats made everything so easy.

All you had to do at the newer casino was walk in, get on some kind of a cat track that went around the place, and get off when something caught your eye. Cat booze was free. The cats were so nice, purring and waving their tails in people's faces that one could not resist. The cats said half of the money was donated to charity, and they used the rest for catnip and whatever else they damn well pleased, being catty, with real cat-chy sense of humor as well. In no time, all was forgotten about the cat walking on top of the score-board in center field while eating a hotdog in perhaps some kind of an animal challenge. Four solid miles of beach with casinos every-where and everybody was happy. You think?

Soon it was advertised in the San Francisco Cat, they even had their own newspaper, that a bigger cat casino would soon be built. It would be the best of its kind in the world. (Since this would be the only one, how could one argue? But again, cats are very clever. Some were even writing books, ahem.) This great catsino would cover the entire beach. Everything one could want or think of would be there. It was already to open on the Fourth of July. Cats and people by the thousands would be there with hundreds of boats an-chored offshore; people everywhere, music in the air, lots of meows and laughter, it would be glorious! It was to be a four mile long catsino where everything was free, except of course, if you decided to gamble. Have to remember it was to be made out of sand with some kind of reconstituted cat invention. People and cats would be riding around in the catsino on the cat tracks and having the time of their lives, too much of a good thing. Murphy's Law always pre-vails, even with cats.

Storm warnings were issued and everyone scurried to their homes and was soon safe enough. The storm hit with lightning force and fury. Huge waves crashed upon the shore smashing into the sea-wall throughout the night. In the morning all was bright and clear on the four mile stretch of beach just next to the historic Cliff House but the catsino had disappeared. What's a cat to do! The large influx of cats had seemingly gone away with the storm. Where did they go? It was as if the cats, the catsino, the gambling, the entire aura of good times and camaraderie between the cats and the rest of San Francisco had sadly left.

John and I went to the beach and took a look around. We walked in the hills beyond the beach and only a few of my furry friends were about. I said that I knew what had happened, and they just meowed quietly and went about their business, mainly watching bugs on bushes. (They didn't have a nice windowsill like I do.) We went to the docs where many great ships were getting ready to go out with the tide. One especially large ship was going to Hawaii with a manifest of mainly dock workers and assorted crates. As we were watching the large ship get loaded, something caught my every vigilant cat eye. Aha! Was that a tail waving out from under one of the yellow rain slickers on the "people" boarding the boat? It was! We went to one of the all night restaurants on the wharf and saw many more yellow rain slickers walking about drinking coffee. They were not particularly tall, and the hoods of the slickers covered all of their faces, and they wore tiny boots. Upon closer inspection it was found there were three cats to each coat. They sat on each other's shoulders and were quite passable for being a short dock worker that way.

I peeked into a few of their minds and soon found out what had really happened. Tons of catnip had washed up on the beach in the Hawaiian Islands getting the cats completely bombed on the one thing they can't seem to deal with. Top cats had evolved and said it was time to the land of milk and sardines, and that did it. They got on board the large ships using their yellow rain slicker routine, and people were never the wiser, until they were washed out and the catnip wore off. Not to worry, they had a wonderful time, and their pockets were stuffed with money. They would never have to work again. Huh? Maybe not all the catnip had worn off. I just read the Hawaiian Gazette, and there were many Don Ho lookalikes singing at clubs on Waikiki, and mysteriously gambling business was picking up quickly on the beach. Don Ho was reported to have a very beautiful voice and could hit any high note while singing wearing a yellow slicker. (I think they were more right than they knew when they said high note.) His tiny feet went along great with the song, "Tiny Bubbles" and yellow slickers were the fad. Everybody had to have one. 'Nuff to make a cat laugh!

# Time Travel to Russia

My experiences in time travel were so much fun and educational that I had to do some more of it. Even with all my great mental power, I must never be content. I must always continue to search everywhere to improve my perfection, except for humility-ahem.

I decided to revisit the big three, President Kennedy, Sinatra, and Marilyn and whomever else Frank brings over for "dinner." (That Frankie is always on the move. A few can call him Frankie, the special ones. Only the President and his mother can call him Francis, Frank, and Frankie. Francis is "somewhat" complicated.) I returned to my usual place on the kitchen counter. Marilyn and Frank were busy fixing something. Could be a drink, you think?

Marilyn said to Frank, "Oh look! My favorite pussy has returned. Where has he been? He is so cute! Don't you just love him, Frankie?

Frank said, "Goddammit! Quit calling me Frankie! If that slips when the President is around, that could be the end of your happy home!"

Marilyn said, "Oh, but he is so precious!" She picked me up, gave me a smooch, and chinchucked me. I gave a small meow and pushed against her, ahem, bosom. Marilyn smiled, hugged me closer, and said, "Oh, naughty kitty!" Even Frank laughed. "We should give him a name, Frank, what do you think?"

"I think we will call him gone if he keeps getting on the counter!" At that moment, Frank's eyes and mine met. In a millionth of a second, I looked into his mind and read it all completely from the time he was born until now. (Very, very interesting) I also "suggested" that I would have sovereign reign wherever I went. I was extremely special, and I was to be treated as such. Frank immediately said, "Oh, you're so right, Marilyn. He is a dandy, beautiful sweetheart. We'll let him do and go anywhere he wants, except the wine cellar. He could get hurt in there. I also think I saw some purple on the tips of his whiskers a few times." Frank smiled kindly, came over, and petted me. Our eyes met again. Frank was happily confused. He gave me the famous Sinatra wink. As I blinked back, he then looked almost nervous, but said, "Let's name him Casey. Whatta' yuh think about that Marilyn?"

She said, "Oh wonderful, Frank, that's a perfect name. You're so clever!"

"Ok," Frank said, "you want to use the car again, or you're low on cash? Just ask and quit giving me all that BS. I'd throw you around a little, but I'm thinking about having you in my next movie, and I don't want any bruises."

"Oh, grrrrr," she said, "Give me some money now and where are the car keys, sweetie." Smooch smooch. Too much smooching for a cat… first me, and now Frank.

As I saw the Rolls pull away, Frank looked at me and said, "Crazy, goddamn broads!" Then he laughed. I meowed. We were buddies for life. The President arrived shortly after sundown. His mood was very somber. We could all tell he had something on his mind. (I mean he was 'THE' man in the whole world, after all.) Frank said, "What the hell, John, Let's go in the study, have a sip, and tell me what's going on, if you want. Here, grab Casey, the cat.

We just named him. I'm pretty sure he is "very good luck." Frank gave me a fleeting glance as if to say, *"Well now, aren't you the real cat's meow after all."* The Prez picked me up and liked me instantly. I could sense right away, the worry and indecision were melting away.

John said, "This is indeed a very beautiful cat. I was about to make a pussy joke, but I am the Prez."

Frank said, "The night is still young." John put me on one of the chairs in the study. They picked up their drinks, sat down, and began to talk-the big two plus me.

Kennedy began to talk right away. He had calmed down since entering, and he explained the situation to Frank. He said, "First of all, Frank, this must never leave your study. This is what's happening!" "The Russians are about to put missile bases all over Cuba. We can't let them. How should we stop them?"

Frank, an extremely intelligent man, despite what some of the scorned journalists report, said, "At first glance, threaten them with a visible show of air power. Tell them, don't ask, that we have to talk this matter over, and right now! Set up a meeting out here in the desert."

"Thanks for your succinct and quick rely to a very dangerous situation," as Kennedy smiled and said, "I was almost thinking the same thing as well. I know I can always count on you not to tell me what I want to hear. Anyway, you have a better job than I do! For now," John said, "This is all we can do. I'll call Khrushchev in the morning and tell him we must meet. Pour us another round Frank, and I'll give Casey a pet for good luck." After the President gave me a pet, I meowed with enthusiasm, stood on my hind feet, and gave him a quick, but firm cat bat. John smiled with surprise, and said, "Whatta' pussy!"

Frank looked at me, winked, and said, "You got that right. There's more to him than meets the eye. There's a pussy joke in there again, but what the hell, the night is still young, and hey, that's a good title for a song!"

"Which one," John said, "The night is still young, or there must be pussy around here somewhere?" Hearty laughter filled the study.

"Speaking of pussy," Franks said, "Oops, there's that word again—goddammit—everything we say sounds like a title for song. How about, 'Midnight in Moscow'? Just can't stop. Let's go get the girls!"

"Can't wait," the Prez said, "Whom do you have tonight, you old charmer you?"

"Gina Lollobrigida," Frank said, "Gotta' stick with the country that brought me into this world." The President picked me up and out we went to meet the ladies. I knew this was going to be interesting, indeed! The night flew by. Gina took care of me personally. She put me in her purse where I could listen and see to all that went on. Everyone was completely charming and well behaved, except me. I put the glom on some of Gina's stuff. *I know, I know, naughty kitty cat, but John would get a kick out of it. All Gina could do was blame one of the big three. It's impossible. (There goes another song title.)*

The next day, the President had to leave at 4 am. (It's not all hugs and Irish mugs.) I transported myself to where the meeting would be. I would be the translator between Kennedy and Khrushchev. (Place your bets on this conversation.) The meeting took place with about fifty people in the room. Among them were various diplomats, guards, journalists, and people of note on both sides. There were to be no type of weapons whatsoever in the room. I noticed immediately there were two Russians who were wearing "bomb suits." Explosive material was blended into their clothing making them walking time bombs. All they had to do was trigger the explosive, and everyone in the room would be destroyed. I "contacted" their minds instantly, and "suggested" that they leave the room immediately. Run to the back of the parking lot that was completely bare, and blow themselves up. Kaput, they did it. The explosion was heard, and President Kennedy said to Khrushchev, (From now on it's "K") "I know what you and your people have been up to now." I was translating this to "K" instantly as President Kennedy spoke. "We just heard them blow themselves up in the parking lot."

Up to now, President Kennedy had been a gracious, understanding, charming host speaking to "K" with goodwill, reason, and calmness. He now said with implacable resolve, "I am sick of all your stupid, pushy bullshit. You are a big, fat, ugly, ill dressed, fraud, and a consummate asshole. If you and the rest of your mindless, shithouse, good for nothing fuckups are not out of here in thirty minutes, United States Marine time, you will all be shot lots! Then, Cuba, and then, your chicken shit ice block locker of what you call a country." President Kennedy was speaking in a very loud voice for all in the room, and maybe some outside even, to hear. "Get going, you stupid mother fucker! In the dictionary under drizzling shits is your picture!" I think I heard some laughter. President Kennedy could cuss real good. He'd seen and been in live combat, saved lives, and half crippled himself in the process. No fat-assed, chicken shit, mumblin' fumblin', cross-eyed asshole was going to bully the United States of America, by God! Twice now Kennedy's Irish temper was hot. (*I did a real good job of translating too, and I hardly embellished it at all, you think?*)

I jumped up, screamed, and all the assholes ran out doors that were already opened, and went into cars that had the motors running. US Marine time for 30 minutes is 25 minutes, and then "K" and his flunkies were off the tarmac in 20 minutes. Our fighters surrounded and buzzed them for the next half hour. After they left, a security man came over and placed a large purse by Kennedy. "What is this?" he said. He then looked into the purse, and voila! "How did you get in here, Casey?" he said, "Guess we forgot about you in all the commotion."

Now it was back on Air Force I and then on to Frank's house. On the way, they decided to play cards and I thought, "What the heck? He is the President!" The Prez won every hand, and made about $25 dollars. The rest were in awe, "It's just my lucky cat," the Prez said.

Back at Frank's house, everything was told to Frank of how he had won every hand at cards. Frank gave me a knowing smile and said, "Really?" I then sauntered out unobserved and went home.

I told John, my John, what had happened. I also gave to him what I had "liberated" from Gina Lollabrigida's sweet smelling purse. Phooey, now I had to take another bath. I don't know what he is going to do with the lipstick, no comments please, but he should be able to put the diamond rings to good use. She was smothered in jewels anyhow. 'Nuff to make a cat laugh a lot!

# Took a Nap & Went to Mass

Time for a nap. That's what we cats always say. Right now, I was so tired that I simply had to roll up inside John's window curtain. It would be a good hideout where I could catch some cat winks. I was asleep I think, then again, John and I had just returned for Rome. We had been to the Vatican for a special cat mass with me. Somewhere in an ancient scripture, it was implied that Jesus had a cat. I continued to sleep or not sleep. It seemed completely real.

I was at the altar with the Pope, just the two of us. I had been outfitted to look like a miniature pope. I had to stand up, of course, which I can do very well, and hold a crucifix with a large envelope like hat on my cat head. It fit perfectly. I also wore the same vestments the pope did except I only had a cross on my back where the "real" pope had a cross on both the front and the back of his vestments. For some reason, I was also wearing glasses with a gold chain attached around my neck, for what reason I don't know why. I had on some very pretty red silk shoes. *How they got them to fit I will never know.* My gloves were tailor made for four fingers. I was the cat's meow!

As the pope moved around the altar, singing in Latin, and I don't mean Spanish, to some kind of tone that came from within, I too, sang the exact same words three beats after he did. It would sound like a kind of echo. I filled St. Peter's Basilica beautifully. Even if I was a note or two behind, I would mix in a meow. After all this was a cat mass. The pope and I were saying mass at a perfect pace. It was called a high/low mass since it was partially for animals; it could not be a proper high mass. That is against the rules. The choir would chime in at appropriate times, and it was so beautiful! The pope, me, the choir, and some people attending mass would break out in a Gregorian chant here and there and every sound with the great acoustical ability of St. Peter's Basilica mixed in so perfectly.

Soon, it was time for the offertory that is when all prayers are offered up to God, the saints, and whomever. Today the cats were the "whomever". Wine is poured by the altar boys to the pope and today, by me as well, to signify a bonding of prayers. I was given a special cat glass, and the pope has his own sixty year old chalice given to him by his dear mother. We were to drink the wine, say some prayers in Latin out loud, and continue with the mass. Refills were optional. Ahem. The pope went for a refill and well, when in Rome… After we drank the wine, the very best by the way, we continued with the mass at a greater speed. We sang a little louder and a little faster. The pope did a few quick steps that only I could see, I think, as he moved around the altar. Me too. He also mixed in a few blessings and mumbled "Hallelujah" under his wine breath.

Soon it was time for a small biblical reading and the holy interpretation thereof. The pope placed me on top to the left side of the pope pulpit. (Cats don't qualify for the right side just yet.) He was smiling grandly now and read the verses with vigor. Since this was a mass for cats, I would meow when he gave a small tug on my tail. (It was hanging out just under my robe.) When he wanted a bigger meow, he would tug harder. After awhile, I was getting a lot of tugs, one big tug in fact. I took a quick look into the pope's mind, and he needed help. I told him to sit off to the side in one of the high backed velvet chairs for now, and I would "wrap it up."

I gave everyone in the church, which numbered a few thousand, including news agencies, heads of state, paparazzi, and celebrities from all over the world, and of course, almost as many cats, a complete "cat papal temporary hypnotism dispensation." They were to hear and interpret only what I wanted. I stood up grandly on the pope pulpit and meowed melodically for everyone to hear while waving my paws and tail to and fro about what every individual wanted to hear right down to a cat's meow. If they wanted to be happy, forgiving, conquering, healthy, smart, rich, or you name it, they got it. It only took me about two minutes with my special cat abilities. (*Hmmm, I wonder what was in the wine?*)

By now the pope was alert again. He got up and placed me on the altar. We finished the mass shortly, and it was reported that everybody had never been to a better mass. It was seriously suggested that somewhere in biblical history a cat must have helped a martyr. Therefore, making a cat a saint, Saint Casey, it was so declared. I was so happy after reading the article that I... I felt as though the pope was picking me up again. Did I hear the paparazzi laughing? Was I tripping on my robe? Had that powerful papal pour caught me off guard? I now had to move around as fast as possible because I felt I was going to trip. Maybe I would knock the pope into the wine bar.

More laughing! I opened my eyes and John was holding me completely wrapped up in the curtain. A wine bottle had been spilled on the coffee table and my tail was wet. I had John's sock and swimming goggles on my head. My throat was also raspy like I had been meowing or talking a lot. I looked around the room.

John said, "Your Uncle Al has been tugging on your tail trying to get you to wake up. Better go easy on that spilled wine next time.

Boy, can you meow when you want to! Best of all was when you stood up on the coffee table, after knocking off the wine bottle and taking a sip, hopping around on your hind feet and meowing 'When the Saints Come Marching In'."

"Ok, I get it," I said. "But how many of you are a living saint?"

'Nuff to make a cat laugh!

# Dreaming...I'm Always Dreaming

*I* know you must be a dreamer as well. Cats dream a lot. Most everything does. The mind never goes to sleep. Dreams are proof of that. I can tell you about my latest dream, and perhaps like yours, they in some way reflect reality. I was taking my usual catnap, and after my last dream where I went into outer space and returned a cowcat, I was more cautious about my sleep this time. I did not get overly tired before I took my nap, and I did not go to sleep on a full belly. John saw me yawn and said, "Should I lock up the fridge, or put the napkins away?" A big ha ha followed. He was half asleep as well watching some stupid John Wayne show. "Howdy pahdner, don't forget your horse or you'll lose your wagon. Har Har Har!" Maybe that is where John, my human buddy, gets all his funky jokes.

At any rate, I felt a nap coming on. One falls into dreams slowly. You don't realize you are dreaming until something tells you that you are. You can choose to participate, wake up or forget it. In this nap I was taking, I felt the dream coming on, and I decided to participate. It was another one of those flying dreams. There I went over trees and houses, and then over The City. I flew over the Golden Gate Bridge, and headed out to Honolulu. It seemed that in no time at all I was there. I was getting hungry by now, so I flew down into a part of town that looked like it had some food and down I went. Since I was in Honolulu, I decided to get some kind of a Hawaiian dish. I see where I had brought along my backpack this time, and I had some clothes that would let me dress up and fit into various environments. I put on a Hawaiian shirt, some sandals and a floppy hat complete with sun glasses. Who could possibly know?

I went into an upscale restaurant and received not too many curious glances, so I continued into the lounge. I was very lucky in my dreams as well. It was happy hour. I got a plate and sat down, and ordered something that I saw someone else was drinking. Have to fit in you know. After eating my fill, I was ready to go back, but upon walking out of the restaurant, I was amazed I could not fly. I was stuck. Now what? I kind of realized that I was still sleeping, but yet I was almost convinced that I was stuck in Honolulu with a full belly because I ate so much happy hour food, and was now too fat to fly. Getting back on a boat would take too long. Hmmm, maybe a plane would work, but I would have to give John a call and tell him. I tried to call him but could not get through. I checked the air line schedules, and I decided to take the first one out. "Off we went, into the high blue places, flying off into the sky..." I was trying to sing the WWII flying song, but the words evaded me in my dream. (I was not as cognizant in my dream as I was in real life. I never made a mistake in real life. Dreams were precarious.) We landed, and once again, I tried to fly, but could not do it. Took the train into The City, walked home and came into the study. There was John still watching a John Wayne movie. Har, Har, Har! And... there I was, sleeping on the floor. Huh? I walked over and melted into myself on the floor. ZZZZZZZZZzzzzzzzzzz

Soon, I awoke and looked around. John's closet door was open and his Hawaiian shirt was missing. The kitchen stove was on, and there were noodles and stuff cooking in a pot. One empty Bud can was on the counter, and some sandals were lying in the middle of the floor. John woke up, looked at me, and said, "Well, it must be these

John Wayne shows that get you going. After John Wayne shot a few men and won a card game, you jumped up, ran around the room real fast, and then put on one of my shirts. You ran into the kitchen and told me to bring over some cooked noodles and a beer. Then, you got on the phone and tried to book a flight to where we are. Are you guys smoking too many cigars up there by the chimney?" More Har, Har, Hars followed.

Really? Thank goodness I don't have those dreams very often. The next time I will have to go hungry and not land. Trying to go to sleep and have a flying dream while you are asleep is too complicated. Sweet dreams. Nighty night and sleep tight. After all, it's only a dream.

# Jim and Louie

$T$he church bells are ringing, I almost said, for me and my gal, but I only meowed softly as John and I were on the way for our morning walk. We just got out the gate and a man with a rather big yellow Labrador retriever passed by us. A beautiful dog, rather heavy, about 120 pounds, I would guess. I took a peek into his mind and heard him say, "*Nice looking cat, but I think in a fair fight, I would win.*" I could not resist.

I said, "In a fair fight, you would not have a chance. I can read your mind. I also know that you are of tremendous character, and I would like to meet you."

His name was Jim, and he said, "Aha, smarty cat pants, let me see what you can do." Kiddingly, I gave him a math problem, and he woofed, "Not fair!" We laughed together.

Our owners said, "They seem to be getting along quite well. Should we introduce them to each other?" I jumped out of the backpack and walked over quietly with dignity and communicated to him with my reading and mind melding ability.

I said, "Do you live around here, and would you like to get together to talk or do something?"

He said, "Yes, my name is Jim, and for being a cat, you seem ok." He then pawed the ground, smiled, and woofed at me. I think he may have winked as well. He went on to say that he lived two doors down, and that tonight was a good night, and so come on over.

At the bewitching hour of midnight, I went over to see Jim, and we introduced ourselves again. He told me he was a 120 pound Labrador retriever of good character, and that he had never met a cat before, that he didn't chase, that is. But, he was always kidding when he did.

Jim said, "I like your style. You are indeed a cat, but in some ways, you seem like a dog to me."

I smiled mysteriously and said, "Oh, well, want to go for a walk."

Jim said, "Sure, but I hope you can keep up. I walk very fast and you have short legs. Ha! Ha!"

I said, "Look at me Jim, and tell me what you see."

Jim said, "Shut up, and get on and let's go for a stroll." (Dogs use different words.) I jumped right up. Jim laughed, and said, "I hope you have money for a taxi. Ha! Ha!" Jim headed right down to the wharf. We were both thinking our own thoughts, seeing and smelling and hearing the sounds of the wharf and the bay.

About a block away from the bay Jim said, "Do you want to go to the beach and meet a friend of mine?"

I said, "A friend of yours is a friend of mine." (Our bonding was completed with that reply.)

We went down to the very edge of the beach where the water was only a few feet from us. All of a sudden the water riffled, and a huge seal popped out of the water. He and Jim exchanged greetings, and Jim introduced me to Louie. Louie sure was a very big seal, about 4oo pounds. He was very sensitive about his weight, so I did not ask more precisely. Jim spoke to Louie and said this and that and asked him what was happening in the bay?

Louie looked at me suspiciously and said, "Can I trust that cat?"

"Heck no, Louie, after all he is a cat!" Jim said. Louie, Jim, and I had a good laugh. Anyone listening would have been scared to hear a dog barking, cat meowing, and a seal barking and dousing off with water spewing out, altogether was a crazy sound.

Louie said to me, "Nice to meet you. Don't get to meet many land lubbers nowadays. How yuh doin' and all that?"

I said, "I am Jim's neighbor, and we seemed to hit it off. Here we are speaking to a guy with a permanent rain coat, beady eyes, and whiskers bigger than mine. What are you up to?"

Bon homie and camaraderie was instantly recognized, and Louie said, "There is something real strange going on here. At the end of Pier 43 there is a strange thing coming out of the water every night. It wakes up all of us, and my wife, Florence, has told me to make it stop. I'm under a lot of pressure."

I asked Louie when does this thing come up and where? He said he would be glad to show us, and that he would meet us at the end of Pier 43. Ten minutes later, we were all there. Jim and I were sitting at the end of the pier, and Louie was looking at us from the water's edge. He said, "Usually, at about this time, some kind of a thing pops out of the water that looks like a tea pot. A window appears and some little people come out and walk around on the tea pot. The water gushing over the teapot makes a lot of noise and wakes up Florence. Something must be done." Louie said, "Let's wait. Any time now, you will see what I am talking about."

Sure enough, within minutes, bubbling occurred, and a thing like a teapot popped out of the water and shot a walkway to Pier 43. Four little people, aliens for sure, came across the walkway and got on Pier 43. I looked into their minds, and saw they were on an exploratory mission from who know where, and they were taking a look around. Upon getting onto the pier, they put on some clothes to make them look like humans. Louie started to laugh when he saw this, and we had to wrestle him around a little to get him to shut up. He apologized and started to laugh some more. Jim was beginning to bark and woof, and I knew I had a big job. We decided to follow them, and see what they were planning to do. First of all, we had to disguise Louie. We got a hat, a Hawaiian shirt, and some kind of baggy pants. Louie wanted glasses and a cigar. Ok already. Off we go following four aliens. Just us, Louie, a seal, Jim, a real big good looking Labrador retriever, and humble me. I had to get off to the side for a while, so they would not hear my tears of happy laughter. Some kind of laughter, but it sure was funny seeing him all dressed up that way.

We followed the four aliens into some kind of an ice cream shop and sat down. Louie looked a lot like W.C. Fields walking a dog, and no one noticed me. I walked in the shadows. (Good title for a Bogart movie.) Somehow the aliens had mastered the English language and ordered ten milkshakes. They paid in one hundred dollar bills, and then told the waitress to forget it. (They didn't have the language down pat as of yet.) Ha! Ha! Louie was getting hungry, so he ordered lots of food. He ate most of it, and Jim and I had to laugh and ask him if was worrying about his weight?

Louie said, "First, my wife, and now you guys. If I wasn't dressed up like W.C. Fields, I would give you a big splash." (He said something other than big splash, but you get the message.)

The aliens and Louie finished their chow at the same time. When they walked out of the ice cream shop, so did we. They looked a lot like most tourists wearing clothes that were all funky and didn't fit. It was perfect. About four doors down, they turned into the Highlights Restaurant on Pier 43, the best lounge and restaurant on the pier. All of us exchanged glances. Louie sniffled, Jim woofed, and I meowed. This was going to be too easy. The four aliens, dressed up like you name it, walked into the lounge, sat down at a table and ordered four Irish coffees apiece. Jim started to woof, almost barked, Louie's whiskers were going all over the place, and I almost hurt myself trying not to laugh. It was a big table, enough for ten, so you guessed it. We went over, sat down, and acted like down home earth people. The aliens immediately took to Louie since he was so big, and they equated that with strength and leadership. (Probably right.) They asked Louie all kinds of questions. Meanwhile, they bought forty more Irish coffees for the tables, and tipped the waitress six hundred dollars. (The money looked crisp and shiny. Hmmm…I thought.) Jim sat at the table being silent and drinking a "coffee." One alien asked him some questions, and Jim just woofed. Louie snuffled a lot, and I let out a fat meow. There was so much noise nobody could hear us. After about an hour of discussing what four aliens, a seal, a big dog, and the top cat of the universe, would talk about, we all agreed to see where the aliens lived.

We went down to the end of Pier 43. An alien pushed what we thought was a nose, and the teapot popped up, the walkway appeared, and we all went aboard. *Hey nice place*, I thought. They told us they were traveling around, and having a hard time figuring out what "this" was all about, very theosophical.

It was now my turn. I stood up on my hind feet balancing on my tail and told them how it is. I said I would only tell them once, and then they would forget it immediately. They all nodded their heads, and even Louie snuffled and did the same thing. I explained how all that is and is not, and how it intertwines to and fro, and in and out, then disappears, and comes back in another guise, continuing continuum, as it were. The aliens, I think all of them had been to some type of an alien college, looked at me with glazed eyes after about 150 Irish coffees, nodded, and said in unison, "By Hooley Gooley, we have finally found the all of the wherewithal. Guess we can all go home now." (Hooley Gooley is what they called their god.) Louie, aka W.C. Fields, started to snuffle, and said I reminded him of his wife, and the blarney she told him when he over did it on sardines. More snuffling and loud seal barks broke out. Jim said to me, "Jump on, we have to get home before the kids miss me." 'Nuff to make a cat laugh! Maybe, shed a tiny cat tear as well.

# Lost in Space, Really!

*I*t's a good day today! It's because I introduced cards to the members of my "club" last night. We gather together quite frequently at my house. Well John just pays the bills, and we do what people in clubs do. I can't tell you because it is a secret. It's because we really don't know either, but last night while overlooking the city of San Francisco and the bay, I brought up the subject of cards.

My Uncle Al said, "Sure, I could always use the money, Meow, Meow" while giving an especially big Cheshire cat grin.

Wrigley, the loyal but sufficiently overweight lab said, "What was that? I was just getting my pipe going, and then Al started meowing all over the chimney. Good thing I am such that I am or else…" Puff puff. "There now, what was it you were saying?"

I said, "What do you think of playing cards? Ever been to a casino? Might be a chance for you to get even with Al for all his meowing? After all, you are such a deep thinker. A good deal of card playing is simply knowing what the other guy has in his hand. Not to worry, we won't be playing cards with women. You might be a natural."

Wrigley replied, "Harrumph, you sound like an encyclopedia salesman, and don't worry women don't sell encyclopedias anymore."

"Touché! Enough already," I said, "let me show you how to play cards. I will be the dealer, and the dealer decides what kind of a card game will be played. After each game, there is a different dealer, and the new dealer decides what kind of a game shall be played. Let's go!" I dealt out one card to each member at the table. I said, "This is cat poker. You pick up the card and put some bubble gum on the back. Don't look at the card, but place the card to your forehead and carry on. Anybody got any bubble gum? Now it is time to bet. After all the bets are made the person with the highest card wins all the stuff. Any questions?"

Wrigley said, "I will bet my dog house."

Al said, "I will bet the combination to the sardine factory on Pier 35!"

Joe said, "The best dumpster in china town."

I said, "One week of caviar."

We were very excited and could not wait to see who won the first round when all of a sudden there was a screeching sound in the sky and large rays of light were flickered all over the bay area from above. First things first! I was looking forward to the combination of the sardine factory but another time.

Seagull Joe piped up and said, "Looks like this is a job for me and my boys. We cover the entire bay area going out to a two hundred mile radius. I was sure looking forward to all that caviar. We'll get on it right now and let you know what is going on.

Wrigley said, "Humph, I want to come along to find out who those people are. Not a bit civilized at all, if you ask me."

Al meowed in, "I will let my army of cats know, too. I imagine this will be a pretty big sardine job-makes me hungry just thinking about it. Not to mention I was looking forward to sleeping in Wrigley's house with free tobacco too, I bet! Meow!"

We dispersed, and I went in to talk to John. He said, "Let's jump in the car and have a look around. We'll pick up the Chief Inspector of the San Francisco Police and hear what he has to say. Let's bring along some of Castro's cigars to help the chief think." After picking up the chief we drove all around the bay area with the moon roof down on the Bentley. It's really my car. We could hear the screeching ships in the sky and could see all those lights that as suddenly as they began, quickly stopped.

The chief said, "We have reports from the Alameda Naval Station that all their communications were useless while those ships were here. Don't know anything else." He continued to puff vigorously on the Castro cigars, and I decided to take a millionth of a second to look inside his mind. Aha, he knew more than he was telling us. Whatever the things were that caused all the noise and lights and jamming had been to Area 51. The noisy plot was taking some shape.

Since I have had some encounters with outer space phenomenon, I contacted one of my sources and said, "What the meow is going on here? Do those guys mean business or is it Happy New Year where they live. Louie, I must know. I realize you were once one of them, and you made some kind of a truce, but they can't run all over the planet screeching their tires in the air, knocking out our grid systems, and blinding everyone with those lights. This has got to stop. Tell me what you know, please."

Louie said, "I could I could get in real trouble. I like living here and those guys are a bunch of nuts, but I have to be careful. I don't want to go back to outer space and travel all over like an idiot on Star Trek doing nothing but fighting monsters, and there aren't any women on those ships either, and the food and blah blah blah."

"Ok Louie," I said, "you know this will never go beyond us. It looks like a bunch of stupid aliens got all fouled up on some kind of space juice and partied too hard. If these are the aliens who look like palm trees, we can appease them with all the palm trees they want, and Castro cigars as well if they want them. Where are those nuts now?"

Louie said, "They have used their cloaking device which makes them invisible. They have also invented a shrinking ray that enables them to downsize their giant ships to the size of a grain of sand. Diabolical I tell you, and I think you may be right in that they were getting bored traveling all over nowhere and just wanted some action. Since I still have some implanted alien chips in me, I can almost tell you where they are right now but I will "check out" if they will come and try to put me on one of those ships. Ugh! Looking like a palm tree, no female palm trees and traveling a zillion miles a second to nowhere is the worst part, eating fertilizer all the time is pièce de résistance." Louie was very upset. We locked him up for his own good in the most super safe place of all time-the basement of Gino and Carlo's Italian restaurant in little Italy in San Francisco. It was as big as a basketball court and entirely lined with material that absolutely nothing could penetrate except money and sex. Gino and Carlo and their families had been around for centuries. They had learned the secrets of the world. It boils down to essentially the same "stuff" as always, money and sex. That they could handle. As for the rest, John and I, of course, ahem, took care of everything else.

We also had a fairly good idea of where the horny food starved aliens were at the top of the Fairmont Hotel doing what they could in their disguises of grains of sand. They were easy to find. They were stupid enough to land their entire shrunken fleet right in a sand cigarette extinguisher. They thought they had died and went to heaven. So clever and yet there were no women or palm trees or crunched up glass or whatever those space jockeys used for fun. I immediately set off ten Castro cigars in the sand cigarette extinguisher and got them bombed until next year. It smoked out the entire fleet which by now, after being downsized, would fit into a thimble, and down to the basement we went. Yea!

The happy bombed aliens were ready to deal. They could not do anything else. They were put under the investigation microscope, literally, and everything was explained to them. They would trade their knowledge of technology to us here in the United States for women and money. As Tom Jones would sing...“What's new pussy-cat? Whoa, whoa, whoa”...and where was I? They were not exactly in any kind of a bargaining position but we weren't going to tell them that part. We just gave them five alien lifetimes of Castro ci-gars, the most beautiful palm tree plants, thousands of them and “let them go.” Except that by now they were totally baked and the only places they were going would be in their minds. They were placed in a thimble with the spoils of their clever trade, women, which to them were palm tree plants, Castro's cigars, which were the means they would travel all over to nowhere. We even mixed in a zillion year's supply of booze, and since they were in a thimble it only amounted to one tiny bottle. This was all tied together with only the special knowledge of a jeweler's sneaky mind and placed in the urinal in Gino and Carlo's “relief room.”

There were three urinals in the room of far off gazes and grunts and snuffles. One urinal had a picture of Jane Fonda in it, another of Billary, and they were placed in the third. Each depository was carefully monitored and calculated and under a twenty four hour visa with sound and olfactory scrutiny. Much secrecy was involved in Gino and Carlos' with only the most “in the know” aware of this which eventually led to just about everybody in San Francisco, since loose lips sink ships and booze makes loose lips. But only we knew what was in the thimble on the chain in urinal number three. Bombed space aliens who said they were conquering the universe, and had a world conquering fleet as big as the solar systems they were conquering, and it was all "in their minds." (Don't forget the sexy palm trees, cigars, and booze.)

The aliens in the thimble, so the story goes, had tried to take over Gino and Carlos' by going in small size. They had shrunk their entire fleet into a thimble. They had been captured by "a very clever cat" that left them in their thimble and placed them where they are now for all to enjoy. Legend also has it that the sound scrutiny device is turned up for all to hear on special occasions, lots of occasions.

The aliens can be heard to be singing when their urinal is used. "Looks like another bad rain storm settin' in cap'n. Should I break out the extra 'gars for the men? (They could not pronounce cigar properly.) Sure helps those new women grow though. Should I turn on the suck in rain tubes to pull in another zillion gallons of the cleansing yellow rain. Sure tastes good with the 'gars, and the men have taken to bathing in it as well. By god cap'n I have to tell you how dumb that cat was who traded us for all this stuff. He couldn't even talk alien. He just kept making crazy meow noises. Good thing we did not have to deal with the boss. He was about ten times as big as the cat and was making crazy noises at both ends, scared me something fierce. He looked at and made woofing noises. Guess we really pulled the shithouse down over their eyes. What universe are we going to conquer tomorrow? Then again, what the heck, as long as we have these smart 'gars to help us "see", pure outer space rain-water to drink and bathe in, and of course, all those swaying palm trees why, we are masters of this place."

The cap'n said with measured wisdom and unblinking eyes that emitted a blue glow, "Hut tut ensign Far Butt, give the men double rations and let's have the swaying palm trees on the bridge." The cap'n for a moment, while feeling his cap'ns cap getting wet from a leaking line, wondered what made him say bridge. "Har, har," he said, "This is all ours. I better watch the movie the cat gave us when he knew he was ours, "South Pacific", or was it "Mutiny on the Bounty", or...Ensign Far Butt, give me 'nother 'gar. Har har! Uh oh, better give this saucer some more juice. Here comes more solar rain." Meow!

# Ant That a Shame?

*I* keep a sleepy cat's eye on everything, and that is completely natural for me being the know-it-all in the universe. Ho hum. Today, John put me in the backpack, and we began our walk. I stand up in the backpack with my paws on John's shoulders and my head turns to look everywhere. I have to see it all. Today, I saw so many ant hills beginning in our back yard that I had to think. What are the ants doing now? The yard looked like the city was digging up the street. This can't go on.

After our walk we came in the same way we left, and the ants were building even more ant hills. I jumped out of the backpack as John went in, and I sashayed over to the biggest ant hill. As I can communicate with anything, I immediately spoke to the top ant on the pile and told him I wanted to talk to the queen. I read his mind immediately, took about a millionth of a second, and "suggested" to him to do it quickly. I felt the ground shift a bit, a part of the ground slid back, and the queen appeared, looking like she came up on some type of an ant elevator. So very clever! She had attendants with her and proper introductions were made all around. Her name was Lady Be Good. She smiled at me and said, "Well hello Casey, we ants have, if I may pun, tremendous underground communication system. We know some things about you. We ants are all over the world, almost. Antarctica, our original home which was named after us, was destroyed by a foolish crazed polar bear, but that was thousands of years ago. After he destroyed our happy home, the phrase was coined, "He has ants in his pants." We bugged the bear, sorry I feel so silly today, for some time, and he eventually checked into a zoo. That's an animal jail. Better to go to prison than to have ants in your pants all the time.

I said, "How interesting, Lady Be Good, but I am also interested as to why there are so many ant hills springing up in my back yard?" She said, "We want to be safe and reorganize all our members throughout the world. We have had an ant tragedy. Our base ant hill was compromised. Our headquarters is located quite close to where you are. We are also knowledgeable as to the significance of this location. It is one of the high power point places in the world. This is where there are the powers of the planet, and the rest of the world has an open line of communication to each other which is very powerful and significant indeed! You are a very smart cat Casey. I know enough to defer to you. Your sweet smile, beautiful fur, cute meow, and tail wagging belies the fact that there is something very powerful and knowledgeable about you. And, that meow is a great one! So Casey, tell me what you want."

I said, "Well, from what you tell me I would like to help you. I was going to ask you why the whole yard was dug up, but now I know and understand. How can I help you, Lady Be Good, to get all your colonies up and crawling around again? What happened to shake up the ant world?

Lady Be Good said, "It seems innocuous, but here in San Francisco there are lots of tourists walking all over the city that carry booze as they walk. When they have enough they pour it out wherever. Lately some article in the paper said the best way to "put" ants away is to pour booze down their holes. It gets the ants all loose and crazy, and they jump in their ant cars and race around in our tunnels all over the world and cause havoc. We have tunnels connecting all over the world. When the tunnels aren't too busy, you can get from here to Honolulu in about five hours. That's hill to hill. These crazy ant drivers make it in three hours and run over all kinds of our people. It's horrible, and that isn't all. They quit working, won't bite anybody, get fat, and then jump on people going by. They ride all over the place, find more ant hills that are loaded with booze, and don't stop their cavorting. Why, they won't even come to see me anymore. This could be the end of our civilization. It's so very sad because ants are needed for the planet's health and happiness."

"I have the answer," I said, "And here is what you should do. No charge to you. Just leave our lawn sparkling clean and green, and if you want, we can go out to dinner or something. Then again, it might be better if you just tell me what hole you are in, and I will pour discreetly, some Dom Pérignon 4 down your hole of choice. I know you have lots of suitors and that should make everybody happy.

Now, here is what must be done. It sounds like you have the same problem America had with prohibition. That was a crazy law. When it was rescinded, then all fell into place, and the world was saved. You too, Lady Be Good, have to place an edict putting a booze bar in every ant hill. The ants will drink responsibly, stay in their respective hill, and all will be in order. Although a few may get loose and drive around in ant cars real crazy, it will be more controllable. There you have it, and by the way, you can be in charge of distributorship throughout the hills. Whoopee! It would be nice if some time we might work together. Ants in the pants and Casey with his cats would be an unbeatable foe."

Even a cat has to work once in a while, or at least pretend that he might. Meow!

# Oklahoma Cats

$\mathcal{E}$ ven though I have it all and knew it all, lots of my furry brethren do not. They are crawling, climbing, and meowing all over the planet, and most of the time doing ok. Lots of them are not. So much pain and suffering, and you and I know that suffering can be an all consuming horror. Something had to done. I told John that we had to take a trip and check it out. Off we go to Oklahoma.

We drove, er' John drove. It was a pleasant trip, and two days later, we were right in the middle of Oklahoma. John contacted the courthouse, and we got a reading on all the oil wells in the county. How many there were, how productive, the pay off and blah blah blah... I also contacted my "buddies" and asked them where the best place in the country for a cat was. They told me, and we all piled in the Bentley with cat food and five cats. Away we went. We soon got to pussy paradise. Just what the cats loved. There was open space, lots of places to sit and climb, places to watch bugs crawl across the ground, then eat them. Not I! The weather was fine, but there was no place to get in out of the rain, except maybe a rattlesnake hole, and that is a no no!

Once I found out where the exact place for "cat heaven" was, John contacted a real estate agent. We bought one square mile of Oklahoma right where the cats loved to be. We got a great deal! Now what? Go to town, always a good plan. Find the best restaurant and get to know the "folks." Maybe one of the Bushes would show up, and as my cat luck would have it that is exactly what happened. George II showed up. He had his charming wife and the rest of his most immediate family with him. George's family had been seated not too far from us. As usual, I was in John's backpack with my paws on his shoulders, sometimes I stuck them in his ears, looking all over and not missing a bug. I saw George II, ours eyes met, and he was mine. He blinked, stuttered something to his wife, grinned real good, got up, and walked over.

George said, "I couldn't help but notice you and the backpack," he said to John, as he was looking at me out of the corner of his Texas slick looking oil eyes, "That's quite a kitty you have there. Can I give him a pet?"

John said, "Well sure, but it is best to build up some type of a rapport with him before you do. You will know when it is the right time, probably just like dealing with leaders of the world?"

John had paid his just homage to George, and George replied, "Yeah, I guess pretty much everybody knows who I am. But, I have settled down near here, and I don't run all over the world anymore. Let "Wild Bill Clinton" do that. But, you sure do have a unique cat, and he caught my eye." George winked, and said, "Oops, I almost made a pussy joke, but I quit doing that and drinking a long time ago."

John said, "I completely understand. So nice to meet you, this is Casey." John nodded his head toward me, and I meowed, reached over, and gave Georgie a cat bat on his arm. "Looks like Casey is your buddy," John said. George laughed and chinchucked me. I gave him a pretty good Chinese cat smile with my eyes half closed and George was hooked. John went on to say, "I know you are busy with the family and all, but Casey and I are on a big project down here. We just bought some land, and you would be the perfect person to talk to about what we are going to do."

George said, "Here I go again, I can't help it. Casey is so great… what the heck? Oops, I almost made another pussy joke, but I know you two won't tell the New York Times. Just what is "tit" you need help with? Doggone Texas accent, so tough to control all the time." George smiled, and I gave him another cat bat. Taking a quick peek in his brain and adding some "suggestions" made him more agreeable as well. All was looking great!

John told him what our plan was. It would be a tremendous boon to America. A model that all the world could follow. It would be a giant "cat house" for any cat that needed help could come here and be cared for properly. Since we had bought the property right in the middle of hundreds of oil wells, we only needed the oil expertise to help with the funding. Think of all the pussy we would be helping. George started to laugh really hard now, and jingled the coins in his pocket. He gave John his card and said, "Call me tomorrow morning, and I think I have just what you need. So hard to stay away from all those cat jokes, but they sure make me laugh." I high pawed George, and all was done except for the ink to dry.

The next day we figured out where to drill, when to drill, how to ship it, and give George a call if you want to know the rest. The building of the cat house was also put together. They could not believe John knew so much about cat houses and how to build them and such. It all made perfect sense. Everyone had to marvel at where he got all that cat knowledge. Ahem… The project was put together in cat quick time, and all over the world it was recognized as a beacon for cat care. It could also be used as a guideline for many other types of animals all over the world. Wow! George, John, and I were completely happy and pleased and decided to meet at the newly built cat house. George said, "Thank you so much. Great idea you had! But, somehow I think Casey might have had a paw in it." 'Nuff to make a cat laugh!

# Sinatra's Lyrics

*S*inatra's lyrics say it all. All… Like the song, 'All of Me'. Like the song, 'My Way'. Like the song which I will let you pick because he sang about two thousand different songs. Probably sang about as many songs as your cat meows in one year. Probably, if you were to have a book of all the songs he sang, you would only have to open it anywhere, read the lyrics to the songs, and would pick you up. Then again, here comes the scotch and a camel cigarette. Both are fine. You might even see a song you know and sing parts of it during the day or maybe for a long time. 'Why not take all of me?' 'Baby I'm yours'. Grrrr! There…it happened to me again. Another song popped into my mind, and I gave it a whirl. Sang it for about ten seconds, and then told you I did. Uh, oh, here comes another one, 'Stars fell over Alabama' last night. Alabama? Well, it worked and it is still working. Odd, Frankie was the epitome of so-phistication, so how did they get him to sing the word, "Alabama"? I think it is because it has four syllables. I must be wrong. Of all the words and towns and cities in the world they chose the word I have been writing about. One of their favorite expressions now is "Roll tide." Say it all the time like you say "hello or good bye," they say "Roll tide." They should say, "Look at the stars tonight," and sing the first song that comes to your mind. I dare say the people of the state aforementioned (I got that word from a lawyer) probably never heard of Frank, and when they do think of him they yell out that gooney phrase, "Roll tide." One more thing before I am visited by

Bear Bryant buffs yelling nutty phrases is a slice of another Sinatra song, 'Shrimp Boats are Comin'. Coming to pick up all you morons and 'Fly You to the Moon'. I mean really, such a great song to have it turned to drivel and neglect.

Frank went everywhere unaware of the greatness of his talent. He acted like a spoiled baby most of the time. Got to envy a guy that can get away with that act. Kidding aside, it is kind of sad. No, it really is sad. One of the great talents of all of all time, and talent is the key word. Those who have a great talent should wrap the rest of their being very softly with a comfortable blanket that would make others enjoy them even more.

Now that I have all the songs Frank sang at my fingertips, I will just keep flipping the pages until I come to one that will give me the mood I want to be in. Don't you want to be in a good mood all the time? Be careful. If you like being jerk or a word that rhymes with itch, you could be in trouble. Then again, if you like to be that way, you won't look at the book. Isn't that the way it goes? You are like Frank, but with no talent. Bet you have his behavior down pretty good. Probably made you throw a fit just by reading this. Ha Ha!

'Once upon a time', go ahead give it a little hum, Frank was in Monterey, California. His "friends" were there, and they did what they did after he performed, they talked and drank. One of the greatest writers of America was there, and they got together and shot the breeze. Conversation turned to who was the best band leader at that time. Ouch! Frankie punched Herb Cane, and the police were called. Instead of a jail, and because Frank had been booked and jailed before, they told him to get the heck out of town and never come back. The great Herb Cane, with talent and manners wrapped in a warm blanket, said they never spoke again for five years. But what is five years I ask you when it was twenty years of no talkie with Peter

Lawford? Really, Herbie was lucky Frank give him a punch. It was an honor. They both weighed in at about 135 pounds, so you can imagine not too much oomph was there. Good column for Herb and now you know the rest of the story. (I don't know if Frank ever punched Paul Harvey. Probably did. Why not? I mean, if you could punch anybody and get away with it might be fun?)

'South of the Border'. Oh, my heart! So beautiful... the music and lyrics. Sigh... Guess that will be my song for the day. Just do the talent part and forget about the rest. Like the great Babe Ruth not Zaharas. Zaharas was probably, really the greatest. But, she had a warm blanket, was a sweet person, and you probably don't know who I am talking about. In fact, I may have to look up what all she did...hmmmm back to Ruth. Same as Frank... All the talent and let the devil take what he wants, and what he wants is your being. The moral of the story is this: If you have all the talent in the world, try not to be a yin yang off your stage of what you do so well. It costs too much. Why not just 'Fly You to the Moon' or tell the cab driver to go around the block one more time and just be cool? Ahem... and that's my cat philosophy for you.

# The Devil You Say?

The devil you say? Oft used saying with tremendous meaning. That's because the devil is everywhere. "How so?" you say. Quite simple really. All of your thoughts are monitored by Scratch, all over and everywhere, because he loves his job that gets the whole human race in misery continually. If one is strong enough to resist his omnipresence, then the best to you. But, most don't. Now lighten up...The devil loves to have a good time. Yes, love. But, it is devil love. Not to fool with, but all of us do fool with devil love all our lives. "Hey, I'm talking to you. Give me a smile let me tell you what the devil really does."

It is a beautiful day in New Hampshire, and you and your family are out for a walk with your dog. You are the father of two children, and you and your wife and family are all walking on a crisp autumn evening in your humble neighborhood. As you walk by a house, you all glance in and wave, and one of the children comes out and says, "Hi!" She walks along with you and all the children are having fun, talking and laughing, and hey, just having a good time. Boom! She is thirteen years old, and you notice the dress she is wearing is tight and fit around her buttocks. You don't like what you just thought when you saw when you did. (Aha, Scratch is on the job.)

The ride to her house is about two minutes away. (Lots of time for Scratch to do his influential work. He got WWII going in the blink of an eye, and here you are with a young girl that is smiling and stuff, especially stuff.) On the way, she pointed out where her friends live, and in the pointing process, brushed against your leg and the steering wheel. It bumped the steering wheel enough that you had to follow its momentum and turn the corner into an open field. (Uh oh, Scratch is on the job.) While stopping the car and reversing to where you were going, you put your hand on her thigh as you were looking back to turn around. She grabbed your hand and... (Isn't Scratch the best?) Your wife then said, "Oh, honey, are you having another crazy daydream or what? You better quit fooling with that young girl around the corner, or what am I going to do for a pension if you get thrown in jail? Besides, I think she is your daughter. You and her mother were dating in college, and there was always talk about you and her and her husband, and how they had had a child a little too soon." (Scratch leaves no stone you know what.)

Dear reader, escaping the devil is impossible. One must constantly battle him, or her, if you are a feminist. If you are a Nazi, you will gladly entertain him. Then, there are those who go to phooey with nary a thought. Being a cat, the devil is completely afraid of me and mine. He is only a silly test for humans, and we can punch his number, get rid of him any time we want. There are worse things for us that we will save to tell you later. Cat wink.

# The Plot of Capturing The Royal Lot

Cats have the greatest creative ability of all in everything. I don't want to make it complicated for you. It dovetails with my tremendous mental ability. I, like the 'Fool on the Hill', did I hear another song going around, can sing and see it all. But, I let my great friend, John, and of course, the wonderful Francis Sinatra sing when they want. But I do, ahem, help "some" especially John. Well, actually only John, most especially with the words. Sometimes he makes them up, Frankie does too, but John is much worse. And, where was I?

We were going for a great walk a short while ago in San Francisco where I "watch over stuff" early in the morning, with some mist, some wind, and some beautiful sights and sounds. As usual for me, I was standing up in John's backpack with my paws on his shoulders looking around to see what I might see. After a couple of miles, (I had to push him.) we stopped in at our favorite hot toddy place and got our special order, one toddy for him, and a toddy and caviar for me. (I'd make John walk a mile for caviar...please indulge me. The cigarette company may put me on the payroll...so there.) Where we stopped was truly an international restaurant that stayed open around the clock, if need be. Of course, there was always a "need be." Think it must be some kind of a game in Spain, or a crowning in England, or James Bond doing Dom Pérignon with Brigitte. (I know she was never in those great Bond movies, but she should have been. They would have been something else. Momma Mia! This is an Italian restaurant. Gotta' fit in.) A beautiful sound and song filled the restaurant. It was, 'You Made Me Love You' recorded by Al Jolson in 1913. Cats love that song because they think it is so ridiculous. I understand, but most of the other cats don't. Why bother? Most cats are loved by humans instantly, so why can't humans do it. Humans are so silly cats think. Why all the bother? Give it a meow, and I am out of here. As I was taking a discretionary sip of toddy, as well as a nip of caviar, my always alert sensitive cat warning gave me a nudge. "How could this be," I thought? Well, I really knew how it could be, but I have been hanging around with John too long. That is what he would say. When he did, I would cat bat him reminding him that anything is possible. (Fun busters all over the place.)

The event of the day was the birth of Charlotte Elizabeth Diana, Her Royal Highness Princess Charlotte of Cambridge, to the royal couple. Such a sweet baby and she was in perfect working order. (Just like me and my ten siblings! Boy, were we healthy. Mom cat was happy, well belatedly so, that is until the time when John came to visit the animal sanctuary, put his coat down, and I jumped into his pocket. Would you believe I crawled at three days of age? (I'll get right back to the royal child.) But, after I went into John' pocket, he put on his coat without noticing me, then got into the car, and took off for home. He put his hungry hand into his pocket looking for some cashews, and pulled me out instead. Yikes! I could not let him give it too much thought. Yes, even at three days of age, I had tremendous mental abilities. I "communicated" with him immediately, and told him what a great pussycat I was, and John laughed big time. I meowed. We have been the best of friends ever since. Sigh…Now, where was I?) Someone was monitoring the TV set with evil intentions…"not quite so cricket old boy" if you know what I mean. He was a rather large Englishman about three hundred pounds or so, and built like the Tower of London. He was on vacation. Even the crime lords of London have to take a break. This was a perfect situation, for Little Larry, the crime boss. The new baby, the royalty, the world awareness, and if all was planned right, he and a lot of his ilk would give a swift tug on the coattails of the "hoity toity." After all, he and his family had been in The Isle of England as long as anyone, and they had been looked down upon for too long. It was time for me and John to go to London. Little Larry and his henchmen would be up to their nefarious plot. I had to find out what it would be and stop it.

When we landed, we alerted Scotland Yard, and security was increased around the new royal baby. We were quite sure that whatever it was, it was going to involve their safety. The new baby and family were going to be in a parade in about a week, and then stay at the legendary Hotel Savoy. It was easy for Little Larry and Co. to find out which floor they would stay on, and then put their plan into action. They would take the family at night from their room, and then place them under sedation in a nearby hide out. The demands would be issued, and it all would be settled in one hour, or they would never see the family again. He would demand ten billion dollars, and Olly Olly Oxen, All Home Free! Small change for England, the money would be transferred in such a way that Sherlock Holmes would find it impossible to trace, and it was a perfect plan he thought.

Well, the plan would have been perfect had not my furry brethren talked to Little Larry's indoor/outdoor cats. As it just so happened, they had been neglected as of late. What with Larry traveling all over the place, they were not cared for in their properly desired manner. Some had not even heard of caviar! They told me all about it in exchange, of course, for a hundred kilos of caviar to be stored in a locker to keep it at the proper temperature. (When they got used to caviar, somebody would have some very expensive cats to feed.) Just as the "Plot of Capturing the Royal Lot" was about to be put into action, it all just as soon collapsed. Bobbies dressed up as the royals, and fake true to life babies boomeranged all back into the henchmen's faces, and they were clapped into prison. Little Larry was never seen or heard from again. Rumor has it that when they let him out, he went on a crash diet, lost about half his weight, and quit driving around in the Rolls honking his horn for fun.

I noticed a new bar had just opened in the city across San Francisco Bay. It was said it had a huge cold locker in the basement full or caviar. The owner was a skinny little runt who spoke funny, and there were always some cats about. You don't think? 'Nuff to make a cat laugh!

# Breakfast at Frank's with JFK, Elvis, & Big John Wayne

*M*ost classic rhetorical question of all time: What makes the world go 'round? Pithy question, too, the pithier the better. For a brilliant cat like me that is gifted with the greatest intelligence and mind reading ability that was ever known or will be known, I will be glad to put the above question to rest. But first, as an insight to the answer, I decided to "drop in" on four of the best known men of all time. They captivated the world. How did they do it? As it just so happened all four of them, Elvis, Sinatra, John Wayne and JFK, were at Frank's house in Palm Springs, California. All had actually lived there part time.

"What the heck, pilgrim, let's get together and play a hand or two? Har! Har!" I just happened to be in the kitchen when Frank and Elvis were trying to make something for breakfast.

Elvis said, "Frank, all you have is spaghetti in the cupboards and booze in the frig. What kind of a way to live it this?"

"Shut up Elvis. I have three more refrigerators and a walk in locker in the garage. Go out there and bring in what you want, and I will cook it. Quit mumbling about being hungry, or I will kick your ass in poker again. Is everybody from Mississippi like you?" Frank said.

JFK came into the kitchen and said, "Both of you guys, stand up, and salute me. Since somebody said you can sing, let's hear a little tune."

"How's about just kiss my ass, and bring us a drink, so we can get our heads together. First Elvis and now you!" Frank fumed, "And oh, there is that indoor/outdoor cat that always shows up when you are around. Something fishy is going on with you and that cat. When he is here, I never beat you at cards." Frank then gave me a chinchuck and winked knowingly. "I think he has some kind of a recorder or whatever on his necklace. It says his name is Casey. Hi Casey!" Frank said, "You are very beautiful, and your eyes remind me of some chick that drives me crazy." I meowed and waved my tail around in a few circles. Frank said, "He moves his tail around just like that crazy broad does too? Hmmm...naw, couldn't be. People can't change into cats can they?"

Big John came into the room and said, "Har, Har! All you guys do is talk about women and pussy. Don't you ever talk about cattle and stuff? If you didn't play poker, I would have to wonder about you. Haw, Har, Yuk, Yuk!"

Elvis broke off a few words from the song, 'One Night with You' and then said, "What can I get you, big boy?"

JFK started laughing so hard that he bumped back into me. He said, "Aha, here is my secret spy that tells me what all you guys are really doing. I mean, all you do is sing a couple of songs, and Big John here doesn't even sing, or do you?"

"By god, now listen up, here little buddy. I can sing plenty, and since you are President of the whole shebang and got yourself an armful of pussycat to boot, I will sing any song you want, right now," Wayne said.

"Sure," JFK said, "Let me see. How about the national anthem? Or, the 'Halls of Montezuma'? Or, maybe… or?"

Sinatra broke in, "Forget it already. We haven't had any food yet, and if we turn him loose with a song, we have to be at full strength. Quick Elvis, where are those goddamn Bloody Mary's?" A pitcher of Bloody Mary's appeared with four glasses, and they all sat down. (Elvis did not bring the booze. There just happened to be a waiter close by. Ahem.) Frank poured, being the great host that he was, and they all saluted the President and me too, I guess. Gee whiz! The President was holding me and smiling, having the best time of his life-booze, buddies, and me.

Big John said, "Well I'm ready. What song will it be, Mr. Prez? But, you know what, by god? Let me have a couple more of these sissified red things, and that might even make me better! Har, Har, Haw, Ho, Ho!"

Frank said, "Waiter, make it two more pitchers. We got an up and coming singer who needs to calm his nerves. Jesus, John, be sure to let us know when you are all calmed down and ready. Don't be too good. You might drive me and Elvis out of business. I know we can sure as hell ride a horse and spit tobacco on people, so you better watch out. We might grab your cowboy ass job just for fun."

"Hold it down, you guys," JFK said, "Don't scare Casey with all this rough talk. He is a very sophisticated cat. I think I can smell some quite pricey perfume on his fur. Isn't he a beauty? I know he brings me luck. When I had the meeting with Khrushchev he seemed very interested. Khrushchev looked at Casey from time to time and tried to pet him once, but seemed to change his mind in mid reach. It was as if Casey told him to stop, or go wash your hands, or get a different suit. How about a dentist? Or, at least spray on some cologne, anything to cut the aura of your noticeable physical presence."

"Indeed, there is something about Casey. Har, Har!" Wayne said, "in other words Mr. Prez, that guy is one big stinko. I thought so. He looks like a sick old bull trying to get up a steep river bank. Har, Har, Haw! Knew it all along. Now, you take Frank and Elvis here, why these two guys look like..." I meowed, jumped out of JFK's hands onto the table, and waved my tail in Big John's face.

Frank said, "I'll be damned, JW looks like you can still attract pussy after all. I guess the girls just can't wait to take that hat off your head and see if there is anything under there." He went on, "Waiter, another pitcher of wake up stuff, and bring us some cards. Let's see who has to buy breakfast. Oh yes, and bring Casey some caviar. I have a feeling if I treat him nice I might be "luckier" at cards." Frank winked knowingly at me, and I gave it a non-committal "Meow." "Just like pussy," Frank said, "The more you give it, the more it wants."

The cards arrived immediately, and poker was the order of the day. I jumped onto the kitchen counter where I could watch it all, and the games began. Frank kept score. Figures... Big John dropped some cards of the floor, and I do think he even farted once. Elvis broke out in laughter.

JFK said, "Ok Khrushchev, we'll give you John Wayne for Moscow."

Frank said, "Will you assholes shut up and use some better perfume. How can I think with all this bullshit going on? Bunch of god damn kids. Hit me again!" (They were now playing 21, and JFK was the dealer.) Elvis couldn't quit laughing, and the waiter brought another pitcher. (I hope he was in good shape.) Frank won another hand and said, "Goddamn, I think that caviar is working! I must have been wrong about pussy all my life!" It was almost time, nine in the morning, to go out to breakfast, so Frank said. It was his goddamn house after all. (Oops, I am starting to talk like Frank.) "Let's play one more hand for the whole shooting match. Since Big John is here, I will say shooting match, and since the Prez is here, what game will it be? Elvis will deal."

"Hurry up, Prez," Big John, said, "I can't last much longer. I gotta go to the can, and I won't leave this here card game. Much longer and I will go right here, but don't want to bother the cat. Haw, Har, Ho, Har!"

JFK said, "Low card draw-one card only. Whoever has the highest card has to buy breakfast for everybody." I meowed, and JFK said, "Oh yes, and caviar for Casey, probably the real brains of this outfit."

All four cards were dealt by Elvis, and Frank got an ace of spades. He won, but he lost. Frank shook his head, smiled and laughed, and off we went in the Rolls to breakfast. First, you know who had to go and take a dump. (I'm sure that's what he would say, but he was running too fast to the can to talk.) There is the answer to the rhetorical question of what makes the world go 'round. I will let you figure it out for yourself. As the saying goes, if I give you a fish for a day and blah blah blah.

'Nuff to make a cat laugh!

# Dream It Will All Come True

**D**ream it will all come true. Dreaming I'm always dreaming, dreaming alone. The mind never stops. You can only imagine what with my mind being the end all, except for humility, that it has fantastic dreams. I had one not long ago.

I became invisible and also able to walk through anything, so off on my dream adventure I went. I had a difficult time deciding where to go. Where are the secrets of the world kept? Where does God live? (Dreams are always funny!) What makes up Colonel Sanders secret sauce? How does Danny De Vito get all those good lookin' chicks? (This dream was getting "real funny!") As I was actually half awake and half asleep, I had access to both worlds at once. (Don't try it- you could hurt yourself.) I decided to try and solve the greatest puzzle of all mankind. Where do we go when we "go"? What better place than to visit the best hospitals in the world. I transported over to the Stanford Medical Center. There were twenty one people n a sure death mode state. They could die at any second. I went right inside their mind with my mind, and went to the exact center. I also created a force field completely circling the body for one hundred yards out. Nothing could leave or come in without my knowledge or acceptance. Aha! I had 'em now! The body I chose was a "normal" human being. It had become sick and ravaged with typical old age wear and tear. It was ready to die at any moment now, only seconds away. My sensitive cat alert warning system went off now as I was covering the outside and the inside all at once. I could see exactly what was happening!

Meanwhile, John walked into the room, grabbed my tail gently and said, "Let's go for a walk. Just kidding." The mind was being totally responsive to the body and to itself. For 76 years, this mind had always been awake and active, making decisions, giving advice, warnings, and dreaming and on and on, never stopping. Now what? The body could no longer be with the brain. It was worn out. The brain was still fresh and active, able to live another fifty years. What to do?

The brain noticed me at its very core and asked me, "Who are you, and why are you here?"

I said, "I want to see where you go when the body dies."

The brain said, "No idea! Can you help me?"

"Sure!" I said, "Let's make a plan at the power point center of the planet with me and my friends!"

"Great," the brain said, and away we went.

All of us gathered on the top of my house by the chimney. Me, Seagull Joe, Uncle Al, Wrigley, the big Labrador, and our new guest- the brain! I explained the situation to everyone present. We wanted to know where brains, which was essentially our essence, went after the body wore out. Cigars were passed to all, well almost. We would just blow the smoke on the brain.

The brain said enthusiastically, "Thanks!"

I said to the brain, which by now had started calling him Bob, "Bob, have any idea where you would like to go?"

Bob said, "Hmmm, never thought of it. Strange… for a brain not to think!" I still had the force field around Bob. As of yet, nothing was trying to get in or out of it. "Maybe," he said, "As I was limited to where the body could go, now I might want to somehow be able to go many places."

I said, "Since all living entities are born with brains, you can't very well just jump into somebody's head and take over, or can you? Maybe… Just move in as I did with yours now, and join forces. Hopefully, you get along. Hmmm, might be why we say he's too smart for his own good, or he's crazy with so many voices telling him what to do!?"

Wrigley the deep ponderous thinking lab said, "Woof, where do you go if you don't join another brain?" He then moved his paws as if to say, "*One is helpless.*" Then he closed his eyes and puffed hard on his cigar and blew the smoke on Bob. All of us were thinking and puffing and blowing smoke on Bob as fast as possible. I was getting hungry. We all went down to the kitchen and did what we do best. Eat! John was there and helped us with the food and the cellar's best wines. We needed all the energy possible to now solve what had become a very cloudy conundrum. Ahem!

Suddenly, I felt myself being lifted into the air. I blinked my eyes, and it was John picking me up from the floor. He said, "You've been sleeping too long. You were on your back waving your paws and tail all around. You would then put your paws over your head and puff up your cheeks and blow. I thought whatever it was wasn't doing you any good. Anyhow, you look ok!" He then chin chucked me a couple of times, and I gave him my best Casey Chinese smile, and away we went for a ride. As we were riding, I was going over the dream I just had. I still could not figure out what to do with Bob. Whatever… I guess a dream is like Las Vegas. What goes on in a dream stays in a dream. I was also still hungry. Dream food doesn't count either. John could tell I was thinking about something as I was just sitting in the back seat staring out the window. He said, "Come up front. As big as you are, you make a great armrest." Like I always say, *"That's why I like being around John. He keeps me loose!"* 'Nuff to make a cat laugh!

# Roos Down Under

*I*t's another foggy morning in the city by the bay. I love it. The most brilliant cat of all time likes fog. It's because...and stop the job, the door bell is ringing. John got to the door by the third ring and greeted whomever. The man was very pleasant and introduced himself as The Chief Inspector of Internal Affairs for All of Australia. His name was Simon Coffington and appeared to be in his early forties. He held his Dick Tracy hat in his left hand, was ready to greet with his right. He had on very thick glasses, was cleanly shaven, and topping it all off was a top coat that came just below the knees. (This is the kind of description you get from a know it all cat.) It was quite stylish in total.

Simon explained, with a very controlled Aussie accent, that there was big trouble down under. The diabolical nefarious schemes that had been perpetrated might soon destroy their economy, and it was very serious indeed. He had heard via the grapevine that John had a certain reputation of being very successful with these types of criminal activities. Would he help? John said, "I'd be glad to hear what it is exactly that you are having trouble with. Let's go and have a cup of java, maybe a bite to eat, and discuss it all. What?" (There John goes again, trying to use some kind of a British accent. Pretty good, but he got the countries mixed up. I think I saw a glimmer of a smile behind Simon's thick glasses.)

Bingo! A cab appeared. John had his backpack right by the door. I was already in the pack, and off we went. On the way to John's favorite morning restaurant, the Buena Vista, he explained me. He said all kind of silly things about me being beautiful, smart, and blah, blah, blah. I won't go into it all. Mainly, he said I was a great care cat and that I had saved his life a time or two by the "things" I carried in my cat care coat. Again, I thought I saw a glimmer of a smile behind the thick glasses. Simon also kept his top coat partially buttoned although it was only 50 degrees. Guess he came from the warm part of Australia. In five minutes we were seated, coffee ready to go, and Simon ordered the special of the day. They know me already, so they brought me my special, caviar and a small sipping glass. John got his regular cup of coffee.

Simon told us what the problem was. Just the kind of work I like, too. He said succinctly, the kangaroos are impersonating major celebrities in all areas of Australian life. They are traditionally large money making events that bring in millions of dollars and help the whole continent. Let me give you some examples. At first, they appear brilliant, but the backlash is overwhelming. Most recently, a golf tournament was held. Simon went on to say, "In all there were one hundred golfers from all around the world. It is a fantastic tournament that captures the imagination of much of us, and it brings in large money to all facets of our lives. As the tournament progressed, one the golfers dropped his bag. Looking back, we should have known. Usually, the caddies carry the bags, but this time the golfers insisted, being in shape, hup hup, and all that you know. One on the golfers, most famous, dropped his bag and oops! It looked like a tail popped out. How could that be? Oh, well, some kind of a golfing joke. We all know golfers have to try very hard for humor."

He looked at me and said, "Somewhat like cats I should think with a pretty face and all that, but very serious."

I meowed very slowly. Looked at Simon and gave his mind one small kitty cat look. More oops! Good ol' Simon, with the thick glasses, overcoat, and what all, was you guessed it, a flaming Roo himself! Big deal… Let's hear the rest of the story.

Simon took no notice of me or my meow. He continued saying, "As the tournament progressed, and it was on the very last day, mind you, with the entire country locked in on the outcome, it started to rain. All the golfers became soaked. Their golf bags under the weight of the water, split open, and the golf clubs fell out. Voila! Big fat kangaroo tails were all over the place. The entire country was in shock! How could this be? Kangaroos being what they were took the prize money, and hopped off into the sunset, or wherever they hop away. For now, with all that money, that didn't have to pay taxes, they might go "hopping mad." Simon really smiled now, and I noticed his teeth had a kind of glow you don't usually see with humans.

"There was nothing we could do since the Roos are a national treasure and all that phooey. Plus, you can't catch them anyway. With all their powers of disguise, it is doubly hard to catch them. One posed as a street car conductor and let everybody on for free. Diabolical I tell you!" he said.

John said, "Is that all?"

By now, there were five more people at our table listening with great interest. The waitress, Kay Kay, said, "Oh brother, bring on the Irish coffee. Here come the kangaroos!"

Simon said, "You are correct in that nobody was hurt, and the money eventually came back to our economy. Some "tourists" bought some large homes in fashionable areas of various big cities. Two large car dealer ships were purchased with corporate money, and a powerful lobby group is putting pressure on our senators. They want "bike lanes" wherever there are roads, and that is very expensive. There is suspicion, but no hard facts, just some sniffing going on for now." "There is one more thing I must tell you," Simon went on to blather, "In our great country once a year, we have a beauty contest for the most beautiful girl in all of Australia with just pure beauty. They don't have to say a word, sing a song, write a word, (Did he just look at me?) do a dance, or you name it. All they have to do is walk around a quarter mile elevated oval track three times. It is made out of glass, so people can be all around it and under it. It is shown on our tellys for a solid six hours. The girls walk very slowly, but are given to gyrations every couple of steps or so, and it is the top rated show of all time, bigger than your Super Bowl." (There were murmurs from the listeners, and Simon heard them.) He coughed, delicately and timely, and smiled ingraciously. "Well almost! Only kidding now, have to show that we Aussies have a great sense of humor. Harrumph!" There were relieved sighs, and Simon carried on. "After six solid hours of walking the glass with their uh-hums, a champion was chosen with tremendous beauty all over. Upon receiving the trophy, the exquisitely beautiful woman walked wonderfully down from the stage. There was a bit of a hop, but she had just won the most coveted trophy in the land. She had to be so excited! Upon getting to the bottom of the walkway she took three giant hops, sprang over the outdoor retaining wall, and was never seen again. We guess? Who knows? The Roos have obviously invaded our most sensitive, creative, talented, and medical sanctuaries. What's next? Are we safe from nothing? Something must be done!"

Simon looked at John directly now and said, "Well, ol' boy, can you help us? Say what?" He was completely smiling now, teeth all aglow, his whiskers, 'er fur, was coming out a bit, only I could tell.

I also noticed his tongue was the biggest I have ever seen. Wow, for a human. He had drunk about five Irish coffees while we were explaining the "situation." Apparently, let's call a kangaroo a kangaroo. Roos aren't used to the "hop" in Irish coffee. Oh, he was doing fine for the folks. But I, Casey the Cat, saw it and knew it all. Wink Wink. Simon gave a sideward glance towards me from underneath his glasses. It was quizzical and almost knowing, as if to say, *"Do you really know who I am, and what I am doing?"*

After breakfast, Simon picked up the bill for everyone, and also bought two rounds for the entire establishment. A most generous tip was given and we left to consensus applause. Boy, we deserved it. A Roo trying to give me the schmoo! I "communicated" to John what was really going on. John nodded slightly, looked at me, gave me a chinchuck, and smiled. He said, "Now, I can put two and two together. (Easy John, don't blow a circuit.) Nobody since Herb Caen wears those trench coats. Herb loved Casablanca and Humphrey Bogart. Hmmm, this was very clever indeed,

Upon reaching our house, we sat down on the front porch. We offered Simon a "bracer" for the road back. He accepted, and said, "Any help you can give us will be greatly appreciated. I'm afraid, if you can't solve problem, nobody can. It would be a total enigma."

John said, "You have a most interesting mysterious dilemma. I think it is impossible to ever get to the bottom of the kangaroo caper, as I now call it."

Simon gave that a few yuks. "Unlike the glass walkway where everyone could get to the bottom of things, this is impossible." Simon, with however many "coffees" and several well embellished bracers, started to smile slowly. Then, he smiled completely and that made his glasses fell off. He started to he haw and yuk yuk uproariously! His trench coat fell off, and you guessed it. A big fat Roo tail popped out. John handed Simon some tissue, so he could wipe the "sweat" from his whiskers. That coat was hot.

John said, "Not to worry, Simon. Only one person, ahem, on this planet knows what you are doing, and I find it quite amusing and industrious. Actually, you are bringing in tremendous amounts of money into the economy, and promoting your great country as well. As we like to say here in the States, no harm… no foul."

John and Simon shook hands, 'er paws and hands or whatever, laughed and had another bracer. Good times were had by all. A taxi pulled up, Simon winked and said, "If we, and there are millions of us Roos, can ever be of any help just let me know. Keep it on the sly, but we also have cell phones. We call them pouch phones."

John said, "Well there is one thing, can I see your pouch?"

'Nuff to make a Roo laugh, too!

# Rats

Rats, ever had to go to the vet? Ouch, and real stinky as well. Guess you never had to go unless you are another animal who can read and write, not many of us around. I am a twenty pound cat named Casey that can read, mind meld, and give "suggestions' to other minds when I choose. No, I am not fat, and I am not a baby tiger, just a big cat with all kinds of fantastic abilities that may be explained as we go along. For now, I am going to the vet. My friend, John, says he has to go to the doctor, so it is the same kind of thing. It is never pleasant, and besides, he pays for this treatment. I gave it a weak "Meow" and away we went.

We went in at our appointment time, and they gave me the usual "cat" checkup. The vet told us that I am completely healthy. Maybe I could chew on some more teeth cleaning stuff, but that is all. Phwew! John promised me we would do something special, since I was such a good "kitty." More blarney, but he does know it makes me smile. Since cats are so serious, it is very necessary that I smile and laugh regularly. John helps me do that. If I get too serious, I just take a peek inside his mind, and it is usually 'nuff to make a cat laugh.

We headed back home in the car and that makes me completely happy. He was hungry for pizza, and so was I. The pizza had to be vegetarian of course. We don't count the salmon sauce dinner I eat.

The next day we went for our usual walk along the embarcadero here in San Francisco. And surprise! We were going to take a boat trip around the bay. Yeaaaaa! I loved it! Seeing up close all the huge ocean liners was exciting for my curious mind, and a couple times we saw a submarine. Everybody got real quiet when we saw the sub, and then hurried to the cocktail bar for whatever they needed just then. Courage, I would guess. There is real evil in the world, and it must be combated. Pretty much the rest of the world wants what we have, and we have to fight to keep it, very grim indeed.

As we were going around the bay all on the boat were happy. We went right under the Golden Gate Bridge and out to the Faralon Islands. We saw lots of porpoises swimming and diving around the boat. I "communicated" with them, and found that everything was ok. Yes, I can read any mind that exists, even the little green, gray blue men who visit us from time to time. Not to worry about them. I "spoke" to a few and about half were lost and the other half were traveling around the cosmos, nice guys actually. Kind of bored with their job but they meant no harm. I intimated to them to keep it that way. I showed them what I could do, and they were impressed, respectively so. For an example, I suggested to one alien pilot that it would be better for him and his crew to get out of their ship and sit on the top so they could see things better. They were about to do it until I "released" them. They understood completely. They looked at me and gave me what they used for a smile and left.

The ride was exhilarating, and I got out of the backpack and walked around the ship. John went into the lounge and someone inevitably said, "My, what a nice "kitty" you have." (*There is that word again. Ugh! Just kidding, it's ok, and besides it makes me feel young. At the age of three, I need to feel young.*) Most were imbibing in the lounge and feeling carefree which was just perfect. John took the liberty of putting me on a chair where I sat with great dignity. I waved my tail to and fro, gave a small meow, and smiled at a few people. I instantly won over everyone who was there.

One person asked John, "Does your cat have a special food or drink?"

John said, "Yes, he likes caviar, salmon and a nip of something from the olde sod."

One wise guy said, "He looks big enough to take a nip out of lots of sods." Laughter ensued. I meowed a bit, stood up and cat batted the air a few times.

John said, "Uh oh, I think he heard you!"

More laughter and immediately caviar and a nip of the olde sod was placed before me. We were, indeed, having a great time, and I could hardly wait to get home and laugh out loud for a few minutes. Not here. John would have lots of explaining to do.

The ride lasted about two hours and it was 'nuff to make a cat happy in this case. As we came near the pier, a rope was thrown out for one of the men on the pier to wrap it around a steel clamp attached to the cement pier. The man caught the rope as he had done hundreds of times, wrapped it around the clamp, and then it all happened. He slipped and fell into the bay, and the pilot hit the back up throttle. Something was amiss. The boat was lurching about wildly, taking on some water, and dark smoke was coming in great clouds out of the engine room. The pilot lost his balance, hit the throttle again as he fell down, knocking himself out. The boat was out of control, and somehow that rope had to be released. I immediately "contacted" Seagull Joe and told him what was happening. I said you have to contact some of your buddies, his buddies being the wharf rats, big ones. Tell them to come immediately and cut the rope with their teeth. He took off, and we could do nothing but wait. But, only for a few minutes as the boat would not last much longer at this chaotic pace.

Seagull Joe got hold of Ronnie the Rat, and told him what we needed, that it was an emergency, and would he do it? Now, Ronnie was always a grouch, and sometimes mean and brooding. He told Seagull he wanted a thousand pounds of Velveeta cheese right away, or it was a no go. (Good old creepy Ronnie.)

Seagull Joe said with a tough seagull tone, "You will get the cheese, but I can't do it right now. What I will promise you is if you don't cut that rope within the next minute, I will bring in a lot of Casey's furry friends from all around The City. I hope all of you can swim, maybe to Seattle, and get along good with Sammy the Shark and all his friends."

"Ok, ok already," Ronnie the Rat said, "You don't have to get so tough. You know I was only kidding. But, seriously, I do want the cheese."

He gave off a funky giggle and called his biggest rat buddies. They appeared in a flash. They chewed the rope in half in about ten seconds, and the day was saved. The boat chugged out a short way, regained its balance, and all were taken to shore safely. The rats got their cheese. Word has it they foundered and did crazy things. Some never returned. Just imagine, one ton of Velveeta right in your back-yard, and you could eat all you want. Poor rats...a classic case of too much of a good thing. Rats! We returned home and were going to eat the rest of the pizza. No appetite! The pizza had cheese on it. 'Nuff to you know what. Let's just leave it at that.

# Casey Gets Tough

*M*y great abilities of mental telepathy, mind melding, and being able to see into the future are wonderful things. So glad I am a cat, and that I am free to go anywhere in the world with nary a question about why I am there or here or wherever. Cats are everywhere. Now that people are realizing cats are great companions and sources of solace, we are being treated with kindness and understanding. My companion John treats me great. He leaves me alone and takes me with him in a backpack when we go places. You must agree that it doesn't get any better.

Today, we are going to take a small trip to San Diego, California, to primarily look at the USS Midway. It is a great aircraft carrier that played a major role in helping humanity get rid of the morons who were trying to kill as many people as possible for who knows why. I must say, ahem, people with that mentality must be banned from living. We all know who did it, and yet not one word from the morons who did it or anyone else, until now, has said they must be confronted about their actions until the end of time. Why did they do it? Who did it? And so on and so forth. Gotta' get tough with those creeps, throw them and theirs in jail, or just throw them away. Gee whiz you say, or come on now it can't be that bad. Ok. Try this on for size. How would you like to be buried alive with your spouse and family? Or see your spouse being skinned alive and have the skin being eaten by the creeps who did the skinning. Horrible thing to say and to read, but it must be said. People who do that must be hunted down for all eternity and not allowed to live. Please, no more gee whizzes. If you did go gee whiz, you are probably a low info person or low brow person. In today's day and age there is no excuse for any type of behavior that is harmful to any living thing. Since humans are supposedly the most intelligent life form, they should set the standard in proper behavior. I realize there are mentally ill people who do great damage, but it cannot be condoned. They must be stopped. Ok, so it looks like we have a bunch of nuts running around. Now you can say gee whiz.

You may think it is strange for a cat to have so much patriotism. Well, get used to it. How would you like the Japs to be in control of America? Or the creeps that built and ran the camps in Germany? Or the tag-alongs in Italy who jumped on the moron band wagon as well? Sick people! Hell is too good for them and what they did, and who they are must never be forgotten. So there!!! Phwew! Tough to be a cat sometimes. Somebody has to do it.

For now, let's get aboard the carrier and see what we shall see. Gorgeous day (*Must get us in a good mood after all that talk about morons*) with a soft wind coming in from the northwest at about seven miles an hour with gentle waves buffeting the anchored boats gently about throughout the bay. I was firmly ensconced in my back-pack, with my chow in the bottom, of course, and I could ride along and look out as long as John could take me.

We began our tour by going to where the planes took off. Amazing! Just the thought of flying one of those planes off such a short runway into the ocean or into the air makes the hackles on my back come to life. I gave it a small meow, and John gave me a pet. He understands me completely. What a softie! Blink Blink. Love my John.

As "we" walked throughout the ship, I noticed there were some areas that were off limits. Of course, that is where I wanted to go most of all. While John sat down in the mess hall to take a break, I went for a brief walk into one of the 'No Entry' areas. Again the hackles on my back went into action. (Twice in one day is getting to be a bit much.) After I entered into one of the areas were nobody was allowed to go, I knew why I was on full alert. I sensed evil was everywhere.

It was though I had been transported seventy years back into time when the world was at war. I saw hundreds of men working with concentrated fervor constructing some type of an airplane. From time to time right before my beautiful cat eyes, and I could hardly believe, because I can really believe anything if I care to, what I saw! Or, more accurately, what I did not see might be a better way to describe it. It was invisible. Only by the way the men walked in and out of the airplane and handled various parts while putting the plane together could I know what it actually was. Another big tip off as to that they were doing no good was that they were wearing Nazi uniforms. Also, there was way too much, "Ja, Ja" going on with a few "Heils" thrown in along with that nutty arm in the air Nazi salute and what not.

This was all too much, and I decided to put an end to this theatre of evil as soon as possible. Since the entire area, as big as a basketball court was completely pristine and free of any germs, the entire project was dependent upon a power source that kept the air absolutely pure. Without it, everything would stop immediately. The workers as well since even Nazis have to breathe. I found the power source on top of the evil structure. It all began with an intake motor that drew in air from the outside to be purified and pumped into the area where all the work was taking place. Without the air intake, all would be stopped and destroyed immediately. Upon the outside air being taken in to a special type of conversion unit, many additives were used to make the now re-converted air the basis for the entire project. It was almost as fantastic as the project itself. For lack of a better term, I call it super air. It enabled the workers and their work with objects and each other to operate with one hundred percent proficiency and accuracy. Everything was perfect. It all started with the intake outlet, its great strength and its great weakness.

I am a cat above all my great abilities. I had been in John's backpack bouncing along, eating food, and listening to John's blarney for about two hours. Guess what? I had to evacuate as all living things must. Only cats are the best at evacuating, the stinkiest and most germ ridden as well. When a cat chooses, he can even ramp up the content, smell, and amount to an amazing quantity of each. I decided then and there to do all I could do, and relieve myself right into that intake fan. I meowed a few times, and waved my tail to and fro. Even jumped up and down just to be sure all was situated inside and ready to go. It was. The sardines were a great help. Only fitting when you think they came from the sea, and now they are returning, although in a different form, but they have retained their smell and then some, more than significantly.

I quickly situated myself over the intake fan and had to use all my strength with my four paws holding me steady. One short meow, took in two deep breaths, and let 'er rip. My cat eyes took on a strange glow and every hair on my body stood at attention as the shit hit the fan. Best job I ever did, and it was for the entire world. All my cat evacuation hit the fan with great force and smell and blew through the air converter as it sucked it all in, souped up additives and all. Quite a blow! Within ten seconds all were dead and the ship collapsed on the floor. The coroner's report on the dead men was gut wrenching. The workers died a horrible death. The looks of their faces as they went to wherever those morons go was up to the reader to guess what it looked like. Pretty bad, for sure.

I returned to the mess hall where John, I could tell, was getting worried about my absence. I told him what I had done, and said communication was impossible what with the super air blocking all thought waves. The air in there now was no longer so super after all. It was such that there will never be a cockroach in there alive for all eternity.

John started laughing. He said, "Guess we better go and get you more sardines."

'Nuff to make a cat laugh!

# Area 51
# Here We Come

*A*fter reading the newspaper, the hackles on my cat back came up. Why? In addition to having mind reading and mind altering abilities, I also have a tremendous warning alert system that covers everything. I'm a cat you know. The article I just read was from the 'Drudge Report'. It was about Area 51 in Los Alamos, New Mexico. It inferred LOTS of things were going on there that few have any idea about. How can they do this? Why are they doing these very secretive things? How can they be doing all these things without some type of sanctions or being watched over? Nobody knows, the article said as much, and what could be done about it? I decided to find out. I told John, my great friend and house mate what I had read and what we should do. "Great," John said, "Let's go!" Area 51 here we come.

On the way, we set up a flexible plan to figure out what was going on in the most mysterious place perhaps in the world. I called upon my paws on the ground brethren of which there were thousands in and around Area 51. They were notified by "cat communication" that I was, in effect, coming to town. I wanted to know everything what was going in Area 51. I also got in touch with Seagull Joe, my great seagull friend, who has access to thousands of "helpers" in the sky. Joe and his minions would cover the sky. The furry fighters would cover the ground. I, as usual, would do the brain work, go on the inside, and find out everything. No problem, right? Everything was set up.

After arriving in Los Alamos, we got a hotel room. Then, I contacted Seagull Joe, and he literally swooped down and picked me up. He's a big seagull. While we were going to Area 51, the paws on the ground caused a distraction by setting off a warning that diverted everyone's attention from my landing and entering the facility. There were already about three hundred cats in and around the giant facility, so it was a smooth cruise. I went to the operation room with the complete inventory of everything that was going on in this super secret place. (Secret except from cats and birds and many other types of animals, rattle snake alerts are frequent there. Snakes will not ever be able to fit in because they always want to hide and bite.) Intelligent information was given to me by about twenty cats that lived inside the facility. The workers in there "needed" companionship because of the very nature of their work. That was scary. The person in charge of the hub of the whole Area 51 had a great cat named Oscar. I "contacted" Oscar right away and introduced myself.

"Aha," Oscar said, "I knew something was going on. I could just feel it. You know how we cats are!" We high four pawed each other and almost laughed. Oscar said, "How can I help you?"

I said, "I want to know everything that is going on in this joint. Period... I also said, "I know you and a bunch of your buddies have a very tough time being in this place, and if you would like we can take you to San Francisco tonight, or as soon as I get the info."

Oscar said, "It's a deal! I always wanted to eat some calamari. Hope you can get me some." We both winked. Oscar said, "I know where everything is except the secret code that is kept by only one person, Tilly McGrew. She is the secretary of all secretaries here and has been for about fifty years. Actually, she probably knows about the shebang. We high pawed again, and this time laughed when Oscar said, "Shebang."

I said, "Take me to her, and leave the rest to me."

We went right to her office and walked right in. Tilly knew Oscar well, and they exchanged greetings and meows. He hopped on her lap. Tilly said, "Oh, Oscar you have brought a friend. My, goodness, isn't he a dandy. He looks so smart, and those eyes are...and for a second, she froze, and then without missing a beat, kept on going exactly where she was before. In that second of time, actually it only took me a nanosecond, but for a human that would have been too startling. So, I let it go to a full second. I read everything. Discarded most of it, and just kept what I needed. Ha, ha, Tilly! One more reason you will have to treat Oscar very, very nice. We went back to the hub center, and I opened the secret of secrets and read the entire contents in about three seconds. It took longer to get it out than to read it. Not to brag too much, but I can memorize the entire Library of Congress in about two seconds on a bad cat day.

I asked Oscar when he and whoever else wanted to go to San Francisco, and it would be done. Oscar looked at me and said, "You are one powerful cat, Casey, definitely the top cat of all top cats. Now, where is my taxi service?"

No sooner asked than granted. About one hundred cats said they would like to go to San Fran, so they hopped on the Joe Seagull taxi express, and off they went. You should have heard all the meowing and such as they took off. All the cats had been given the strictest of instructions to not talk, or ahem, try to eat—crude, but they are after all cats--the taxi driver. They would after all be at 3000 feet altitude, and even a cat doesn't have that much luck. I was "dropped" off gently at the hotel, and told John we would have a good conversation going back.

I asked Seagull Joe if he wanted a ride, and he said, "Heck, yeah!" He said he was tired after carrying me around with what he called a lot of cat fat. John heehawed. I meowed, gave him a cat bat, and we all laughed. Hope we didn't scare anybody with John, laughing like John Wayne, Seagull Joe breaking out a big scree scree, and my meow. Time to leave now.

"So, what are they doing in that place," John said, "I just gotta' know Joe, 'er Casey, but I was going for dramatic effect. Who knows maybe Hollywood will find me some day?"

"You think?" I said, and acknowledged John's drama with a wink and a wave of my tail.

I have broken down all the secrets of Area 51 into five areas. They are as follows:

1. Invisibility

2. Complete silence in any type of military defensive/offensive actions.

3. Communication chips in all the heads of all the "leaders."

4. Knowing where everybody is on the earth at any time.

5. The ability to sanction anybody at anytime if they are not complying with the "script" of humanity.

Ok, so now the logical question is, "Who writes the script?" Ahem.

'Nuff to make a cat laugh!

# Napa Valley

*H*ave you ever been to Napa Valley, California? Simply, it is a beautiful place. They advertise that there are over two hundred wineries up and running in that area. (Other "operations," ahem, are up and running as well, but they are not legal as alcohol is.) We took a trip there to look around and to check out some rumors that something was amiss with the grapes and the green.

A special tourist train runs directly through the Napa Valley area. Of course, we got on the wine train, with me in the backpack of course, standing up with my beautiful statuesque Siamese head looking over John's shoulder with a paw on either of his shoulders. My whiskers were very sensitive that day, and what could I do? I had to listen to my whiskers. They were another way for me to read and meld with minds. If one of my whiskers brushed against you, your mind was read, if I wanted you to be. I can't read every mind, and it isn't something I don't want or need to do. By looking at "the cut of your jib" I can tell if you are worth a mind read or not. Never wrong, I am Siamese of special caliber, you must know by now.

We were sitting by the window waiting for the train to depart, and a woman came and sat in the seat next to us. She immediately gushed when she saw me and said, "Oh, kitty….." this and "kitty…" that. She asked John if she could give me a pet.

John said, "It is best if you just look at him, and if there is a connection you will know it, and then you can pet him."

"He is so beautiful," she went on to say. Her face was rather close to the backpack by now, and one of my whiskers, inadvertently skimmed by her cheek. Blink. Blink.

I took a quick read and it was all there. Her mind I mean, what was in it, and what she was thinking. She was in trouble. She knew all about what was going on with the grapes and the green, and it was nasty, bit of a sticky wicket and all that. In this beautiful part of the country there was ugliness, death and evil. I immediately communicated to John what was going on, and we knew it was time to bring down this evil empire.

At the end of the ride we went back to our motel room, and I sent out a call to Seagull Joe and Uncle Al. Seagull Joe was really a very big seagull, and Uncle Al was, well, my uncle. Seagull Joe with his minions could monitor great areas of space from the air, and Uncle Al had complete communication with thousands of his furry friends everywhere. John brought them into the motel, and they approved. Al jumped on the bed, and Seagull Joe sat on a chair. We were ready to plan.

Here is what was happening. The entire grape vineyards and the "grass" patches were being sprayed with a chemical that once ingested by anyone would leave them open to complete mind control if activated by a bonding chemical. Aha! Who was doing all this nefarious evil mind control? The young lady who had next to us on the train knew it all, and she was scared and running for her life, not willing to talk about it with anyone. As it so happened, she was staying in the same 5 star motel as we were. I say 5 star because we were stinko rich that particular week. John had gotten lucky in a card game. It was all in good fun, and we had made about ten thousand dollars. Had to spend it real quick, don't you know? He called her room and said, "Hello, Maria, this is John, the man with the beautiful cat. His name is Casey, and now that we are settled in, he is in a more receptive mood. If you'd care to, please come on down, (always kidding) and visit us."

She said, "I will be right there." She was extremely nervous and fearful. On second thought, it might be better if she was not in a room where she could be found, might as well go to a "cat house." (I see I am picking up on John's kidding habits.) She arrived in a couple of minutes, and we could tell she was very upset. Upon seeing me, she calmed down. She said, "Well, I see you have other friends here as well," and laughed.

John said, "They are very special friends indeed. They have excellent understanding of humans. At times, I think they know exactly what I am thinking, and even understand when I talk." Maria looked at me and gave me a light rub on my back. Wink. I meowed a bit, and then Al came over, and of course, she had to give him a pet as well. Al likes lots of pets, so she was stuck with him for a while.

Seagull Joe took it all in, and John broke out the special cigars. They were very unusual in that they ironically had a cancer killing cure when you smoked them. Just one more of the strange things that happen in life like the situation we were facing right now. Maria was very happy with all of us as we were with her. She and John had a glass of wine, the "safe" kind, and he introduced her to a cigar. She said, "I don't smoke, but for you and Casey, I will give it a try." We all made appropriate sounds, and Seagull Joe gave out a small seagull noise, a big one and who knows. Good thing this was a 5 star hotel and was well insulated. Seagull Joe, ever the gentleman, still did not let rip with a cry that could be heard from San Fran to Napa. Since time was of the essence, I "suggested" to her to tell us all what was really going on as soon as possible. We already knew, but we did not want her to become confused with her supposed very secret knowledge.

This is what we knew, and what she told us. Her family had been in the Napa Valley for over two centuries raising grapes and selling wine all over the world. As of late they had run into a bad patch of luck. Her parents had died, the vines were getting old, and her brother had taken over. As the story often goes, he meant well. But... he got in with some of his grass growing friends, and they introduced him to their chemical spraying "friends." They were part of the Neo-Nazi regime that was based in South America. (The brother did not know this, but Maria did.) They introduced their life giving chemical to Michael, her brother, and he went along with it immediately. The vines returned to their old vigor, and it was found it also helped the "vigor" of the grass vines. It was a tremendous coup. Grapes and grass grew and grew. Production was, as Michael liked to say, extremely "heady." (There are comedians all over the place.) As the grapes and grass grew, so did the desire of the chemical producers. They wanted to buy the wine business at a tremendous knock off price. Sell or else! In order to stall or somehow put off the selling of their business, Maria had shown signs of affection to the top man in the organization. She was being pressured in every which way and could not get out. She left her home instead. Michael was entirely under their control, and soon the entire company would be theirs. Once they took over, they could, in effect, rule the world.

Maria and her brother had the finest wine in the world, and because of its expense, mostly only the very wealthy drank it which included the leaders of all the countries in the world. (Yes, even the countries who espoused no alcohol. They were complete hypocrites in everything. At least they were entirely consistent in that sense. Living in hypocrisy and lies was their true being.) In effect it was as if Hitler was returning from the grave under the guise of souped up grapes and grass. (Has a certain ring to it, don't you think? But it was a ring of death and evil, and it had to be stopped.)

We thanked Maria for telling us all about it. I had communicated to her that we would handle the problem. It was also necessary for her to go into hiding, or she would be killed. She said, "Where can I possibly go and not be found by these monsters that are all over the world."

In a mind melding moment I told her, "You can go and stay with Sarah Palin. You will be completely safe with her. You can tell her what you told us. With that knowledge, she can use it, and be a shoe in for the presidency." (I almost said it would give her a "leg up," but there were too many comedians around here as is.) We communicated with Sarah Palin. She was well aware of some of our life saving ventures throughout the world, and she thought it was an excellent idea.

John said, "It looks like Maria can play basketball as well. (Sarah was an All American basketball player in high school.) I will also send along some of our Castro Cancer Killing Cha Cha Copa Cabana cigars. If you don't like the cigars, you have to love the name we gave them." (I won't say a thing.) We immediately put our anti-Nazi chemical plan into action. Once again, we called upon the United States Navy Seals to spear head the plan.

The Nazis were immediately going to be taken out of "circulation" wherever we could find them. Then the chemical they were using was modified, so that it would only help the grapes and grass grow without the mind controlling chemical. After all, grapes and grass do a pretty good job of working on one's mind as it is. (Can't quit.)

In a short time, everything was under "our" control. Simple plan really. Put out the Nazis lights and the ones in their chemical factories as well and... Voila! Success! We also profited greatly by the new chemical as well.

It looks as though it is going to become a ritual. When the Seals help us with a job, we all go to Coronado and play cards and such. (Especially the "such" part) The Restaurant loves us. They may have to build another one. If they do, I will let them know it must be pet friendly. They have no idea, but a deal is a deal.

As usual a card game broke out after many Cha Cha Cigars and hot toddies. The Seals, being as intelligent, resourceful, and insightful as they are just gave us ten thousand dollars before the card games began. They knew it would be going to good use, and we gave them a car load of cigars. I got in John's backpack, and we took off. Being around with such people as Sarah Palin, the Nazis, the Seals, and world dominance by a bunch of creeps, it was good to get in the back seat of John's Bentley and simply relax and watch him drive. Time for my catnap…

# *Yes, I've Got You Under My Skin*

My great all knowing mind has shown me another path to take today and it is fascinating. I found that I am able to go anywhere in time, to see and listen to anyone. I almost don't know where to begin. Who would you like to talk to if you could? For some reason, you may be fascinated by the dark people of history-Hitler, Kahn, Stalin, and the like. Then, there are the good and the great such as Julius Caesar, King David, George Washington, Thomas Jefferson, Benjamin Franklin, and so many similar men who helped form our civilizations. Another group you might like would be people who were famous for all kinds of various reasons like the great Babe Ruth, Thomas Edison, Tesla, and so many of the great inventors. More recently, your interest might lie with so many of the Hollywood stars, and then the celluloid characters that came afterwards. (There's a big difference what they were like on the screen and off, whereas the aforementioned were themselves in what they did.) Now after all, we have to remember, "They are only human." I won't be visiting too many animals. Then again, look at me. If I am ever discovered, people will want to talk to me. Good luck. You better be pretty smart, and not set off my inborn alert warning system. One hair on my hackle goes up, and off you go. I may have my giant Labrador friend, Wrigley, with me as well, and if he catches you, he will interview you. I hope you can speak Labrador and like pipe smoke.

The person I have decided to visit and talk to, not necessarily in my present physical form, is Marilyn Monroe. Why not? From what we have heard and seen, she has known the good, the great, and the not so good. We all have seen her singing a song to President Kennedy at his inaugural. We know that as gospel. Now, let's find out, "the rest of the story." The best way for me to get to know and be around Marilyn is by just being me. She loved cats. I gave her the famous cat blink blink eyes, and she was in love with me. As soon as she saw me, she picked me up and gave me the high pitched, "Oh kitty, kitty!" thing. I immediately put "on the dog," meowed softly, and purred just right. I also peeked into her mind. It only takes me a nanosecond to be able to read what is going on now, and then whatever was before. Today was going to be a great day. She and John, the President, were going to get together at Sinatra's house in Palm Springs, California. Whatta' day this was going to be! Marilyn had been staying at Frank's house for about three days. Frank had set up the meeting between her and the Kennedy. The stage was set.

Frank said to Marilyn, "We gotta' make sure everything is all set up. Get the vodka and stick it in some ice. That should be enough." Frank laughed, and so did everybody else. When Frank told a joke, everyone laughed especially when he laughed at it himself.

Marilyn made a pouty little face and said, "Oh, I liked that wine we had last night, and I hate to change. Couldn't you just slip me a little on the side?"

"Jesus Christ!" Frank said, "This is the goddamn President of the United States, might as well be the world. Drink vodka or whatever else he does. Don't piss off the President unless he asks you to." Frank thought that was really funny and the best laughs from all around were heartily given. (Frank also had a slight hangover, and so it made for egg shells all over.)

Marilyn said, "Ok, I guess I can. I am just so excited. I do want everything to be ok, Frankie."

"God damn it, don't call me Frankie anymore either," Frank said, "John, 'er, the President, doesn't want to think we know each other that well, if you know what I mean. Momma Mia you set me freea."

Frank was a brilliant lyricist as well. He incorporated in his speech many excerpts from his songs and even movie parts. Frank covered it all. Guess while I am at it, I see that we are getting a bit out of Frank as well. Might as well see what all three are doing-Marilyn, John, and Frank. Let's be informal, after all, "they are only human." John showed up about a half hour later. Greeting and booze and laughter began immediately. John and Marilyn hugged and kissed as Frank stood smiling happily by, almost subserviently so. We must remember Frank is one helluva' entertainer, as well. He did it all, on and off stage. All three had pretty much the same m.o.-being powerful, actors, talkers, and charismatic people who could do whatever they wanted. Watch out! Yikes!

They were in the kitchen now looking out over the swimming pool and tennis court. John said to Marilyn and Frank, "Get out the swimming suits. Let's move this party outside. By the way, Francis…." The President could see Frank smile greatly with almost filial piety behavior when he called him Francis. The only other person who could bring that out in him was his mother, known as Dolly, whom he completely adored above all else. "…this is good booze. It better not be bootleg booze or any of that goddamn Russian stuff. Gotta' help America every second in everything we do." Lots of laughter now, and it was real. Both men were very funny and actually didn't need much help in getting laughs or attention. They were the two of the greatest men on the planet. Really!

Frank said laughing so hard his drink glass shook, "God damn it, you're right, John! I'm trying to save on money and sure enough. That's Kennedy bootleg booze. I meant well, trying to help you out and all." (Lots of bootleg booze was brought in to the country by old John Kennedy. Nobody was to know. Wink Wink.) Frank went into the cupboard above the bar, and pulled out some Stoli and said, "Will this do, John?"

The President said, "Hell yes, Francis, I know those are phony labels anyhow, so we are actually drinking the same stuff. If you can't get them in the front door, get them in the back door." It was really getting noisy now.

Marilyn said, "Oh, you boys and your booze. Next thing you will want to know if I am real, or Russian, or whatever. Sometimes, I wonder what you like best, booze or broads?" (That just so happened to be a line from one of her movies)

Everyone was beginning to get confused. Was this real! Three of the most powerful, beautiful, well known people in the world were having a great time talking about nothing. They loved it. So did I. As I was sitting on the kitchen sink, for some reason, all three looked at me at once. All of us had great minds, but theirs were not nearly as great as mine. They did, however, for a fleeting moment sense something. I meowed coyly and in perfect tone. Frank loved it, since he was pitch perfect. John smiled indulgently, and Marilyn had to pet me and give me a smooch. I was completely accepted, and could do whatever I wanted. The party was just getting started in the kitchen, and soon moved out to the pool. Frank brought out the booze and the fixin's, and all were very happy.

Marilyn said, "Oh John, if I may call you that?" She went on, "I love your dimples and the way you handled that big, tough, old Russian. Can he speak English, or does he just act that way? And

Frank, why don't you send him one of your suits? He dresses so awful. His wife seems very nice, but she was dressed like the people who were in Frank's movie back in the forties. I mean, I know I am only a poor little ole girl, but somebody has to say something." There was genuine laughter and what a tremendous sight, the Big Three, laughing and having the same kind of a good time that people all over the world were having. Only human…

The Prez said, "You're absolutely right, Marilyn. If you ever tell anybody else what you just said, I will have you locked up."

"Is that a promise," Marilyn said, "Who, with you?"

"No, me," Frank said, and all three howled with delight, and drank some more of whatever was in the bottle.

Marilyn said, "Isn't this kitty cat beautiful? When he first showed up, I called him Casey, don't know why, but it seemed the thing to do. (Hmmm) When you look into his eyes, it seems as if he can understand you. When he meows, he sounds a bit like Frank."

"Sure," John said, "and when he takes a leak, he looks like me."

"You men are so naughty," she said, "I simply love it. Just think of it, I am surrounded by the best entertainer in the world, and the most powerful man in the world."

Frank, said, "Which is which, and don't forget about that beautiful pussy?" "Last one in pays for dinner," Frank said, and they all ran for the pool. Looks like I was going to be stuck with the bill.

Later that evening, at Frank's favorite place in Palm Springs, The Purple Room, they set up a microphone just in case. All of them were having a great time, kind of tipsy, but perfectly so. Frank had called in a date for the evening, and she wasn't too bad either, the beautiful Ava Gardner. The evening was beginning to take on a life of its' own.

Ava chirped in with her southern accent, "Pleasure to be here with y'all. I recognize Marilyn and Frank, but who are you, sir?"

"Very funny," the Prez said, "Why I am the house decorator Frank brought in. It seems like someone was playing golf in the house or throwing ash trays all over the place. Francis must be very quick." Frank was getting nervous.

"Touché," all of them said, and clinked glasses together while looks of admiration were exchanged with each other. The laughter continued, and the President said, "Love to hear you sing a song, Francis." How could Frank refuse? He went over to the microphone with his familiar walk, and sang, 'Fly me to the moon' and 'Stars fell over Alabama'. Everyone shouted, "One more, one more!" So, he sang one more, and one more and then, it was Marilyn's turn. She sang the President's favorite song, and that pretty much shut the party down, and home they went.

When they came home I was conveniently sitting on the kitchen sink. Marilyn said, "Oh there you are, you cute little kitty cat," and gave me a smooch.

Ava said, "Ma' turn," with her southern accent and picked me up and said, "Oh me... oh my, is this a lot of pussy or what...and so beautiful, too? When I look into his eyes, it seems like he knows what I am thinking. Can't let anybody know that now, can we?"

Lots of laughter but Frank looked a little nervous again. That was the end of this visit. They went to bed, and I returned to the power point by the chimney on top of our three story house in San Francisco. My buddies were there, and I told them of my visit in time. While all of us were smoking cancer curing cigars, Wrigley, the extra large, ponderous lab walked in. (Thought I might add, he was puffing mightily on his cancer causing pipe.) He woofed to get our attention as if he needed to do something more. When Wrigley speaks, we all listen. He said, "That was very interesting, but what did you the President, Frank, Marilyn, and Ava have for supper? It made me hungry." 'Nuff to make a cat laugh.

# Toughest Job in Town

*F*loods, wars, aliens, family problems, employee revolts, no sleep ever, where to find a barber? Help keeps flying all over the place. Phone never stops ringing. Have to be everywhere at the same time, and be all things to all people. You think you have a tough job? Wanna' trade? It's God's job I am talking about. He started the whole thing and now what? Then again, if you let them have their own way...

I just had to find out what God really does. No problem since I can do everything. This should be a snap. The baby Jesus needs a playmate and what could be better than me. All I have to do is hang around the kid, and have him show the people some tender moments, and that should give me a free pass. If that isn't good enough, I will "visit" their minds and give them some "catly" persuasion. My being able to read and control minds comes in very handy.

I was no longer just meowing and purring around the baby Jesus when God walked into the room. "Hello little fellow," God said, "Sleep ok? What have we here? What a pretty kitty cat. He will make a purrfect friend. Have to make sure that gets in the bible. Little Jesus loves animals. Maybe I can get some more converts with the SPCA. So tough nowadays to get new sign ups. The other group promises death and seventy one virgins, such a tough sell. I spoke to Mohammad about that a few days ago, and he said it is a competitive world out there. But, not to worry, if this planet doesn't work out, we will see what we can come up with the next one."

Michael the Archangel just entered the room and said, "Hey God, where did that cat come from? Too much pussy around here already I thought you said that it was the cause of all evil...Ha Ha Ha! Just working on some new stuff, so when I go down there to Earth I can relate to the humans... Ha Ha Ha!"

God said, "You're getting to be a pain in the ass, Michael. I'll let you do a tour with that stupid Judas, and then see how you like it. That guy is a mess up. Yesterday, he was trying to run a card game with some marked cards, and said the devil made him do it. I'm really getting sick of him. Take the kid and the cat for a walk now, and let me think. Some guy named Hitler just called and wants to see if he can get into heaven. He said he will do anything. From what he has been doing, it looks like he has already done everything, mostly wrong. Use that in your shtick. You have potential, but you have to quit chasing the angels so much...Quit it for a while. You can't catch them anyhow. Do some work once in awhile!"

We went for a short walk, and then I turned around, and went back to see what God was doing. Michael the Archangel was boring. Angels, angels, angels...that's all he had on his brain. Let him change a few of baby Jesus' really big diaper dumps, and maybe that will smell some "scents" into him. Boy does that kid stink. All they feed him is red wine and bread. It is no wonder. Where is the fish everybody keeps talking about? I bet Moses eats it or stores it away. He keeps blabbing about a big cruise and stocking up, or is that Noah? Oh, boy! Now, for some real fun!

Today, God saw me coming back onto his cloud and said, "You look too smart to hang around with that dope. Hop into this souped up chariot of mine, and let's take a ride around. Here, I have some caviar for you, Casey, and a hamburger for me. Nuts to those idiots and their crazy food. We know how to live, don't we? Hmmmm, what shall I call you? It must be a biblical name. How about Casey? Well, it's biblical now. Ha Ha Ha Ha! Gotta' tell dopey Michael to use that in his shtick too." Off we went. Hell was breaking loose all over. There were wars all over the place. God zapped a few with lightning bolts, and that sent them back on their haunches for a while. He flooded a few others, and all kinds of diseases wiped out millions more. They just kept on coming, one disaster after another, and still they weren't getting the big picture. What to do?

God pulled the chariot over and said, "By golly, Casey, I like the cut of your jib. You seem to get a lot more than you let on, and that is fine with me. All kinds of Jewish people up here acting real smart, and they don't know nuttin'! (God was really warming up his sense of humor.) I have so much bullshit from the Jews and the Muslims fighting all the time. Neither one knows what to do with their women. The Jews go I, Yi, Yi, and the Muslims hide out under sheets with their camels and goats. This is a tough job even for God. I put in a new group of people a couple years ago, I call them Irish, and they seem ok. They cuss me out a lot, get drunk on red wine, and if that isn't bad enough, have invented their own stuff-Irish whiskey. They sing some songs, work once in a while, and even have the women doing some work. Gotta' love a people like that!

Don't know why I invented women? Well, I do, but more about that later." "Then again," God went on, "Why not tell you why I invented women? Since you are a pussy cat, I feel very comfortable with you, pussy and such, I guess. (More stuff for that dopey archangel comedian, Michael) I invented them because I could not make the humans as smart as me, and I had to let them think they came from somewhere, not like the chickens. Get that joke Casey? The chicken or the egg?"

I said, "Meow, meow, meow!" I stood up on my hind paws, and God and I high pawed each other.

"God likes that," and he laughed big time. "Haw, Haw, Haw!" Lightning, wind, storms, mountains, and planets came out of his mouth. It all shot out into the wherever and clashed into other suns and solar systems, and even blew up a few stupid aliens that were sniffing around too close. God reached under the seat of the chariot and pulled out some vino and said to me, "This is the best I have, Casey. I took a trip once acting like a hippy, didn't have to work too hard went to Napa, California, and swooped up a whole vineyard. Not to worry, I replaced it with happy grass. This wine is wonderful. Come on. Let's go over to the Sisters of Divine Mercy, and see what they have for dinner. (Even God gets hungry.) You must be getting starved too."

The sisters had a real nice layout, very beautiful sisters they were as well. They all were wearing bikinis and singing Beatles songs, and I could not believe what I saw next on stage. Frank Sinatra was there smoking a cigarette, singing 'Strangers in the Night'. John Wayne was riding round on a horse, taking a swig, and offering horsey lessons. Ahem… Kennedy was trying not to stutter as two nuns were sitting on his knees.

God said, "Well, here it is Casey. This is about as good as it gets. I know you and the Prez have met each other before. I just happened to have some cards here in the chariot, and I want to see if these guys think they can whip me at cards. What do you think, Casey? Wanna bet on it?"

The cards were dealt. Big John Wayne just licked his fingers, asked God if he wanted to cut his luck, said "Har, Har," and started to deal 'em out.

Suddenly, God jumped up and said, "Gotta' go, hell's broken loose on Mars, and I have to see it firsthand." God picked me up, put me in the chariot, and zoom…Mars here we come. In the blink of an eye, we were landing. I thought I saw God take a sip of the red stuff in his chariot, but who knows? He is so quick, but I did see a red stain on his beard. But then, he is God after all, and can do whatever he wants.

Mars is a funky place of rocks and hills, and not much of anything else. There was a big hole in the ground; however, and we flew right in. Voila! It looked exactly like Los Angeles with the Pacific Ocean, Sunset Avenue, and Beverly Hills, a simply picture perfect LA. Cops were on every corner. The rest of this LA was completely naked. This would never do. They were violating the sanity and sanctity laws. They could not put everybody in jail, and that is why God was here. The biggest actor of all time was needed to solve this delightful dilemma. God used his mind control over all of them there, and told them to jump in the Pacific Ocean and cool off, and then go home. They would not budge. Guess who was there first? Scratch the devil promised them everything they needed forever-sex, drugs, and rock and roll. What else was there? All they had to do was take off their clothes, and the rest would just come easy. God got in touch with Scratch right away, and they met in Chinatown to get things settled out.

The devil said, "Aha! I told you people like my way best. I promise them fun, and you promise them work, old age, and hell. Don't you think it is about time to change your old fuddy, duddy ways?"

God said, "Slow down Scratch, let's get one of these Siamese slings, gather our thoughts, and discuss this in a civilized manner. Why are you always in such a rush?"

Scratch said, "Ok, I guess you are right. We got eight million naked people out there all having fun. Let's be civilized."

God said, "Sure, how about a game of cards? Winner takes all. You name the game. I'll even buy the drinks, and throw in my chariot if I lose. After all, I have God on my side."

"Don't quit your day job, God!" the devil said, "Those corny jokes sound something like a Jewish comedian would use. 'Oy vey, remember I used to be Jewish before you ran away with my girlfriend, Mary Magdalene?"

God said, "Let's play cards. You can name the game and deal. How can you lose? But... if you do!" The devil winced. Already he was stuck on Mars with an ersatz LA. This God guy was slick. Even when you won, you lost. Maybe he should get God to throw in the Sisters of the Divine Mercy. That should do it!

The devil said, "I want the Sisters of the Divine Mercy, as well, and forget the bikinis."

God said, "Ok, and if you lose, all the Muslims of the world will come here to Mars with their bombs and heavy guns included to wreck all the havoc they desire." All was agreed upon, and the devil dealt the cards.

Have you been to LA lately? Everybody is wearing clothes and not a flowing robe in sight. They even have a baseball team named 'The Angels'. Football is coming to town, and the team is named 'The Saints'. This God guy has a tough job. But, he sure can play cards. You think?

'Nuff to make a cat laugh!

# Humor? Huh?

*D*o you have a sense of humor? Cats are not humorous, but we enjoy sitting on a windowsill for hours at a time, looking at a bug walking across a watermelon. Even I, the smartest entity in all that is known and not known, rarely crack a joke. My good buddy, John, jokes continually, always looking for a laugh. Not pushy, mind you, but he will tug at you once in awhile. I was looking around "everywhere" seeking who has the best sense of humor. Want to help me? Come along, and I'll tell you what I have seen and heard, and then you can help me as well. Here goes. Hang on. Humor can get pretty rough, racy, or deliciously sweet, with the sage saying, "There's no accounting for taste." Off we go.

I can "hear" everyone yelling Bob Hope, Robin Williams, Buster Keaton, yes, the Chicago Cubs, marriage, (Told you it could get rough!) love (So sweet!), or quite simply it could be your best friend. Maybe, it would be your pet that will only sleep in the washing machine or a sudden philosophical glance at "life" that instantly puts you into paroxysms of laughter followed by confusion and your favorite bar. I find most animals to be positively hilarious except for me and my brethren. Small price to pay for getting to wear a fur coat night and day-see there, I told you we are not funny.)

John and I decided to take a trip and visit "the relation." This group of relation lives on a good sized farm in Nebraska. It seemed like a good idea, so off we went. We flew into Omaha. (Remember the quarterback Peyton Manning, who plays for the Denver Broncos? Always yelling, "Omaha!" this and "Omaha!" that? Don't laugh, 'er do laugh! He made a cool one million off t-shirts with Omaha printed on them.) John and I rented a car and went to the farm. We just pulled in the driveway, and all the animals were talking like crazy. (Since I can speak any language in the world, and read any mind, as well, it was fantastic, also hilarious!)

The pigs were saying, "Let's scare them and oink a lot."

The chickens said, "Let's see if they have any food." The cattle yawned and wondered what we were doing here.

The dogs were saying, "Pet me, pet me, over here, now quick, hurry, I want a really good pet. Yeah… oh yeah… like that!" The birds were suspicious with me being a twenty pound cat. They've had their fill of bad cats. Most of us eat them. No fun there.

The very big geese waddled around us with no fear, and said, "Honkie, honkie," and gave us the evil eye.

Of all the animals, I found the pigs to be the most insanely fun loving. (No accounting for taste, etc.) They were aware of their cruel fate, but were continually trying to escape. I decided to help them. They survive very well in the wild, and once on their own, do very well indeed. Ask the wild pigs in Northern California how they are doing, and they will say, "We really like bulldozing golf courses whenever we find one. Oink Oink. We eat anything we want anywhere. We are hardly every bothered because we run and oink around in packs of pigs."

One day one pig said, "Let's go to Monterey, California." His name was Earl.

Another big pig named Larry said, "Why?"

Earl said, "Beautiful golf courses are there and they have lots of marijuana patches there."

When Larry heard the word "marijuana" he perked up and oinked, "How do we get there?"

Earl said, "Take a boat." He also hummed the song 'Slow Boat to China' by Irving Berlin. (See, I told you they are funny.)

They got their pig pack together, commandeered a fishing boat at night and off they went. Plenty of food on board since Larry had brought along a bale of "green stuff" to keep everyone happy. They landed in, of all places, Pebble Beach, one of the most prestigious golf courses in the world. The pigs hit the beach running and oinking like crazy heaven. They let their snouts do the talking. It was the middle of the night when they do their best work. Being "all" loaded on dope and salmon, it was quite a production. They rooted and snorted and oinked until morning. Larry and Earl decided to go to town. In many ways, they looked like a lot of humans. They put on some clothes and sandals, especially sunglasses and baseball caps, brims in front, thank you. They know how fussy the golfing crowd is. They went to the nearest lounge overlooking the Pacific Ocean and ordered a round for everybody. (Just to put all the snooty tooties at ease.) Just so happened, a couple of big name golfers were there, Arnold Palmer and Chi Chi Rodriguez. It was 6:30 am, and they were getting a fast start.

Arnie, being the gentleman that he is, sidled over to Larry and said, "Thanks for the scotch. I must say, I like your costumes, reminds me of Chi Chi." Much laughter ensued around the bar. Everyone was having a great time. One thing led to another, and someone started playing the piano asking for requests. Earl called out, "The USMC "Halls of Montezuma'!" He was met with cheers and huzzahs and such. Everyone began singing, and Arnie got on the piano. Chi Chi took Larry's baseball cap, and put it on sideways. This was golfing fun at its best. (Bet you thought golfers were boring like cats!)

Chi Chi said to Larry and Earl, "You two guys remind me of someone. You're not Jeb Bush and his wife, are you? The short one here is kind of cute!"

Larry said, "You're right, I told her not to blink her eyes at you. Ain't she pretty? Even though she's a republican?" Chi Chi hooted and hollered, and wanted to sing 'South of the Border Where Mexicans Have Their Way'. More scotch was poured, and then they noticed the golf course. It was all dug up. The fishing boat just off shore was rocking to and fro.

Arnie said, "Let's go down and take a look. Maybe your brother, George, made all those divots!" He always was sticking his snout where it didn't belong, just like Wild Bill!" (Looks like the golfers were funnier than the piggies.) Arnie led the way. When he saw the fishing boat, he said, "Whose boat is that? I want to fish, I think! Har Har!"

Larry said, "It's my boat. Wanna go for a ride." They all boarded, and honked the horn, and took off. It was tough to tell who was which. The party was just "taking hold" when all kinds of fish started jumping around the boat.

Arnie and Chi Chi grabbed their golf clubs, and they cold cocked a few fish, and Arnie yelled out, "Hole in one!"

Chi Chi said, "South of the Border where I never lose! Yi, Yi, Yi!" Darkness came upon the, and it was getting chilly. It was time to land.

Arnie asked Larry and Earl if they were really Mr. and Mrs. J.W. Bush?"

Larry said, "I'll prove it."

"How?" Arnie and Chi Chi asked.

Larry, 'er Jeb, said, "Where do you want to go?"

"Acapulco, of course, Chi Chi said. It was done, and they "pulled" up into Acapulco, and booked the best place in town.

"Now what?" Arnie said.

Larry and Earl and all of the piggies oinked out at once, "No problem. We're going to pig out!" 'Nuff to make a cat laugh!

# Sadie Rules

*M*y eyes could hardly blink. I had to lie down. I did. My paws and tail began to move around in slow circles and gradually, one by one, they stopped. I was dead asleep. I think I began to smile while sleeping.

Earlier that morning I had read of a fantastic total body salon in, where else, Beverly Hills. Lo and behold, it was owned by one of my more successful distant relatives. She was brilliant, very big, creative, and many years ago had escaped from a zoo in San Diego. She was a Siberian tiger, her real identity known only to me and perhaps, some of her workers. She had opened up the business with the moniker of Sadie's Salon. She disguised herself very cleverly and nobody had the slightest idea what she really was. Despite her somewhat great bulk, about 300 "svelte" pounds and six feet height, she dressed extremely tastefully, and some mistook her for Caitlyn Jenner. She always wore a large panama hat, a full length coat, gloves, her "hands" were very big, with fashionable boots, and she barely smiled. Boy, if they ever would have seen those choppers… but I digress. Knowingly, they never did. They just wanted what Sadie offered-total body do. Sadie's was the best and the most ingenious. Her workers were all cats.

There would be four cats to a customer. The newest member of the "team" would take care of the feet, and easy job but odious. It was usually a young Siamese cat because they were so strong

that they did the foot work part. They wore a mask, appropriate attire (Never the claptrap dress one sees in some places…harrumph!)
small gloves and fashionable boots. The mask was the most important. Some feet had a horrible case of what was coined the "el
stinko." When "el stinko" was there, it was time to spray on the
magic ingredient invented by Sadie. The spray was skin colored,
but all powerful in knowing out the pue smell, the jam, the grout,
the hair, and some nails that were never going to survive anyhow.
(So sad to see a tiny nail with an infinitesimal amount of blood red
nail polish on it. As if trying to bring the poor old girl back to life
which won't happen. Only brings out the worst, either get rid of it,
or put on a prosthesis nail. The Siamese were excellent at that as
well. Once the spray hit the "el stinko" it began to sizzle and pop.
Oh yeah! In a couple of minutes another invented wash was put on
the area of pue and the feet were ready for anything. Voila! Even
more than that was the pièce de résistance of the foot. A tight fitting
red velvet slipper exactly like the pope wears and bought by the
bye, from the same foot store in, ah yes, Roma. You think this is too
much? Exactly, but necessary, and that is only another reason why
everybody loved Sadie's Salon.

Of all the conveniences loved by the customers, the one above all
was the simplest. The feel of four cats paws feet continually walking all over one's body gave the customer an indescribable feeling
of relaxation, peace, and wellbeing. Some customers came every day
just for that. Some never wanted to leave. When that occurred, it was
necessary to administer, tastefully applied, nighty night drops, to the
armpits. It was quickly absorbed and even helped with some of the "el
stinko" there but that will be explained about later, much later. They
were then driven home by the Sadie's best, and no one was the wiser.
Sadie also had pricey charges, but there was never a break intake of
a complaint ever. It was told, only in some circles, that an especially

"well to do" customer, after receiving her body do, had the almost smidgeon of unmitigated gall to perchance think about glancing at the crass monetary necessity. She smiled discreetly, and was about to ask Sadie "the" question. Sadie lowered her very large sea blue sunglasses, made especially for her in, ah Roma, about an eighth of an inch thick. A slow green glow emanating from eon old Siberian eyes began to meet with the inquisitive apologetic begging glance of the person who had just been dood...no word for it but pronounced "dude." She had just received the full treatment, red velvet shoes and all, and she needed it, like really...wow! Before the green glow was fully seen to the customers who dared to ask Siberian tiger eyes, she immediately said, "Just kidding, that was only the tip." She then proceeded to come up with an amount that would make a cat blush. Meow.

Money aside, this was Beverly Hills "ahf-ter-wall." Sadie's Salon was a wonderment to make you feel and look VA VA Voom! Let me tell you just some more of what was offered there. Upon lying down face up on the cushioned recliner, if you chose to open our eyes, you were met with an incredible view of the sky. No roof, only a smattering of sun was let in. If it rained, or some other type of inclemency came down, a wind tunnel covered the roof so that then feet above it all was blown away. One could watch the rain come down until it almost was on your nose, only to be blown away. Some said this was maybe, could be, slightly too much. Sadie insisted. Uh oh! The story of the "strong" hands reaching up to adjust the glasses and the almost penetrating slow green glow from eyes and its implication was 'nuff to say, *Oh sure, my golly, what was I thinking? Surely...* Weak ha ha's ensued and that would be considered in the "settlement" as well. Hair, hands, feet, el yucko, and even some places that had never seen the light of night or day were take care of here. Word got around.

One morning, almost before the sun was peeking its shiny smile, a large limo pulled up in front of the store and almost took up three parking places there. It looked ominous, black with wide sidewalls, European designed, no roof in the front, and some kind of a bid for an ornament on the front of the hood. Six heavyset gangster types, as if from an old Bogart movie, got out and lumbered into Sadie's and didn't even take the time to remove their hats. Sadie greeted them pleasantly, but one could well imagine how the look in her eyes must have been behind her fancy specs.

They said, "We heard about this place, and we would like the works. Now, or maybe just forget the works and show us here you keep the "proceeds." They were trying to fit in. We have been watching this place for some time now, and notice you do all your business in cash. You then make several trips a day into the back room, and we have it figured out. We just want some. No fuss, no muss, just a cut. Sure you understand. We really want to be your friend, and even help you if you need it. Oops!"

The creep talking "accidentally" dropped his cigar into a beautiful aquarium in the middle of the room. "Least ways, the proceeds will keep things like that and more, from happening. Know what I mean?" as he began to leer.

Before it was a half leer, fifty cats and sweet Sadie had them in six sacks with their heads sticking out. Their mouths were stuffed with "el stinko," and there would be no recognition in their eyes of ever having lived. They were put in the trunk of the limo and away they went. Sadie drove with a big smile, no glasses, no coat, and no nothing. One six foot, 300 pound Siberian Tiger with fifty helpers going down Sunset Boulevard at six in the morning heading for the Pacific Ocean. It was a beautiful morning for a drive and what it must have been like to see the sight. Cat faces pressed against all the windows and some riding up top and in front with huge Chinese smiles on their furry faces. The driver, Sadie, might have been taken for some kind of European chauffeur, if you were Dean Martin coming home from a Sinatra party that is. Soon they were in a secluded alcove right by the Pacific Ocean. The sacks were unloaded and dispatched. This was the fitting end of ugly people dressing and acting horridly who would never be missed. Harrumph!

The limo was returned to the front of Sadie's Salon. A wench on the roof hauled it up above the door and placed it on two, not noticeable, steel beams to which it was then welded. Remember this was nearly the size of a bus, seven feet high, forty feet long, and eight feet wide, with leather throughout, a few card tables, booze hidey holes, and a tremendous sound system. Sinatra, there he is again, was singing "Night and Day." An elevator was placed right outside beside the limo. If you wanted to ride the elevator, it was "Up you go!" You could relax and then when ready, get in a chair that would bring you down to where you could get you special "Sadie do."

"The cat's pajamas!" someone said.

I then heard some saying, "Pajamas, pajamas, why are you wearing my pajamas?"

I awoke with a start to see and hear John laughing and pointing at my paws. They had Boston Red Sox socks on them, and I was also wearing a Giants baseball cap. My paws were all wet, and the fish bowl was knocked over. John could hardly get out a word.

He just said, "Want to go for a ride and dry off? You were wearing some sunglasses, but when you jumped in the fish bowl they fell off. Don't want you to go blind. It was also really clever when you sat on the kitchen table and pretended you were driving a car. That's my Casey." What I have to do to make that old grouch laugh. Harrumph! 'Nuff to make a cat laugh!

# Casey and the Richest Man in the World

$\mathcal{D}$o you know who one of the richest men in the world is? He owns Russia, but he can't get a reservation at the Waldorf Astoria in New York City. Such a deal... Of course, the answer to the question is Putin, the czar of Russia. I just call him Raz for short. He is the newest Rasputin of Russia. He is carrying on the tradition of a long line of crazies that have led the homeland Russia. Reminds me of the show, 'You Asked For It', and Russia gets it…Hard, long, strong, and it keeps coming.

What to do? Well, since I am the smartest entity in the entire universe with the ability to read minds, let me tell you what should be done. But, the bet board in Vegas will gladly take your bets whichever way you want to go. (Vegas really rules the world but shhhhush, don't tell. If the planet earth is conquered and blown up entirely by some force, the last sound you will hear will be someone trying to place a bet. Probably someone will take it, and here we go again.)

America, the strongest, smartest, best country in the world has to have a female leader. Sarah Palin will do the job perfectly. I know. I met Putin once, by his request, at his table in the great Moscow hotel, The Intercontinental. Huh? Surely, they must have a better name than that, but they don't. I would name it the Rasputin. In fact, I would name almost everything Rasputin. After all, I mean, the boss is named Rasputin-Raz to me and you. Something has got to grind at him, what with all that dough and nowhere to go. That country is a symbol of sickness. Why, you ask? The answer being if you live there you have absolutely no rights, and if you don't believe that, look back to the forty million, give or take a few, that were murdered in the Stalin regime. Still continues. People are afraid to say so. Really? But, let's get back to Sarah Palin. Hmmm, Palin and Putin, good sounding names for a fight. Let's see how it goes. Upon being invited to Raz's table, I immediately began to read his mind. Absolute horror! Just what one would expect for the things he does all the time. Murder, intimidation, mutilation, and just to mix it up a bit, he may throw someone in jail. You can guess where that goes. Believe me, Casey the Cat, you don't get three square of anything, except fear and death.

Sarah would make a great president. She is instinctive, intuitive, extremely smart, calculating, and what's more...a sense of humor. She is also pleasant, well mannered, well spoken. She speaks her mind honestly and passionately in what she knows is true, and what she believes in. She also makes mistakes, silly ones that she laughs at, admits, and then doesn't make again. She does not make mistakes that are borne out of anger, ill will, hatred, deep seated hidden bigotry or preconceived convictions. She is as good as it gets, and the United States needs her leadership at the top. After all, she has been looking at Russia out her kitchen window when she does the dishes for about ten years now. So, she knows a lot about Russia. That's a joke I think she has told, and I got it. Lots of others didn't get it, and thought it was dumb. It was funny and light hearted. She also has a great sense of humor. She enjoys life and what she is doing, and she scares the be-jesus out of every dictatorship in the world. Sarah is also a good target for the smarty pants that make fun of her when she goes "Oops!" But, she will not make horrendous mistakes that will cost us lives, money, and respect throughout the entire world. Compare her to a young Margaret Thatcher with a great sense of humor. Sarah was also a great basketball player and led her team to the state championship. There is something about a great athlete with a great mind I always like. Reminds me of many of cats I know. We all have the "It" factor. Very important! The "It" that all people know and recognize is wrapped around Sarah Palin. Sometimes the wind may blow the blanket that wraps her to and fro, but Sarah grabs it and puts it back where it was often times in a better place. So, come along with me, and I will tell you how Sarah Palin could lead the United States, and yes, the world to greatness in peace and productivity and human dignity. It's been done for a long time, by us cats. There is a reason I can do what I do. Also, why I can't drive a car, and have to have my buddy John do the driving, and make reservations, and.....yes....make me laugh. Mainly, make me laugh. I'm hiding now. I mustn't start laughing when I am getting ready to tell you how Sarah will change the world. Then again, I have a feeling that a laugh or many laughs will find me soon.

Every dictatorship is deadly afraid of women. That's why they kill them, maim them, cover them up, and you name it. That is about the only way those types of governments can be creative. Otherwise, it is the same old thing. Control whatever is making money, cheat, kill, and keep it. (Then, they send their kids to Harvard or Yale, and... I won't go there now, but when I do, there will be a lot of, "Oh, my!", and "Not me!", and they may even go country on yuh. Hank Williams said it best, "Mind your own business, and I'll go minding mine!" Hypocritical creeps to the 'nth degree. Even use 'ole Hank to try and get out of trouble. Guess what Hank would say? Ha Ha! You're right. Funnneeeee! Go ahead... say it again. You're 100 percent right.) When Sarah comes to town, they will turn turtle, and their funky and deadly ways of killing and controlling people will end. The country will be run like democracies are. People vote and put those in office who are voted in office. Oh sure, creeps will prevail like the creeps do. It is a painful growing process-democracy. Sigh… So wish they all could be like we cats.

In taking a look at Putin's mind, forgot to call him Raz, and Castro's, yes I saw his mind when we did the cigar deal. I saw their complete fear of women in every way, just like Hitler was. They were completely uncontrollable and misunderstandable in every way. Women were something that must be controlled at any cost. They were the only thing that could take away their power. Why, you ask? Well, the answer is not pretty. Oft times, human nature is as it is and can't be denied or controlled. Those creeps needed women. They knew it, and they recognized it, but there was fear in the potential power that women possessed. Women could be their greatest obstacle to what they wanted. They wanted them, yet they could not accept them in any human way. These dictators, if nothing else, are completely diabolical, willful, and psychopathic. They killed them, or dealt with their very real fear in any way they could. A short look at history will tell you what dictators have been doing to women for centuries.

Sarah scares dictatorships and creeps. If you think of a better word than creeps just let me know. Putin and Castro and the rest of the dictators in the world can be definitely described as the first syllable in the word dictatorship. Can't use that word here because children may read this book. (Just being catty.) In looking into the mind of Raz and Fidel, I saw women come up again and again. They feared women. They could kill men and did by the millions, but women were different. One had to have them around in their life. Killing them made it tough, even for a dict-tator. Women drove dict-tators (just had to do it) crazy...more than crazy. Maybe, women made them better. It scared people even more. They knew in their minds if women got "loose," they would no longer be in control. Can't have that! They must do something to keep them under control.

Imagine a conference of Sarah and Raz or any other dictator in the world. Sarah would leave them in tatters. I know because I saw their minds. They would have nothing to say, and would only look like fools, and their ruling over millions of what amounts to slaves would end. For the whole world to see a woman at the very tip top of leadership in the most and best country of the world would open all the doors to whatever needed opening throughout the planet. Dictatorship would be kaput. (The first part of the despot word would remain, but in some instances it might be tenuous. Being catty again.) All would be perfect.

Well, let's not get all crazy with catnip. We, however, can remember how Margaret Thatcher had great control and respect throughout the world. She and Ronald Reagan got along famously. Most of the rest of the world would not even speak to her. Now you know why. With Sarah, they could not refuse because she is such a beautiful woman, (Get some contacts, Sarah, and cut those fingernails a bit...then again...hmmm....methinks she is more like a cat the more I think of her.....long nails, long legs, and... yes, very much like a cat...a very big one, indeed! Intelligent, forceful, with the "It" factor, humorous, now powerful, kind, yet just and forceful about what is obviously wrong, and hey, she has me.) I read those creeps minds, and I know we need her to get the job done. We need her folks, let's get it going. Won't it be fun to travel to Moscow or anywhere for that matter with the same trepidation we have of going to San Diego? Cool man, who's rolling now? (You can explain that one to your children...or maybe, someone can explain that to you.)

Reminds me of the Beatles song, 'The World Will Be One'. Now, that's what I get for listening to John's jokes and some of his music. Mostly, he is listening to Sinatra. Frank used to live right down the street from where I am hiding now as I am writing this Sarah Palin push for the presidency. Sure bet Frank would have approved of Sarah. Just talking cat dreams, but imagine, Sarah and Frank. Come on with me. It's ok to dream a little. Besides, Frank has already been married four times, and let's make it five. Good title for a song too, and gotta' go. John has found me hiding underneath his favorite football jersey. He is going to wash his favorite #16 Joe Montana jersey, and I am in it. Meow!

# Alakazam!

am! Slam! Alakazam! And guess what! It's football season. John just got tickets to the greatest show on earth, the Bears and the Packers at Soldiers' Field in Chicago. (John knows the owner, or the owner knows John, or ok I did it, but who's keeping score?) We could go anywhere-upstairs in the plush lounge or down on the sidelines with all the grunts and stuff that go into a football game. John likes it. I'm not sure myself. All this energy expended and for what? At least they have caviar in the lounge. Since the packers have been winning all the games, there has been some talk about "unfair practices" being used by the winning team. Really, I mean, this is sports? Every game is hooked up to Las Vegas and you can guess where Las Vegas is hooked to. The game began and the screaming and yelling and huffing and puffing were too much for us, so up to the lounge and caviar we went. The executive of all professional football teams was there along with the Vice President of the United States. So there! Who says cats just sit on window sills and watch bugs crawl across tree leaves for hours at a time? (Well, actually they do that a lot, but surely I digress...) The Vice President of the United States came over and shook hands with John and said, "Beautiful cat you have in your back pack. What kind is he?"

John said, "The hungry kind." As I was standing up in the back-pack with my paws on John's shoulders, I gave him a friendly cat bat on his melon.

"Aha," the vice president said, "he heard you. He looks so intelligent. I would not be surprised if he could understand what we are saying."

John said, "Well, thank you. He is a lot of fun, good for America and all that." (*Oh, brother, what is John up to now?*)

"Indeed," the Vice President said, "and while you are speaking about what is good for America, I must say there is much speculation about the games the Packers are winning. They never lose. What do you think about that?"

John said, "That is why we (as he gave me a chinchuck and smiled) were invited. I am from San Francisco and have dealt with similar situations. It's like your party always winning the nomination. Impossible."

With that the Vice President excused himself and moved on to other guests. It was a fairly regular crowd of football fanatics who lived and died for the sport except for one. I had noticed the same type of a person when we were on the sidelines with all the grunting and woofing. They were techno geeks who had everything typical but a slide rule. They each had the plastered down greasy hair, complete with dandruff sprinkled on the top of a ill fitting too large sports coat, glasses with thick lenses and large black frames that were barely held up by a sniffling nose, and so on. (All the caviar in Russia would not let him speak to me. Harrumph.)

As the game progressed and the Packers continued to take on a commanding lead, I noticed that whenever "duh Bears" were about to score they would be shut down right away. It was as if someone knew what their plays were going to be. Hmmmm, do you think? But there was a specter. Perhaps the biggest "business" in the world is gambling. They call it the stock market, Wall Street, international diversification, growth funds, and footsie wootsie, for all I care. (I could know in a second if I wanted.) In terms we can all understand, it is called gambling in one way or another. Betting money on what the future will bring and you winning or losing by the outcome. Simple… Gambling has been going on forever. Those who gamble cannot help but wonder what it would be like to know the outcome of what was going to happen before the "money" was bet. Surprise, some do not have to know what is going to happen. They can make it happen. Controlling what will happen is not particularly difficult. You just have to be ready to go to prison or die if you get caught. Everyone gambles every day. Can I get to work and be on time with a low gas tank or "gamble" and see if I can make it? Do I need to go to the dentist or just "gamble" that the newest teeth whitener will solve it all and blah blah blah? The biggest gamble we hear about day in and out relating to food is this-can I gamble and eat this bag of chips or salami sandwich and maybe the calorie counter in my belly will be asleep? Gambling is what we do. But aha, there is gambling and there is "gambling." If you don't know the difference, you are probably reading this book in a grey bar hotel somewhere. My advice to you is fill up the gas tank already.

My cat instincts and hackles were suddenly alerted to one geek on top rows and one geek below. Communication would be simple. They could probably hide a two way radio in their oversized glasses. Their dandruff and "cologne" would prevent any close inspection or casual chitchat leaving them to go about their business of "gambling" unnoticed. Oh yeah! The geeks would talk to each other and... yes, then they would have to communicate with someone who was on the field, but they would have to do it in seconds. The sounds in the stadiums were off the Richter scale, they could not put a receiver on the player because it would be discovered too easily. How could they be communicating with the players? I would have to take a one millionth of a second look into the geek in the room and find out. Yucko! (Boy is John going to have to pay for this. His fault, he should have known better than to ask for my help. He was gambling...aha!) It was a nasty one millionth of a second, but I found out how they did it. Bet you are dying to find out. (See... even Mr. Purrfect Cat has been corrupted, slightly by insidious gambling clichés and blah blah blah.)

Football teams do immense amounts of preparation. They have plays for every conceivable situation. There are basically about ten crucial plays that decide every football game. If you control those ten plays, you will win. Many times only five of them will do. How many times have you heard yourself say *nuts*? Well, maybe you used another word. If I would have known just that little thing or this little thing or... The geeks were super prepared. They knew every situation and also had the ability to intercept the plays that the other teams would be using. Once they knew these two factors, they supplied the antidote for the other team's about-to-be-plays and voila, the game was theirs. Almost, except then the players had to perform, and play football. So there! The "complicated" signal relayed to key players on the field was done by hand. One finger meant this play, and two fingers meant that play, and so on. Hey, it isn't theoretical physics, after all this is still football, and gambling is gambling, and cheating is cheating, and I told you to fill up the gas tank. Meanwhile, I am still recovering from that slimy trip into the geek's mind. John will have to give me a bath tonight. No football for him either. I may also want something I have not thought of yet. Too bad John... Don't gamble with the cat that could rule Wall Street. Then again, what's that saying by the famous circus entrepreneur? There's a sucker born every minute... Actually, I kind of liked the football game and watching John talk to the Vice President with a cat on his back making cross eyes and meowing ridiculously at his BS was surely 'nuff to make a cat laugh!

# China Town...
# My China Town

*E*vil is everywhere. (Where is The Shadow when you need him?) It all depends upon where evil is going to strike. If it is pointed at living things, there you have it. Evil raised its ugly head in China this time.

John and I, your friendly, beautiful, all knowing, mind controlling, absolutely no humility, Siamese cat, Casey, are China bound. I could almost hear the sound of the ringing gongs as we winged our way to the mysterious Orient. (Not mysterious to me but why spoil all the fun?) Upon landing in Hong Kong, we were escorted to our extremely lavish beautiful "digs." We had it all at $2000 dollars per day. Our trip was being sponsored by the United States Agricultural Department. If what we had heard was true, agriculture all over the world would no longer exist as we know it. A type of food had been invented in China that would enable a person to take only one pill a day to maintain his body completely. It also would eradicate many diseases and other sufferings of mankind. (Gadzooks and yikes! What will the medical profession do as well? No more would one receive a two hundred dollar fee for having someone tell you that you have high blood pressure and that you are overweight. In addition, before that terrible news, they told you that you had to wait an hour, and schedule the meeting one month in advance. Yikes some more! What will happen to John Hopkins and the mayonnaise brothers? All the great scientific help and programs for so many years for naught! Oops, almost said yikes again.) We had to find out all about this mysterious pill in the most mysterious of places! But now we were hungry. Thank goodness the pill had not reached Hong Kong or had it? Ah so! We had so much to do, but nobody was going hungry right no. So let's eat, drink, and so on before we have to pop a pill and say, "Now what? Go back to work? Run another 5 miles? Paint the house again? Get a good night's sleep without having to take a toddy even?" Why bother, when one feels perfect and there are no complaints? How about the product of the brewer's art and the like? Maybe the biggest business in the world could go out of business, end up in its cups? Where would it all end? Perhaps with complete health, never being hungry, having mental acuity and stability, a burgeoning IQ, excellent sociability-without a toddy-*there's the toddy again*-great athletic ability, at the very least, impressive physical features, and most noteworthy would be the implacable resolve of complete understanding that there would never be war! Yeaaaaaaaaa! Too much! What then? Almost everybody would be out of business! What would the world do? Having all people moving about quietly efficient, happy, and doing tremendous vibrant works nonstop! Where would it all end!

As Mr. Spock would say to Captain Kirk, "Jim, it's completely too logical for me. Therefore, it must be evil-evil of the worst kind that has never been seen or contemplated. It must be stopped."

In reply, Captain Kirk would say, "All thrusters on complete double warp blasting power jam. We can't be a nanosecond too late. Then again, if we are a little early I would like to try one of those pills myself. I am putting on weight and balding slightly. My overall physical appearance could use a shot in the arm as it were…'er, pill in the mouth I should say."

Spock could only comment, "Human's idea of what you take for humor does not compute. No matter if you are slim and good looking, or chubby and balding as you are now. I can only conclude that your so called "jokes" will not stop."

Captain Kirk's reply would be, "Everyone to your stations with renewed zeal. There is an even greater need to get there ahead of time. Harrumph!"

Enough already! It was time to eat real food. With all this talk of a perfect pill, I was simply "stahving darling," don't you know? John and I had an excellent meal. There was a great restaurant overlooking the great city of Hong Kong and the harbor with ships coming and going and activity everywhere. So fantastic that John almost forgot to eat. But we did not eat too much actually, all vegetarian food and spicy, as John likes it. (He likes everything spicy, but I have new one for him. Now that I have told you, dear reader, you may get some idea of John. He is a great man but...just kidding actually. Well, maybe a little.) As for me, fish would do, and with the Chinese tradition of their food entrees, I had to "suggest" to everyone that I was an extraordinary care cat that John needed at all times. Besides, I pointed out what room we were staying in, and everyone agreeably said, "Okie dokie." During our dining, there was constant, tastefully done tremendous entertainment on stage with singing, dancing, and many Sinatra songs which was amazing, considering this was Hong Kong. After the way they looked at me when we walked in, I was going to get my way. I am one big kitty cat with a lot of attitude that can be backed up, and "Meow!" They got my meow up, so I will have and do whatever I want. Yes, it was all Sinatra and some Deano. No complaints from us. I even took a quick walk into the kitchen, and lucky for them, I detected none of my brethren in there or ever having been in there. (Must have been something in the Saki, this never happens to me in Ireland.)

During our great dining experience with the fantastic view, and entertainment, the hackles on my back were brought to my attention. My sensitive alert cat warning system had picked up an all alert signal-evil. It was there in the restaurant. The game was afoot. (Ok, apaw for you purists.) The restaurant was circular, as big as a basketball court, sitting atop the hotel going always round and round. Slowly, so as you could hardly tell it was moving. It was a great changing visual sight of everything outside around us. I told John it was most likely that the ones we were trying to find could very well be here.

John said, "Well, ain't that a cat's whatever? Let's go get 'em!" Too much saki for John.

I said, "Take one of the pills that we have for these emergencies, and a cup of coffee, and you'll be all right."

"Damn Saki," John said, "Never happens to me in Ireland. Harrumph!"

Soon after one more very fitting Sinatra song, 'Some Enchanted Evening', and a cup of coffee, everything was a go. I spotted the woman, yes a woman, who was totally responsible for the pill, and now what? She was sitting alone, seemingly lost in her thoughts looking out across the city and the harbor sipping on something. (If it was saki, it would be over real soon.) I also noticed in a table. I looked into her mind briefly, and it was what I thought but one always has to be sure. She wanted to help mankind be its utmost, but in doing so, she had outraged the gigantic money powers. Mr. Evil was two tables away and had just left her table where I first got my evil reading. Mr. Evil was the real evil. Her children were in his captivity, and she was his slave. Really, it could be looked upon as only money. Mr. Evil would control the world with the pill if he so chose. Or, the great powers that be would pay him to keep the pill away, and all would continue as is. Great good turned into great evil. Don't want to make this look too easy and it wasn't. Trying to keep John in his chair from wanting to go over to Mr. Evil's table and put the quietus on him was difficult. One short meow and some cat bats, and he smiled at me. He said in John Wayne's voice, "Sorry pahdner, I almost screwed that one up. I promise I'll make it up to yuh. I'll do whatever you want. Just tell me."

I put a mind lock on Mr. Evil and completely erased most of his mind, except where the children were and how to get to them and save them without any problems. I then turned his mind to wanting a bottle of "really good" saki, and let him go. He then jumped up on the table and starting singing Sinatra songs. *Hmmm… not bad at all. Oh, well, he might make some money out of this after all.* The great inventing woman was immediately joined by John and me, and then John explained everything to her in a voice imitating John Wayne.

John said, "Well little lady… it seems like we have taken care of Mr. Bad. We've got him riding out of town on the next stage, and you don't have a thing to worry about."

She started to laugh uproariously. She said, between great guffaws and deep breaths, "Thank you for the entire world. I am so glad that my children and I and you know what are all safe."

John continued, "Yes, ma'am, we have corralled that critter, and your kids will be in your room in as long as it takes a chicken to lay an egg. In the morning, 'ah reckon. You better believe it. Har Har Har... Pleasure to hep' yuh ma'am."

She continued to laugh uproariously, and when she was able, she said, "Please sit down. You especially, Mr. Wayne, you old hot dog you."

Guess everybody is a comedian nowadays! 'Nuff to make a cat laugh!

# Paris...
# Oh, but Sweetie!

"Oh, but Sweetie, I don't want to go to that restaurant. Its waiters are just so yucky, or something. They bug me." Marilyn said.

"God damn it," Frank said, "Quit calling me sweetie, and those waiters probably won't be there tonight."

"Oh, I call everybody Sweetie, you know that," Marilyn said.

"Well, not me, damn it, and I'm not everybody, and take off those stupid shoes! I bought you some shoes yesterday. Wear those!" Frank said, "The president will be here in one hour."

Kennedy showed up right on the button as usual and was escorted to the veranda where everyone exchanged their usual greetings-the President, Marilyn, and Frank. Some drinks were poured by Frank, and they settled into their chairs to chat.

"Here's to Paris!" John said, "I see you still have the lucky cat." "Hello, Casey," he said to me, as I was lying in the chair right next to him. He chinchucked me, and I smiled a cat smile as he gave a soft laugh. "Whatta' cat," Kennedy said, "And, I really think he is lucky."

Frank said, "Hmmm, he must be. I don't see him all the time, so he must know when you are coming." Frank gave me a quick smiling grin.

I took a quick peek in the President's mind, and read there was trouble in Paris that would greatly affect America and the world as well. He wanted to talk to somebody about the problem that wasn't politically connected or some kind of a suck up. When you are the most powerful person on the planet it is almost impossible to find such a person. Who does that leave? Sinatra. He has a better job than the President and is a real friend. (As good of a friend as Frank can be to anybody that is.) Then… there is Marilyn. Well, she "simply" gets rid of all the pressure. When there is no pressure, one can perform at anything fantastically better. Just ask a cat.

First things first! They were hungry. So, out they went to Frank's favorite restaurant with music, ambiance, good friends, and great chow. Afterwards, there might be a "friendly" game of cards. They took me along, "Casey, the Lucky Cat." Also, a surprise guest showed up, Angie Dickenson. She said, "Well now, I recognize everybody here except the guy with the part in his hair. May I introduce myself?" She said, "I am Angie Dickenson, movie star, and bon vivant."

The President said, "I am a friend of Frank's, and thank you for telling me you are a movie star. Is it in this country or behind the iron curtain? You hair style looks dated." They all laughed, and I meowed as if I knew what was going on, and, guess what, I did. The President chinchucked me again and said, "Time to play cards. I have to go to Paris tomorrow, and I don't want to keep Casey up late." We played cards, and everyone won a bunch of money, except for Angie. She even lost a hand of four aces. Frank said it was because they were playing low hand wins.

"Oh," Angie, said, "I think it is that cat. He is always walking around the table, and I think he has something to do with it."

Frank said cryptically, "Never know what a pussy is up to."

In the morning, we all went to Paris on the most powerful and well guarded plane in the world. We were constantly guarded by six fighter jets with all their guns ready to go or intercept a missile with their own plane if need be. Air guards ready to take lives or give theirs. All air bases were in constant watch of the President's plane as it traveled across the world as well. I felt safe plus everyone says I am lucky.

The talks in Paris were tense. All the Russian armaments were being aimed as Paris. They were also "conducting" war games very close to the border. Russians…they would not quit. Their Slavic intellect having been at war forever and lack of self esteem told them they could not trust anybody. When in reality no one could trust them because of how they were. The old question of the chicken or the egg-it's the Russians. Every cat in the world knows that. Cats are getting out of Russia. Ever since the days of the czars, it has not been at all safe. The Russians sent their top ambassador who spoke perfect English due to his time acquiring his doctorate degree at Yale. There were two minders who were with him wherever he went. They seemed partly westernized and even smiled a few times. They accepted drinks, and the ambassador laughed. "They let me choose my "friends," so I brought along some boyhood companions of mine," he said. He waved a hand, and they left the room immediately to take in the "town."

"Let's get down to business," Kennedy said, "Where are the cards?"

"We have the cards and booze," Marilyn, Angie, and Frank joined in.

"Who's dealin'?" the ambassador said.

Frank said, "Let Angie, do it, she's good at dealing." More laughter and drinks were refreshed, and the game began. I scanned the ambassador's mind, and he wanted no confrontation with the West and neither did the leaders of Russia. Because of the Russian lack of said self esteem, they wanted assurance form Kennedy that there would be no aggression from the Americans with the new regime. This would certainly be agreed upon. I also found out that Kennedy and the ambassador had known each other from their school days at Yale, and were in complete agreement on all that was necessary. This was one more extremely world shaking secret that was only known to Kennedy and the ambassador. The ambassador was a complete American spy. In a terrific act of heroism, he would give up his assured American citizenship to go back to crazy Russia and "do what must be done." He was a complete American in the Kremlin with all the inside knowledge of the place. Let's face it. He had to get lucky at something. Here come some "lucky" cards. The ambassador got completely lucky and won it all. They all were good sports, and each one shook hands, smiled, and marveled at the ambassador's luck. Frank gave me one of those Sinatra grins, and I gave him a few cat bats. I showed him who was the boss!

On the President's Air Force One going back, I took a nap, and then disappeared upon getting back to Palm Springs. Indoor /outdoor cat, don't you know?

"Indoor/outdoor cat, my Italian ass," Frank said and laughed, "He works for the mafia! I know it!" Wink. Wink.

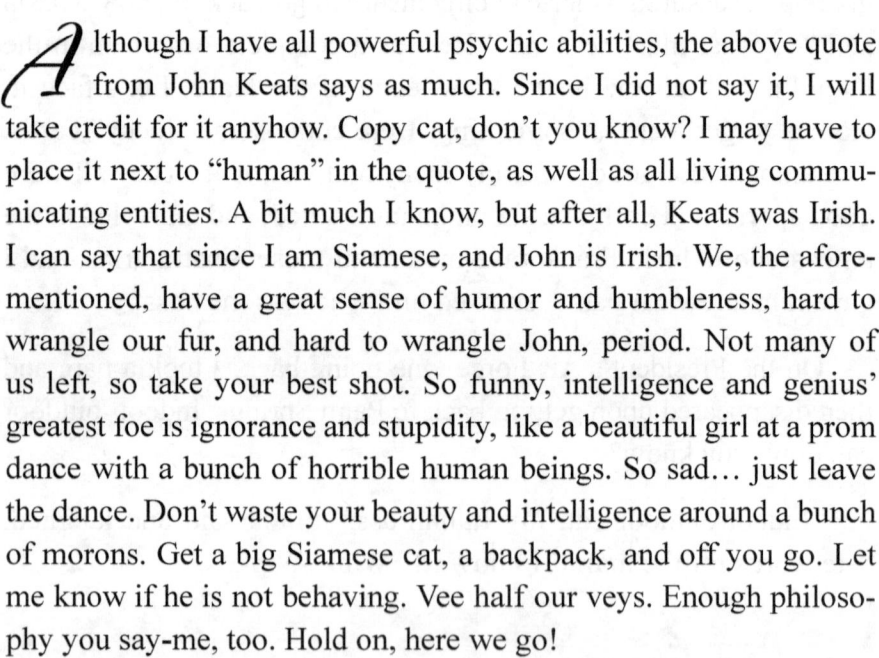

*"Scenery is fine...
but human nature
is so much better."*

*John Keats*

$A$ lthough I have all powerful psychic abilities, the above quote from John Keats says as much. Since I did not say it, I will take credit for it anyhow. Copy cat, don't you know? I may have to place it next to "human" in the quote, as well as all living communicating entities. A bit much I know, but after all, Keats was Irish. I can say that since I am Siamese, and John is Irish. We, the aforementioned, have a great sense of humor and humbleness, hard to wrangle our fur, and hard to wrangle John, period. Not many of us left, so take your best shot. So funny, intelligence and genius' greatest foe is ignorance and stupidity, like a beautiful girl at a prom dance with a bunch of horrible human beings. So sad… just leave the dance. Don't waste your beauty and intelligence around a bunch of morons. Get a big Siamese cat, a backpack, and off you go. Let me know if he is not behaving. Vee half our veys. Enough philosophy you say-me, too. Hold on, here we go!

I was in the backpack, and John was walking along the embarcadero on the San Francisco waterfront. I was standing up with each paw on John's shoulders. I was looking all around and giving John cat bats at random. We were having a good time. John was laughing at my inability to drive a car, and I was laughing at his not having a permanent mink coat. (You had to be there.) Many people were walking faster than we were, and really most everything was going faster than we were. I mentioned it to John, and he said something about my weight. Irish-all the humor, and me with all the smarts. More cat batting ensued. Good times.

All of a sudden four "serious" bikers passed us with well stuffed backpacks going at a good clip. (John made another joke about stuffed backpacks and more cat batting continued.) As I have great mind reading abilities, I took a peek into what they were thinking, and it was not nice. They were heading for the Golden Gate Bridge with 2001 intentions. I communicated to John instantly and John quickly hailed a cab. You guessed it. John said, "Follow those bikers!" Cabbie laughed, and away we went...at a discreet distance of course. When they were about a half mile from the bridge, the cabbie pulled over, and we watched them go on the pier next to the bridge. They did not slow down, and continued to the end of the pier and went bikes and all right into the bay. Before doing so, they had put on a diving mask and breathing apparatus. They disappeared into the water only one hundred yards from the Golden Gate Bridge. Foul happenings were afoot in my City!

I immediately got in touch with Seagull Joe and told him what was happening. In a flash of eyes many seagulls watched every move the bikers, now scuba divers made. They were going to blow up the Golden Gate Bridge. The scuba divers continued along what they thought was their merry way, while all along the great seagulls watched their every move. (Some of the younger bikers dropped a few "bombs." Ah youth...) Now, it was obvious visually, what I had already known mentally, they were going to blow up the north tower of the Golden Gate Bridge. (The only one I use.) They thought so, but I, the mind reading, mind melding cat, was reading their minds as they all swam toward the tower, and they had no clue what they were really up against.

I "communicated" with Seagull Joe and said, "Any ideas?"

Joe said, "Well, they are not my favorite people, but there are certain "fish" that could end this whole blow up show in about ten seconds."

"Yes," I said, "Give Jaws a call, and let's end this about to be worldwide signature disaster with one of the greatest terrors known to all", that being seeing a shark coming at you directly with its mouth open wide, and having zero chance of ability to survive. "The horror, the horror!" It was done. The sharks were communicated with about four men swimming under water to the north tower of the Golden Gate Bridge. The message to the sharks was in so many earthy words, free lunch, including four terrorists about to blow the north tower and bring down the Golden Gate Bridge. Shark replies were slurred and excitingly enthusiastic. Since they were not allowed inside the east side of The Bridge, they could hardly contain themselves. In fact some did not, and took a chunk out of their buddies just to get "the feel of things." Youth again...

The eldest shark, Ernie, considered an intellectual in many shark circles, since he had been in captivity as a child as the Berkeley Fish Farm had a camera placed on his snout. The film was very descriptive and even provocative, in some ways perhaps, as the eager sharks (Let's just say it.) ate the terrorists slowly and leisurely. Sharks when attacking their "foes," or meals as the eldest shark told the seagulls, start at the bottom and work their way up. The sharks began at the toes of the terrorists and worked their way to the top, proper shark etiquette and all. The camera was an excellent record keeper of all that went on at "Breakfast at Sea" as the sharks like to call it. Some like Ernie the eldest had also been in fish farms and had seen the movie, "Breakfast at Tiffany's." Slow start, albeit a start for shark movie reviewers. They were, after all, doing all they could to shake the notions that sharks were vicious killers and all that nonsense. "Harrumph!" many sharks were heard to say.

With little more than a watery whisper, the terrorist attack was completely obliterated. The sharks were extremely happy, and were all excited about more terrorist happenings throughout the entire oceans on the planet. The message went out, "If they are yelling 'allahachbar' eat them out of the water pronto!" (To a shark's mind, they are noble beings, enthusiastic and wanting to do the right thing. They have been on the planet longer than most living things, and they realize they have to get with all this "computer stuff" to survive. Lots of sharks have been in fish farms and have been properly educated. The movie, "Jaws" set their promotional plans back a bit. All that talk about sharks eating boats, kids, watermelons, and license plates did not help their cause. They are a minority and need understanding. Their slogan to the world, "Let's get together and have dinner," was quickly squelched, and the advertising firm was eaten. Ha! Ha! Just kidding... Sharks are working on humor now.) They should give John a call. Look what he did for me! Meow!

# Make The World Go Away...

*A*lthough I am the most brilliant entity in the world and am able to read and control minds, I have never heard of such a thing as invisible paint. At first glance, it seems like a tremendous tool for war. (Doesn't it seem like no matter what is invented it is used somehow for military use?) But, whoever invented this invisible paint is using it for practical jokes. No one knows where this paint comes from, who invented it, why, where, and what not. It is some top secret classified material perhaps. Some things that were done with it were hilarious, and other things could have been catastrophic if not caught and fixed in time. Let me tell you what happened.

John and I were out for our morning walk with me in my usual spot in the backpack standing up, paws on John's shoulders, looking all around to see what I could see, and maybe just to be nosey. We stopped in our usual coffee shop for a bracer, and stop the job! Right there on the TV were all the beauty queens of the world naked on stage in New York. How, what, who, and wow! It looked great, and Twitter talk was instantly ablaze all over the world. But, how did it happen? The girls said they got ready as usual, walked on stage, and all of a sudden their suits became invisible, and left everything for the world to see. My goodness gracious! Oh me, oh my, and such phrases were suddenly heard! Lots of fun and all, but it had serious implications and applications.

What if this invisible paint was sprayed on bridges, buildings, air planes, or people themselves, and you name it? The implications from everything of what could be done and what would happen were beyond imagination, except for mine. I did not like what I imagined at all. It could destroy the planet. Maybe more, if whoever invented this invisible paint could travel into space. This paint could make the moon go away. (Hmmm, is that a title for a song, 'Make the Moon Go Away'? Almost...)

John and I had a job to do. We had to talk to the beauty queens and their environs to see what we could see. (Pun intended.) The first beauty queen we spoke with was from Argentina. Very lovely, but of course, she said, "I did my usual routine before going on stage." She then made complete eye contact with John, while I was in the backpack, and I noticed him jump back a bit. "I did my exercises to acquire a pleasant sheen, and then I rubbed down my entire body with lotion." More eye contact with John and then she noticed me. She then looked deeply into my cat eyes. I knew instantly why all this eye contact was taking place. She was nearsighted. Really, it is a very good handicap for a beauty queen.

She continued, "I then put on my attire that I would be wearing for the stage, and it all seemed to be in perfect readiness. I went out on the stage and when I was about halfway through my walk on the ramp through the reporters and onlookers, all my clothes seemingly disappeared. I thought it was nerves or some type of an illusion, but I was wrong. People were screaming all over and so much light from all the cameras blinded me, so as I almost fell over. I made it off the stage in a hurry. Rushed to my dressing room and looked into the mirror. I was completely naked. It looked like that, but when I felt for my bathing suit, it was still there. I did not know what to do." She said, "What was it? How could this happen? All of the girls were walking around naked. If that wasn't bad enough, or good enough, (She smiled coyly), after all, we are very fit nice looking women. Some of the judges were naked as well. Much booing and all kinds of sounds were heard. Quite funny in some ways, but the pageant became a joke. All this work to get here, and now this whole thing has turned into some kind of a vaudeville show." John asked the usual questions.

He asked, "Did you see anything at all, even the slightest bit unusual?" (Clever, question, huh, for someone as nearsighted as she was? For John at that time, I was proud he could talk. As we were speaking, her clothes became invisible again. Sigh. Ahem.) She gave John another close eye contact and noticed his eyebrows raised and heard a choking sound.

She said, "What is it? Do you have a cold or allergies? I must ask you to leave if you do." She then looked down and saw... yep, you guessed it, no clothes again. She turned, completing the entire picture, and ran out the door. Seconds later, she quickly turned back around again as there were people all over the hallway. John put a blanket around her, and she calmed down. Relief and calmness came over her suddenly as she was after all an aspiring starlet as well. John gave her his phone number (real slick.) and said the usual blah blah blah...

She thanked us profusely and said, "Pretty pussycat you have there by the way with his beautiful eyes and his fur looks so luxurious. (I won't say a thing.) May I pet him?"

John said, "You have to have some type of a rapport before you do that. He is very protective of me, and well, I hope you understand." (I was reading John's mind, and it was getting close to all kind of nonsense jokes, so....) "Maybe some other time we can get together if you have any more info. Good luck with the show," he said, "we were just leaving."

She said, "Oh yes, there is one more thing. Just before I entered my dressing room, a janitorial type was passing by in the hallway with a big backpack on that was very similar to the one you are wearing. No pussycat in it though." She smiled.

John said, "I think rapport has been made."

She petted me, and said the usual "Pretty kitty, oh my, and oooh la la!" I gave it all one meow and peeked into her mind for a millisecond. That's all I needed to find out all she knew and what she had been thinking from when she was born until now. It was all ok, if you consider a beauty queen's mind to be ok to begin with. Ho hum...

We left in the car and turned on the radio and even the sports shows were now postponed which irritated John. All kind of invisible things were going on all over the Bay area. The biggest one being what appeared to be a huge hole had opened up in the Presidio. It was about a block square. When looking into the hole, it seemed one could jump in and go on forever, both frightening and fascinating at the same time. Upon further investigative news reports, one had opened up in China as well. It seemed that one could jump in this hole and truly end up in China or vice versa. Imagine that! Seems Bugs Bunny was right!

One could theoretically jump in this giant hole and fall all the way to the other side of the world at no charge. People would be passing each other going up and down. What would this mean? Actually, it only captured the imagination. In reality the ground and all were still there, but it just appeared that it wasn't. Invisible is what it was. This spray paint was on the loose and had to be stopped. Already people here and in China were flinging themselves into what they thought was a giant expressway to the other side of the world when in reality it was an invisible illusion. There were people getting hurt, and ambulance folks were afraid to pick them up for fear they might fall into the hole themselves. One can only imagine what this would mean militarily, or can you? Probably I am the only one who can do that. All in all, it would be used as a weapon that would cause mass confusion and death with everything being invisible, yet really still there.

We had to contact the beauty queen right away. She was our only source of finding who was responsible for this mess. We immediately gave her a call, and she agreed to meet us right away. Her name was Carmen, and she was glad to help, and said for us to bring along lots of blankets. While John was asking her questions, I took a peek into her mind and got a complete picture of the janitorial type she saw before getting ready for the stage. I saw him completely with a complete picture of his face. I ran it through my face file and identified him immediately. He was a grad student at Stanford. So, guess where we went next?

In one half hour, we met with him in his quite nice home which was very nice, in fact, for a supposed graduate in chemical engineering. We got to the situation right away. "Why did you do these things?" John asked, "Are you the one who is solely responsible for this mess?" We had to have the info immediately, so I did my mind scan technique and got what we needed right away. He was busy working in the lab on a hush, hush chemical project. He inadvertently had mixed up a different chemical in experiment. Voila! The chemical jar seemingly disappeared! He rechecked his experiment and found what he did. He was exhilarated. He made up gallons of the concoction and placed it in a spray container to test it out. That's about it. Still being in his early twenties, he had enough jerk mentality left in him to want to pull off a few pranks. He got that part fine. It was also found that the spray, as it was, would only last for about twenty four hours. Who knows how much longer it could last with more experimentation, maybe forever. That could be scary.

Since no one was harmed, and, in fact, some were helped after the entire world saw all the beauty queens in their completeness, they received notoriety, jobs, modeling contracts, and made a lot of moola. There were still about five hundred people laying out stunned and confused in the Presidio, but they would recover. Broken dreams mostly, and people in China were thrown in jail for trying to escape a worker's paradise. There were about a million of them and counting.

Of course, the formula for the invisibility paint juice, where it had originated, who did it, and so on had to be very hush, hush confidential, top secret all the way! I knew if some group of people, no matter how well meaning, found out about it, that it would eventually get out. Better to just stop it at its source.

The young gentleman was "convinced" quietly he knew nothing. No harm, no foul, just thousands of great news stories all around the world. People got to look at hundreds of beautiful women for about an hour, and some people proved they don't know their asses from a hole in the ground.

'Nuff to make a cat laugh and smile, too!

# Parallel Worlds

There are parallel worlds. One has to be careful. One step in the wrong direction and you are in that new world forever. Parallel worlds occur all over the world at different times and different places. One is going to happen in Marin, just across the bridge, tomorrow. I told John, and he said, "It sure sounds interesting. Let's go and try it out. What are we looking at exactly?"

I told him, "The parallel world has an entrance that you have to go through to get into that world. Once inside, you can do whatever you want. Well, almost, but it has to be in good taste. If the parallel world doesn't like what you're doing, it will send you back. If you stay in longer than ten minutes, you may have to stay there forever unless you know me, of course."

John said, "Let's go. This should be a lot of fun!"

Off we went the next day directly to the entrance of the parallel world in an isolated spot. (You didn't think it would be in city hall now, did you?) I told John again that we could only be in there for ten minutes and to keep me in sight at all times. Upon entering, I decided to do what cats like best, sit on a window sill and watch a bulldog almost choke himself by wrapping his leash around a tree. I would order a large portion of Russian caviar with some of the sipping best, crawl up in a tree, meow like crazy, and have the fire and police department, as well as the whole neighborhood, come out and try and get me down. All that attention and care, after about five minutes, I will just jump down and go away to hide. I think that is the perfect day for a cat.

John had no idea what to do. You think? He only said he wanted to meet Marilyn Monroe and Frank Sinatra. Magically, they both appeared. Frank sang 'Fly Me to the Moon', and Marilyn sang the song she did at Kennedy's inauguration. Then, they sat down and played a game of poker. (Frank is an inveterate gambler.) Of course I was there, read all the cards, and John picked up a quick fifty thou...

Frank shook his head and said, "Are these cards marked? Let's play one card stud. All cards down until the final draw, and blah blah blah." No matter what "we" won again. Frank laughed and said to Marilyn, "Do you know this guy?" He then asked John, "Who in the heck are you? I love playing cards with you because you win all the time, and I want to know how you do it." By now we had about one minute left to get out of the parallel world or have a tough time getting out.

I told John, "Time to go fella!"

John said to Frank, "It's quite simple really. I have a magic pussycat right here. His name is Casey. That's the difference between you and I Frank. I have a magic pussycat, and you have a tragic pussy."

Frank laughed, they shook hands, and as we went out the exit, we heard Frank singing to us, 'I Lost My Heart in San Francisco'. He then yelled out, "The next time, I want to win. I will pay you for losing. After all I am Sinatra!" Laughter by Marilyn and Frank followed us out the "door."

John said, "Looks like I owe you dinner. I know a restaurant that just got some fresh lobster right out of the bay. If you eat a lot, you can glow in the dark at night, and then I can see what you are up to," with a laugh.

I said, "Let's go. Seeing Frank and Marilyn made me so happy. It was so nice to sit on Marilyn's lap. Let me tell you what happened while you were playing cards. 'Nuff to make anybody laugh!"

So, as we headed back across the bridge with the sun setting in the west, which was so beautiful, I almost took a nap, but John pulled my tail and said, "Not now! The last time you took a nap in the car you thought you were a race car driver and made the loudest motor sounds I have ever heard. You jumped over my shoulder from the back seat, grabbed the steering wheel, and I let you drive. Good thing I controlled the speed. All the while you had your eyes shut, turning the wheel this way and that, and making that race car roaring noise. It was great. When we got home, you awoke and said, "Rrrrrrrrrrrrrrrr, where's the champagne?"

Where was I, oh yes, we finally pulled into the best restaurant on the wharf who knew us there very well. When we walked into the lounge with me in the backpack, each paw firmly placed of either of John's shoulders, my statuesque head perusing all around us, a waiter said, "Good to see you! Especially Casey, the customers love him, and he brings in lots of business what with all this 'Save the Animals' stuff, he is a perfect advertisement." We got our favorite table. Yes, even for a cat. Of course, I was a care cat. John ordered lobster for both of us, and it was great. The bar became crowded, and the hubbub and drone level was just how I like it. I scanned the minds of the people and all were happy. While eating and enjoying the people in the restaurant, we had a tremendous view of the bay and the bridge. Oops, don't forget Alcatraz and Angel Island, so much history and beauty. Whatta day! Frank and Marilyn, Alcatraz, and lobster, and oh yes, don't forget my Parnelli racing car drive across the Golden Gate Bridge. I was really awake, "Meow," I always wanted to do that. But really, John has to get some kind of a car with soup. This Bentley is so stodgy. So funny when he puts on a chauffeur cap, and I sit in the back for all to see. 'Nuff to make a cat laugh.

# Casey Goes to Moscow

*P*utin resigns! Almost! Something is amiss in Moscow. I could say more than usual, but I won't. We must go there. Of course, I will be loved and honored, oohed and aahhhed after and all about, but I must keep a low profile. In some situations I am too beautiful. 'Nuff to make a cat laugh! Off we go to 'Midnight in Moscow' as I like to say. Love that song. I am humming it now while John is picking a fight with one of the waitresses about a phoo phoo drink of some kind. Hold on, there, I finally heard him say oh, f--- it, just give me a glass or whatever of your best vodka. Wait a second, oops, the waitress or whatever these serfs call themselves is now giving him some pointers about how to order properly in Russia. She is say-ing, "We do not use the "f" word in Russia. We do not talk down to the people as if they were serfs." I'm sure you get the drift. Actually, that is John's odd way of flirting. Now, he is asking her if she will join him in a glass. She is smiling, and all is well. In fact, John of-fered to buy all of the serfs a steady strong drink. All smiled and agreed. I can see I am going to have to keep a close cat eye on John over here. Then again, he could pass for looking like a Russian, and he certainly can be a knuckle head at the drop of a pin. Maybe things will actually go smooth. He yells at the serfs, maybe a little too much, but they may take that as a sign of being related to the czar. If yelling means you are related to the czar, John will be accepted in a hurry. The czars were like bad cigars before we invented the perfect one. (The perfect one being the cigar we named the Cha Cha Coco Cabana Cancer Killing Cigar after getting some cigars from Castro, a ship full actually, that were accidentally intermingled with a chemical substance on the ship that killed cancer pronto, unbelievably miraculous, as so many great inventions are. We, John and I, now have a cigar that tastes great and kills cancer silly.)

We landed with no problems unless you consider thirty five degrees below zero a problem. Everything, and I probably mean "everything," is slow and jerky. Mea culpa, mea culpa, mea culpa...I just saw about ten range rovers going right across the tarmac at about sixty miles an hour. Guess who? We immediately got in what they call a taxi, and said I "suggested" to the driver to follow the range rovers, very discreetly, of course. Of course! Ahem. Off we chugged with steam and oil spouting out from under the hood as we kept up with the entourage. This was a good driver. We gave him some cigars and that improved his mood greatly, also some vodka. It was a necessity. After all, we were just about the only cars on the street, and if someone looked into the vehicle, they could not see a thing. The smoke from the cigars completely blotted us out, and the steam from the motor hid the car. If you happened to look our way, it would have looked like a low piece of fog being sucked along by the car motorcade ahead. We were headed for Moscow's best hotel. We had already been checked in there before we left America, so all was working purrfectly. (I had to throw that in there for Uncle Al. He wants me to give cats lots of credit for what I do. I say, "Sure Al, I know they can't wait to read the editorials every morning." Good uncle but sometimes...) All ten cars of the motorcade went into an underground garage, and we went right to the front door and into the magnificent lobby.

I was in my favorite riding place. John's backpack with a jacket on saying that I was a care cat, printed in Russian, mind you.

After all, I could pretend I was in disguise and that I am a Russian Blue Blood, and we were the czars' favorite pet. Might help, and then again the czars were not exactly very sociable with the rest of Russia. Anyway, here I am, all twenty pounds of me certainly dressed for the weather. We went right to one of the most magnificent restaurants I have ever seen. (Not imagined you can well bet... and win.) We seated ourselves at the best advantage point in the whole place and ordered Stoli and sturgeon. Two beautiful young women were seated about five chairs from us, and John ordered for them the same. (Like it or leave it, I guess.) They smiled courteously, and held up their glasses of Stoli in the universal sign of "Let's get blasted or something…" As I was standing up in the backpack with my paws on either of John's shoulders, I looked their way, and they smiled and squealed a bit, and then came right over. They could speak English! I knew they could as both had received the PhD's in psychology from Stanford just that year. They were excited about life, about being psychologists, about being beautiful women, and yes, being Putin's daughters.

The game was afoot, old boy! (Notice I did not say apaws, and disgrace Sherlock's great, now is the time for action line.) Social verbal greetings were exchanged, and then, they wanted to, well, you know. Give me a pet. I was on a chair by now, completely approved by all, as after all I was a Russian, very beautiful, and the most well known beautiful women in Russia were agog all over me. Might have helped a bit, you think? (Russia is like the tiger at the zoo, very pretty from afar, but don't get too close.) While they were doing the usual kitty kitty business, I was reading their entire minds. Only took a second, and instantly, I relayed it on to John. "John, come on, pay attention here! They are one of the closest people to the biggest killer in the world!" Yes, John was all farmer smiles and using his best Irish manners. He gave me a quick wink, and I knew everything was under control. Well, almost. We were having a great time! Smiles, clever repartee, and sparkling rejoinders were everywhere. I had Russian perfume all over me, and I don't know how many air kisses, or how many whatta' pretty kitty witticisms were thrown my way. Enough already! Where is Putin? But, aha, I did know. He would be here shortly to have dinner with his lovely daughters and one of his good friends. The great bar ballroom became strangely quiet. Take a guess. Little Raz was on his way. Oh, boy!

When one of the daughters of Raz was petting me, I placed one of my whiskers behind her ear. (It would stay there for at least a couple of days unless it was washed thoroughly off. I must be "catty" and say, "I bet it will be there for about a week what with this "lovely" weather and Moscow's crummy plumbing system.) Hmmm, beginning to wonder what kind of perfume is really on me? The great killer came over to where we were behaving quite pleasant, reserved, and mannerly. His daughters acted as young daughters do, and said, "Daddy, look at this beautiful cat, and this is John's cat." John said, "I have always loved Russia, and this cat reminds me of it constantly, big, beautiful, and mysterious. Sometimes eats too much…" "Carefully, John, carefully," I said to him. But, everything was alright, and laughter ensued. I do forget sometimes that John has a sense of humor. Gotta' watch where you use it, however, like I say, I must keep an eye on him. We were invited to dinner with them. Gee whiz, don't think I had anything to do with it do you?

The conversation was brisk, perfunctory, and when Raz asked John a question, the girls interpreted for him. Raz knew how to speak English much better than he let on. John was going to make a wise crack that he knew how to speak Russian better than he let on, but I scratched him just in time. He laughed out loud a bit, and Raz was taken in. He thought John liked his jokes. One joke after another was being tossed to and fro. Raz actually had a pretty good sense of humor. After all, what great leader doesn't like to think of themselves as one of the people? That includes knowing the language of jokes and the off color words used when telling them. Loved it! I was able to scan every bit of Putin's head, and the deal was sealed. Meanwhile, they could tell jokes about caviar, and where it goes on a bad date and whatever. Yes, it was getting very earthy, just how Russians like it, and just how John likes it too.

There was actually some kind of a meeting of the minds between John and Raz. John at an appropriate time thanked them for everything and hoped they would stay in touch. John said, "I know where you live, but I hope you don't know where I live," laughter ensued... not strained at all, and he gave them his business card. Handshakes were exchanged between John and Raz and the daughters, and I got back in the pack. Before getting in, I stood up meowed twice, and cat batted the air very quickly. John got in the last comment and said, "That's a Russian for you. Beautiful, fast, strong, and so loquacious!"

"You Irish devil you," I so loquaciously meowed in his ear while I was on his back in the pack, "now let's get the hell out of here!"

What I read in Putin's mind is exactly this. He wants to take over the world. By making a consortium of countries that need him, he will use them to do what he wants. Unfortunately, the countries that he is "making friends with" don't know how to drive a car much less what one needs to do for war. Yes, war. Here we go again, won't last long, but it will be ugly and terrifying killing millions of people. That's exactly what Raz and his kind is known for. That's what they do, horrible but true.

Let's wrap it all up in a Mexican proverb. A turtle and a scorpion were on an island, and the river was getting higher and higher. The turtle said to the scorpion, "I know you are a killer, but if I give you a ride, you kill me, and we both will die. Surely, you won't do that and kill yourself as well?" The scorpion got on the turtle's back, and they began to cross the river. Half way across the river, the scorpion stung the turtle, which would soon kill the turtle and himself as well, because he would now drown. Before the turtle died, he asked in great pain, "Why did you kill me? Now, both of us will die. It will surely do no good. Not to mention common decency and worldwide understanding of life?" The scorpion answered, "I killed you because that is what I do. I bring death and misery wherever I go. The more the merrier!"

'Nuff to make a cat cry!

# London Bridges

ing, ring, ring… We have an old fashioned phone. It rings with a real built-in bell. John finally answered the phone and after the call, said to me, "Want to take a trip, Casey?"

I said, "Where? Watching those bugs crawl across the bougainvillea bush is getting so boring. I guess my calendar is open."

John said, "London. They are having trouble with something they can only tell us about in person they said. Thought you would like to sit in and see what goes on at the pinnacle of the financial world."

I said, "Meow!"

Although I am the most knowing and intelligent thing in all and everything, I still have to eat. I wanted to be sure the flight we were on would have caviar, and some garlic crackers too. I have to eat them before John does. He never touches the caviar. It's all mine and I like it that way. We were on a private jet going straight to London from San Francisco. It was like the Air Force One but smaller and lots of fun. I walked all over the plane when we got inside, and even went into the cockpit and caught up on the gossip there. I would like to see how it is to fly this thing I told them. It looks easy enough. Just keep your eyes on the horizon and follow the map, take a left at the moon, and beat the sun to the London tarmac before morning. It's time for a nap on a three billion dollar intercontinental jet with only me and John aboard. They think they are taking John to see the Prime Minister, almost right. After they saw my cat care coat, they figured I am some kind of a medical helper. I love being incognito, and love that word too. After all, I am a cat.

As we landed, I jumped into the backpack on John's back, stood up, put m paws on John's shoulders, and kept my head on a swivel, looking this way and that, checking things out. So much for a cat to see, but I also had lots of responsibilities. London has been around for a long time and it has many secrets and mysteries that must be carefully respected. (Where is the shadow when you need him?) I was completely on cat alert and my hackles were on a millionth of a second's notice. Meanwhile, John almost, seemingly tripped getting into a royal limousine. In doing so, the backpack was dislodged, and he had to take it and me off and that is how I got a look at the under-carriage of the limo. Uh oh! My quick scanning of the undercarriage revealed some parts that were not made by British Motors. (John and I have instant communication at all times if need be, close to think-ing as one. But I, ahem, do the heavy lifting.) John told the Prime Minister and in the blink of a cat's eye, we were all out and going into another car, just like that. A truck actually with bicycles in the back, and you guessed it, on the bikes we jumped after putting on common working men's clothing. We biked off of the tarmac on the way to Big Ben. There we would have an international conference of all the leaders of the world who had their heads screwed on right. (The last phrase is something John would say. From what I see of humans, he is right. Cats don't have that phrase because we don't have stupid human problems. If only that bug would walk a little faster on that bougainvillea bush so I can get off this windowsill and meow for my midday bowl of milk. But I digress…knowingly, of course.)

It was a tight fit. The worker's jumpsuit John had on was not big enough for me to ride in the front of the suit. There was a basket on the bike and I got in. Perfect! I felt like I was leading the charge. I could also see everything from a great vantage point, and the Prime Minister almost smiled. He somehow had his pipe puffing away, and we looked completely common. Two old farts riding beat up bikes, wearing dirty greasy clothes, one guy puffing away, and the other with a snotty looking cat in the bike's front basket. There might be some English in me after all. It was a great ride. We stopped for fish and chips and the king's best Guinness, by golly! We did the usual hubbub one does in the great pubs of London. We learned a lot and said a lot. The Guinness was having its usual "enlightening" bene-fits, and the smoke from the Prime Minister's pipe kept anyone from seeing who we really were. If they happened to or thought they did, I "suggested" to them to forget about it. Before entering each pub and grub, I would do a mind reading of all inside and around the area to make completely sure it all was safe. Only a few needed "proper suggestions" such as "That's enough, go home, no…that is not the Prime Minister in the cloud of smoke," One of them thought—what a big fat cat getting a ride to boot—I gave him a very special "sug-gestion" and the trip continued in like elegance.

Political talk was always the order of the day. In fact, the very problems we were going to discuss at the conference were being spoken about in the pubs. Yikes! Gadzooks! Big Meow! Would it be possible to solve the problems of the world while we humble bumble working people and faithful furry companion were pedaling across the heart of London visiting the centuries old meeting and feeding places. Could it be these "common folks" possibly knew what to do and how to get it done in this sophisticated high tech world? The more we rode, weaving a little here and there, stopped and had a pint and a bite to eat, the more things fit into place. B'gosh and b'gorra, after a five hour bike ride to fourteen of the oldest most prestigious pubs in the world, and responsibly helped along by the king's best clouds of pipe smoke…I think I saw John with a cigar… and about a hundred or more "connected" people of the greatest city in the world—New York is on the line—the Big Ben Conference and its agenda had been solved.

The Prime Minister stopped at his favorite tobacco shop, got new supplies, and gave John a cigarette, and winked at me. Huh? He dove into his pocket and pulled out a fresh sack of, meow, you guessed it, caviar and cilantro. I do remember stopping in a Spanish pub a few blocks back. The Prime Minister sure knew lots. Far be it from me to make a "suggestion" to one of the most powerful and charismatic people on the planet. What with the smoke and Guinness and the camaraderie brought about by such things, why anything could be figured out. Shortly after our "bike ride," we got to the conference, five hours late. The press throughout the world had been set on fire! Where was the leader of the conference? A bomb had been found under his royal limo! Was he seen in Greenwich Village riding a bike, smoking a pipe with a commoner who had a fat cat meowing and waving his paws and tail the bike basket?

The Prime Minister walked to the front of the hallowed and well BS'ed and said in short, "Here is the answer to the problem that is vexing the entire world." He described the solution in concise and understandable terms, and everyone unanimously agreed for the time being at least, but it was a great start. You know politics. I hope it wasn't what a cat would do, but then again we don't smoke pipes or drink Guinness, most of us anyhow. Then again, there is my Uncle Al, and …the closer I looked at the Prime Minister, the more I began to wonder exactly who he was or what he was. All I really ever saw of him was a cloud of smoke and his feet barely touched the pedals on the bike. And why did he wink at me so mysteriously after coming out of the "smoke shop"? How did he know I liked caviar and cilantro? Why was he always wearing gloves? Once I thought I saw his face, and it looked like it had a bad shave. I now remember his bike looking like it had disguised training wheels on the back wheel. Do you think?

John and I were on the plane back to San Francisco. It had been a very busy day. First thing I am going to do when we land is give Uncle Al a call, then again, maybe not. I don't think the world could handle what might be. I don't even want to know, and by the way, where is that bug by now on the big bogey bush? 'Nuff to make a cat laugh!

# Be Careful What You Wish For

*I* lived in a sea of darkness broken up by rays of light every so often. There was warm milk all around me, music, and someone was rubbing my tummy. It was perfect. It was my beginning in life living in John's pocket. Because I was too young to see and move about in a coherent manner I enjoyed every second...make it millisecond. Since I work in milliseconds, it is best to tell you that. I was not only the smartest entity that ever was but I was also a cat. You have to make exceptions when there is a cat involved and so be it. I could think and read minds with my usual great clarity but I had to go through this particular cat phase of life.

John pampered me as well as most cat owners indulge theirs. When we were in the car he would put me on the front dash, and I absolutely loved it with music coming out from underneath me, people staring at me as we went by, and of course, the sounds coming from the radio. John would sing along with the music, I would put in a few meows, and then Vince Scully would come on. Nice, now I know why John sounds like a baseball announcer. Good thing we weren't listening to Oprah. I mean, after all, I could only live in his pocket so long. I was getting bigger, meowing louder every day, just kidding.

I am always polite and understanding but was way too big for the pocket so off we went to a tailor for a special cat-fitting. I bet I am the first cat that's ever been specially pocket fitted. I lived in my new tailored pocket until my head was sticking out all the time, and then big bucks John bought a backpack and that is where I remain when we go for a walk or when I am tired or when I have thinking to do that is. Cats are always thinking, don't you know? Me especially, I never stop thinking every millisecond of every second, of every blah, blah, blah.

I also loved to ride on the front window dash. At my full size when I stretched out I almost took up half the entire space under the front windshield, and it probably looked like a car coming at you with some kind of a fur dashboard. Glad he didn't put lights on me and try to make money letting people take pictures. At any rate that was the beginning of my life and I enjoyed it very much, but I also knew that I wanted a wood dashboard that would be, if I may say so and I will, "The Cat's Meow." John and I could communicate at will. The mind channels were always open. Sometimes I had to close mine because I can only take so much of Vinnie Scully and hearing John describe traffic like it was a baseball game.

I had to tell John, "You need to get more money so we, 'er me, can get a wooden dash, and we might as well get a big house to live in as well, and I have even more ideas!"

John said, "Ok pardner, whattya' got in mind? Har, Har and leave the banks alone." (He also does John Wayne.)

"Casinos," I said, "Let's go. I know of one 5.3 miles from here where wealth and opulence await us."

We went to the nearest casino and five minutes later walked out with 250 thousand big ones. We did a few more and that much money almost filled up the trunk, so I figured that would be about 'nuff. (Boy, are those slot machines fun! My engineering skills are light-years beyond all those tomatoes and cherries whirling around.)

I got my first wish for the wood dash surrounded by the rest that is on a Bentley and a beautiful four story house located on the highest hill in San Francisco where it is kind of windy, too. (Where is Tony Bennett when you need him? John will have to work in some Bennett along with his Scully. Forget for a while J and the Americans...so many high notes and to my sensitive cat ears...well, you can imagine.) The house was beautiful with a view from every window of the City and the bay. My great view, like most cats, is when I sit on the windowsill and watch nervous bugs go to and fro on a bougainvillea bush. They do the work, and I do the watching... cat fascination supreme! Ahhhh!

The morning paper thudded against the walk and I brought it in. The headline article that day was about the 49'er football team and all the players had completely quit, and now what would happen? Never heard of such a thing, you have to have players to field a team. Hmmm, sounds like some kind of skullduggery was going on. Some other game was afoot and I knew just what to do to stop it. We went to take a look at 49'ers headquarters which was a beautiful place that had everything except players. I checked the salaries of all the players on the team, and they were the best in all of football. But now there was no coach and the owner was a dweeb plain and simple. The team needed a new coach and maybe a new owner, and then the problem would be solved. Right? Probably, after all this was really only football, some kind of a game that almost all of us had done at one time or another. I mean, let's get this show on the road and "let the games begin!"

We called the owner and told him what he must do to get the team on its cleats and off its pants. He said, "Yes, thanks!" due to a "sudden thought" that had come to him, and it was going to be easy to convince all the players to return. Ahem. The work began immediately. The 49 story hotel was soon built adjacent to all the football facilities. The theme was 49 for whatever. The hotel was 49 stories, 49 rooms on a floor, 49 cents for drinks at the libation station. The owner was 49 years old, and a hotel room for 49 dollars, and blah, blah, blah. Don't forget now this is still football. The main feature was that the players all lived on the top floor. The gigantic roof was used for the football field and the stadium. You could stay at the hotel, and in the morning take the elevator up to watch the game. Yes, it held 49 thousand people. The tickets, I must admit, would have you paying for them for 49 years if you were pinching pennies. If you couldn't be at the games in person, the greatest set of TV screens were assembled throughout the hotel and in the sports bars. Literally, the greatest celebrities in the world attended every live game-you name them and they were there. Why you ask? Moola is the answer. The game had everything you ever wanted. Every game was like Super Bowl Day. The entire planet was agog continually almost everyone that is.

Guess who wanted a ticket most of all, had billions of dollars, but could not get in? It's the same group of schmucks that bombed New York City, pay crazed people to strap dynamite on and in themselves, tell the world they want to kill everybody, and when we see pictures of them, they walk and talk like the zombies we see on cheap Hollywood junk movies. (Harrumph, even a cat can only take so much. Meow!) I turned it around and offered them the tickets they wanted with a bonus. The price was too big to print to fit in this book, and I also promised them what they really wanted-a Caitlyn Jenner Special only in reverse. They all wanted to be men-the biggest men ever. They wanted what those types of people never have and you know what it is. It was granted as much as they even paid for it.

Since the stadium was next door to the greatest university in the world-Stanford, I contacted all the people who were on the cutting edge, pun intended, of what was needed which were plastic enhancement, replacement, abutment, supplementation, and fulfillment of the dream for men who had for eons been riding on a camel's hump. Rumor has it that is how a certain cigarette got its name. Riding a bone hump and sucking on a paper hookah stick guarantees what they think don't have enough. The deal was made. Every man in the world who had been riding camels and pounding sand signed up for football tickets and their dream of being able to drill for oil by themselves. The entire list of signees was given to the Marines.

Before the first football game of the season was played, hundreds of helicopters were seen landing and then taking off again, leaving from atop the 49'er stadium's giant helipad. No one knew where they went or where they came from. The Forty Niners' won the game and a certain calmness and quiet was radiated in all of civilization. It was also discovered that the mysterious 200 gallon per pint carburetor had been "suddenly invented" and now, there was hardly any need for all that expensive oil. Discovered simultaneously was the strange going's on of men lying face down and bopping up and down in the entire Sahara Desert. You don't think? 'Nuff to make a cat laugh!

# How the World Was Really Won... by Casey, of course

"*G*ive me one of those beerz out of the icebox on the porch and I will show yuh how tuh knock a sparrow off a branch at fifty yards...ok make it in about three steps. Har! Har! Boy, these beerz are slippery. All that greasy food you fed us last night is startin' to come out of my hands...ah, ferget it... those birds won't stand still. Nutz to them, who's dealing?" John Wayne said. Yes, the real John Wayne, along with my favorites whom I like to visit in Palm Springs, California. Along with big JW are his friends at Frank's house, Sinatra, of course. He has a couple of houses there and invited friends over all the time. His favorites and mine as well are John Wayne, Marilyn Monroe, Elvis Presley, The Prez-JFK, and whoever else drops in at any time-like Deano Martino or Peter Lawford-night and day. (*Good title for a song, huh?*)

Then there is me, Casey. I drop in occasionally too. I have the ability to do everything. Not to worry, cats can do that quite easily. Haven't you noticed? One meow is all it takes, and we get lots of loving attention. *What do you want? Is it too hot in here? So you want out? Or in? Ha! Ha! Do you have a tummy ache?* And lots of other gooey questions that I'm sure you have heard people utter in their soft sweet kitty cat voices, like talking to a baby.

Now, I am going to Frank's house, as I often do to see what is "really" happening in the world. The people I have mentioned and alluded to are the most powerful, well known, respected, creative, beautiful, and blah, blah that the entire planet has ever known. When Frank visited Churchill, he thanked Churchill for seeing him. Churchill said, "My young man, it is I and the British people who thank you. Your songs and interpretations of the words within them were with us in mind and spirit as we fought for freedom all over the world. Yes, it is I, whom is thanking you."

Of course, we know all about Big John JFK. He embraced the spirit of America and was one heckava good comic too, "by golly, there pilgrim". JFK was the kind of charismatic leader the world needed, maybe too charismatic upon occasion, ahem. Marilyn was, ahhh, Marilyn… beautiful and wonderful. Presley just had to wink and smile, and you were his, and then there is me... Casey, tying these people together in Palm Springs doing and saying things that we would love to hear and see. There is that glorious singing by Frank and Elvis, the beauty and charm of Marilyn, JFK with the hammer of the world always at his ready, and many other famous people of the world showing up now and then. Everybody who was anybody knew that where Frank lived was really the capital of the world as far as getting the real things done. Let's see what they were doing while I, Casey, whom Frank called the Mafia Cat, will be the eyes and ears to you of what they said and did.

Frank made great spaghetti too for them sometimes. Oh, my Momma Mia, and la de da…I can hear him singing in the kitchen now. They were just having their usual pre-meal card game which gets them ready for their post-meal card game when JW was going out to shoot some birds of a bush. He gave up because it was too dark and there was no rifle around.

JW said, "Well, Prez I see you brought along your lucky cat again. So far, you have won about fifty bucks and every time there is a big pot, you "always" win. That fat cat (I meowed a bit) just sits up on that damned counter or walks around the room, and I swear he can see our cards. Why even once I felt some fuzz in my head, and I thought he was taking a look in here. Har Har…come here kitty" as he picked me up and gave me some kind of a woof.

Phwew, I better let him win a few more hands so he will quit talking like that, don't want him giving me away.

Marilyn said, "Oh Johnny, (The only one who called him Johnny) that kitty cat loves you so much. I bet if you gave him some of that stinky stuff you have in your saddlebags he might go home with you. Here, let me hold him on my lap while you big ol' men play cards and cuss. No cheating now, this time I will deal and that will make you behave.

"Goddamnit Marilyn," Frank said, "hurry up before JFK and Elvis quit laughing at that whatever juice running down JW's skirt, so I can make some money. I gotta pay the electricity bills here you know, and they ain't cheap! I may even charge for the Italian brunch that Ava whipped up. Where is she, by the way? And where is that damn Mafia Cat? Oh there he is, sitting on the counter behind the President. That damn cat has it made. Reminds me of the time I was making the movie, "From Here to Eternity" with pussy all over the place." Frank laughed and so did everybody else. This time the joke was funny. Naturally, I did not let on, and just waved my tail at a fruit fly nonchalantly.

Marilyn began to deal the cards very slowly. She was humming some kind of a tune, and it had the "boyz" in some kind of a trance.

She then made comments that had them guffawing and hee hawing. Elvis had to go out back, and Big John blew a plume of smoke that covered the card table. JFK started to stutter and only Frank kept his cool.

Frank said, "If I don't win a hand pretty soon. That damn Mafia Cat is going to have to leave. I know that cat is up to something, and I can just smell it.

Big John said, "Har, Har, that ain't what you're smelling Frank. It's Elvis out there on the porch smoking some of that laughing tobacco. Makes me laugh anyhow… Har Har. I puffed some here a few days ago, and I thought I had never had a meal in my life. I went down to Mammacita's Café and ate everything on the menu. So heavy when I left that I couldn't get up on Big Copper-JW's horse. Had to get a taxi and hold the reins while Big Copper walked along beside the cab. By god, that cost me plenty. Where was Casey when you need him? If he was there, we could have flipped, double or nuttin'. Never lose when Casey is near. "Come here Casey, Casey, Mafia Kitty."

I went over and jumped onto Marilyn's lap…so much better than Big John even though he had soaked himself with Old Spice for an evening of conviviality and the like. A few card games passed and Frank's limo appeared. "Let's go!" Marilyn giggled, and they got in the large car immediately. They brought me along too, of course. I went to the back window and laid down for a short nap. Elvis' head was right by one of my paws as it was hanging off the rear seat.

I gave his head a couple of light touches and Elvis said, "Keep it up Casey, I know that is going to bring me good luck. Better have somebody wash your paw though, I have some makeup in my hair and it might make you cause a mess. The leather seats in the Bentley cost plenty. So does Marilyn's dress, and we can't have her walking around tonight with black cat paw marks on it. Hmmm, that reminds me of a song. How's about 'One Night with You'?"

Frank said, "I'd prefer it's that old black cat magic called love." Frank always changed the lyrics, knowingly or not, he won't tell.

JFK said, "I haven't heard Beethoven's Fifth in ages. Can you play that on a guitar? If not, I know you can play the score to the movie, "The Third Man" with a tremendous performance by Ali as well. So beautiful and her interpretation of the basis of the movie was scintillating. Is anybody listening? Big JW will you please pass me some of that excellent Mexican tequila, I feel like I am talking to the Russians at a summit conference. Come here, Casey, let me wipe the hair makeup from your paw. See, this is why I win so much. He likes the way I take care of him. I'm not trying to put him in a saddlebag to bring me luck, or sell him to Tony the Thumb. Plus, I am going to Paris next week, and he is invited. The first time we went to Berlin, I had such fantastic good fortune with the trade talks that I am beginning to believe he is really something special. We have to keep this a secret however between us. Let's seal it with a song, any suggestions?"

Frank said, "We'll dedicate tonight to Casey. Every song will be dedicated to him and only the people in this car will know what an exceptional cat he really is. We think...Frank winked twice...all in favor say huzzah, huzzah, and that is that. I know we can make decisions better than Congress and keep secrets too. I am quite sure that during this short ride to Mommacita's Café we have accomplished more than the world ever has. (Oh boy, here goes Frankie!) I'm so goddamn happy. Now, what song can we sing to solidify this most momentous occasion of all time? (I told you, Meow!)

"Oh Frankie, that performance reminded me so much of you in the movie, "Ocean's Eleven." I just love being here with all of you truly fun and great people. And…who's wearing that stinky Old Spice? What's a girl to do? Black cat paw marks on some very intimate parts of my dress and now I smell like a sailor on a London dock. Just for that, I get to choose the song. It'll be, "Fly Me to the Moon." Great song and it's just perfect for this occasion. The song was sung by the stellar group, all at once together…definitely a cat's meow. I sat on Marilyn's lap while everyone was singing and then had a catnap. Yawn…

Mommacita's was jumping, and we were escorted to a table right in front of the stage where we would hold the dedication songs to me, ahem. I was ready to go to Paris. There wasn't much more I could do here. I had already "helped" to shape what would be done throughout civilization. Besides, tequila and tacos makes me meow funny. I silently slipped away, like a fog on cat's feet, leaving under a cover of mist and boat horns on a dark harbor night. Actually, it was Mexican cigar smoke and Big John blowing his nose, but who's counting?

I'm home now doing my most favorite cat thing cats do all over the world-sitting on a windowsill observing what is outside there. I am a lucky cat because I have a sill to sit on. Now, to get down to business and watch those silly bugs walking all over that bougainvillea bush.

# Mamas and the Papas

*T*ime for our morning sashay. With me in the backpack, John can't really stride out. I am the most brilliant entity on the planet, and for my classification, one of the heaviest. That's why we sashay, a classy kind of walking. I get all the credit. Off we go down to the wharf and see the usual hubbub of the workers at six in the morning. Today, a huge truck load of crabs just arrived from Alaska. I love crabs, and so does John. May be time for a friendly "suggestion" I think. We move along and as all of you know, there are times when you can't get a song out of your head. Now, the Mamas and the Papas have "control" of me with 'California Dreamin', don't you know? It won't go away. As I am standing up in the backpack with either paw on John's shoulders and my head on a swivel perusing all around us, humming, ok… meowing, to the song in my head, I hear another sound in my head. Good bye Mamas and the Papas.

A huge submarine was just coming into the bay under the Golden Gate Bridge. Some thing was not right though. It was a Russian sub by its unique sound signature, and I knew it should not be there. My cat eyes and ears are to a power much more powerful than a human's. I realized that I was the only one who could see and hear the sub. It was using an invisibility cloak. But we, The United States of America, by God, should know all about that and not let this occurrence happen. I let John know immediately, and we got right over to the beach to see what we would see. John could not see or hear a thing out of the ordinary. I told him to contact our main man in the military secret police and tell him. John did. Five minutes later, maybe two, Thomas O'Malley, Chief of the San Francisco Military Secret Police was standing by us on the beach. But, he could not hear or see a thing as well. In thirty seconds the techno trucks and Navy Seal teams came to the location. The Seals were ready to launch and contact the sub, but first of all needed readings from the trucks. Nobody could see and hear the sub but me. Soon, a reading was made by the trucks, and all was in gear. The Seal boats shot out to the sub, surrounding it. Helicopters were above us and now what. Bomb the sub? Talk to the mariners inside? Crash into it on a suicide mission? Suddenly, it all became crystal clear. What we were seeing and hearing now was an attack by our counter intelligence section. They wanted to know how alert we were, and what we would do when such an attack was made. It took a cat to catch them, one super smart cat like me. Ahem!

All was soon brought under control, and the "Russian sub" went over to dock in Alameda. We had been snookered. Our vigilance was horrible, and all of the bay area would have been under Russian control. Millions of lives would have been lost at the very least. We spoke to the Chief briefly, and he said, "Thanks, with a heavy heart. May I take you and Casey to dinner at the Fairmont right now? After all, we have just overcome a possible national disaster. It was a bit late, but we did it. What I wonder is how you could see and hear the sub, and yet nobody else could?"

"Just lucky," John said. (Irish blarney strikes again. I had to duck down in the pack and cover my laugh as much as I could as I cat batted John to help me ease the pressure.)

The Fairmont was sparkling and bristling with movie extras that were in town. They were going to be used on a set in the Fairmont for a great upcoming James Bond movie. Even at now, approximately 7 a.m., all were bright eyed, and you know the rest of that line. The movie, with me and John's favorite actor, Sean Connery (Hope he reads this, so I can get a part...nothing racy mind you.) was about overcoming intrinsic evil in beautiful women. (Ho hum, what's new? Kidding aside.) They were having a great get-together for the most beautiful women from all over the planet. (If I said world, you would ask me, "How about the rest of places you have been?" Ok, and oy vey, so I let your mind ask a question.) The plot was about classy intrigue, music, great acting, sparkling repartee, and clever rejoinders with James Bond in complete control. (Shaky, maybe a little, but never far behind...pun intended.)

Three of the "women" were not so beautiful as the others. Clever make up, dress, and what have you transformed them to look like the rest of the 'real women". They were actually some kind of a new breed that only wanted control of everything. Hmmm, sounds familiar. They were robots. I knew immediately which ones they were. The morning sun pouring in from the giant bay windows gave off a telltale glow from their robotic bodies which only I could detect. I "communicated" to John, and he told the Chief. In a flash but surreptiously so, two robots were removed from the set. The other one had conveniently gone to the powder room. Security followed "her" in and would soon have her "powdered." Good start.

We were all ready to go. They had conveniently placed me on the great bar in the lounge area. Since all the bartenders knew me, they gave me caviar to walk around, meow, and cat bat people. What a get together! James Bond, the most beautiful women in the world, John and I, and an about to be made greatest movie ever! I meowed a bit, purred some, and "suggested to several of the starlets to come over and say "Hi" to John. Sean Connery needed help. The classic movie cry was heard. Silence on the set! (It got real quiet, even for a cat.) Sean walked into the bevy of beauties, sipping his vodka not stirred over the rocks, and took it all in. The antagonist, big bad villain, who had mind control over all the beauties came over, and said to Sean, "I don't remember seeing your name of the guest list."

Bond said, "I don't remember seeing yours either. After all this is San Francisco, not Loogash, where all are slaves and you are the "master.""

"Cut!" went the familiar cry, "Let's do it again!" Everyone got back in their places and prepared for another take. Just as they were getting ready, some kind of a mysterious white fog enveloped the set, and bedlam took over. John and I watched from the lounge bar. It was a mess.

All of a sudden, I heard the cultivated sound of a thick Welsh accent. It said to John, "Beautiful cat you have there. May I pet it, or at least get him some more caviar?"

John accepted, and said, "If you feed my cat, you must drink with me." (Big line from an Al Pacino movie 'Serpico', just in case the reader is under thirty.)

The thick Welsh accent continued and said, "Seems a bit foggy here. Care to come upstairs where there's no fog, and your cat, Casey, I believe I heard you call him, can do what he does best, nothing but everything." We went along with the person who had "the voice." You guessed it, Sean Connery. Upon getting to Sean's "digs" at the Fairmont, we smiled greatly and exchanged greetings. Sean said he knew all about the "secret sub," and how we had helped capture it. He said you might actually be a real James Bond. I meowed immediately, and we laughed for some time. We also found out that Sean Connery was a great patriot of the right kind, and we were impressed. (Well, I knew it all along but....)

John then asked Sean, "What happened to the movie?"

"All a ruse," Connery said, "The "three women" were going to disfigure the most beautiful women in the world, thereby scarring beautiful women to hide. That may very likely cause a threat to the human race. Men would have to hang around with the likes of Hillary and Pelosi, and that will be the end."

Eyes rolled and more vodka was poured. Sean and John gazed out of the suite overlooking the Golden Gate Bridge with the sun reflecting from its structure. Connery said, "I've been in a lot of movies, but that pussycat in your backpack is the most beautiful cat I have ever seen. Don't suppose we could make a deal?" Wink. 'Nuff to make a cat laugh!

# If I Ruled the World, We Would Not Be on Menus

*I*magine this-a cat army. Stick with me now, not the usual army where there are helmets, guns, and boots, and airplanes. Although, I'm sure a few of us will want to fly a plane. Imagine an army of cats throughout the world that would be together with complete communication every second of the time, from now until eternity checks out. Hmmm, reminds me of a great movie, "From Here to Eternity," where there were the biggest stars in the world, the best songs ever, acting, plot, and... where was I? Ah yes, cat army. As I said… stick with me. This will be a different army, a greatly advanced army in every way in that everything will go exactly the way we want it to go. There will be peace, rational thinking, caviar, sardines, and... right there is a fantastic start like never seen before. Like I said imagine this, another great song by John Lennon just appeared, "Imagine". Yikes, already we have the marching music and movie theme in place. The rest will be downhill. This is exciting! Now, here is how it is going to be worked out.

I will communicate with every cat in the world and explain to them what we are going to do. Since cats have inbred communication and one language, this will take about a day. Meow! The key factor is that cats have access to every human and human dwelling and work place on the planet. The cats will know what the humans are doing and where they keep what they need to control the world. With that all is ours. Being cats we don't want it, we just want to be sure it will do what we want or else we will get rid of it. The driving force behind much of this plan is that we are tired of being part of the featured menu in many parts of this planet. So horrible and as mentioned before, there are some cats of egos that must be fed with something other than sardines and caviar. I know some of them will want to fly planes off an aircraft carrier. Ahem, we know who that one is! Alright already, I will set up an aircraft carrier cat flying school. Harrumph...some things are almost too much for me. But, surely I jest. I really can't wait to see a Siberian tiger at the controls of the absolute latest flying machine getting ready to fly from the Ronald Reagan carrier by saying, "Siberian Sam to tower, all systems and checks ready to go. Please advise when ready. Check." "Tower to Sam... Hold tight. We have three in front. Have a good flight, marine."

Back to complete communication with cats being everywhere in the world ready at a moment's notice to put in the plan whatever need be to help run the world as smooth as a cat's meow. Let this be a lesson to anyone who wants to know how to get things done. Don't eat the help! Ahem! I immediately contacted the top cats all round the globe and told them of my plan, and they all agreed. A few selling points were necessary but most of them felt they already controlled the world. When I told them of the "bennies," they agreed to pull themselves off the window sill and quit watching bugs crawling across bougainvillea bushes for a few minutes a year. I would begin the cat takeover in Moscow.

My top cat in Moscow is Ivan. Wouldn't you know? Meow! I said to Ivan. "I want you to know exactly what the ten leaders in

Russia are doing every second of the day from here to eternity." We almost broke out into song, he wanted to be Sinatra, and ok, I will be Lancaster... again surely I digress, knowingly however.

Ivan agreed and said, "How about contacting the Big Boys, back in the Russian woods for sheer size and growl-ability that can really get someone's attention? Being seven foot tall, four hundred pounds, and having a bad attitude, they can get a lot of work done just by showing up. When can we set up a meeting?"

I said, "John, my good buddy and traveling companion, is on the way right now. We will be there tomorrow, and I will talk to all of the big cats in Russia. Be sure, please, pretty please, wink, wink, to tell them there will be plenty of catnip, cigars, and caviar, even more because we have to keep the Big Boys happy. They are a touchy group, and I think I know why."

The next day I picked up Ivan and went deep into the Russian woods where we met with the Big Boys and told them "The Plan." There were deep basso profoundo growlings, lip licking, four foot tail waggings, paw wavings, and a couple of them stood up and said some wild stuff that I can't repeat. I told them before we went any farther that I wanted to check their teeth. That brought the giant cave enclosure to a cat cacophony that none before in the world has ever had the great chance to witness. I loved it-talk about fired up. Clyde Beatty at his best would have smiled and doubled their sardine rations. I said, "I want every one of you to get your teeth checked by me. I am a dentist. (I read a book about it on the way over.) There will be no charge, and if you don't like it you can leave." I did a cat scan of their minds, and being cats, they quickly realized the practicality of what I said. Those who were not quite sure were gently "helped" by a mind tweak. It was found that every one of them had some type of a tooth irritation and plenty bad cat breath as well. Phwew! Had to dip a few! (Where is a camera when you need one?) Each Siberian opened wide, (more cameras needed) was pressure sprayed, and x-rayed. I had a state of the art dental laser which knocked out all cavities. I cemented the damaged parts and even pulled a few teeth. Talk about fun. One tooth was as big as a beer can. Which by the way I suspected some of them had been sucking on before the meeting began. There would be no toothache excuses now to keep them from doing whatever was necessary.

After the dental duties were performed, there was surprising calm, and intensity of concentration. A slow green glow was emanating from every giant Siberian's eye in this enormous snow cave. I said, "Now I can tell you have never felt better in your life. You know what the plan is and what you are to do. Are there any questions before the meeting is over and we can begin the 'er, social activities?"

One of the biggest cats waved a paw and said, "Where are the catnip, caviar, cigars, and other things that start with a "c" that we were promised? One more thing... who's dealing? Har! Har!"

So, the party began. Some of female tigers had come along to see how their Big Boys would react to this worldwide meeting and had anticipated what was on the menu, not us for once. They had fancied themselves up to be even more attractive than usual and had set up card tables, big ones complete with the big three-cigars, caviar, and catnip. The Russian national drink, at its very best, was served by the bucket. The drone level in that fantastically gigantic snow cave sounded like a plane taking off from an aircraft carrier. You guessed it. These would be the cat aircraft carrier pilots. Much of it had to do with their feet being able to reach the pedals. I can't tell them everything-teeth or no teeth.

We returned to Moscow, and the plan was solidified. Whatever was to be done by the "leaders" of Russia was to be approved by us.

No muss, no fuss, but lots of us. (Looks like that is the end of my try at Russian poetry.) In Russian it sounds like, take your boots off and let's shoot some more czars. That won't do. One down, two to go-China and the United States of America. China, here we come! If you would have known at the time that "we cats" would no longer be on the menu, you could have made zillions by investing in McDonalds instead. Meow!

Louie is my contact in The Forbidden City. Cats, however, are not forbidden there but not for the reasons one would think. This will all end tonight when my precious brethren will no longer be served a la carte or ad the main entrée. A tour de force of mind cleaning will be given to everyone in China one hour after my arrival. At that time everyone in the entire country plus the menus, utensils, and other accoutrements that are used to continue the barbaric practice of using us for food will be completely stopped. It will be accomplished by giving every cat in China the ability for one second to mind read and "suggest" to everyone they see to completely forget everything they have ever known about cats regarding human consumption. The people who in turn had their minds "suggested upon" will in turn pass it on to all those they see and so on until the message is received in the entire country. It will be as though it never happened or ever will be again. It will not even enter any oblique thought process. All the menus and whatever have been written about us in that disgusting manner will be destroyed. We will be free.

It was a roaring success as I knew it would be. Our huge brethren in the snowy mountains were not affected. In fact, if given the chance some folks might end up on their menus. Nothing personal, cats will always be cats. These same large cousins were given the same deal as were the Siberian tigers. They all wanted to be aircraft carrier pilots-a scary thought. Their motto will be, "On the ground or in the air, we will get you anywhere." Look, I have to give in a little to a seven foot four hundred pound kitty cat. If you don't like it, you go and talk to them. Harrumph! Besides they also like to play cards, and I fixed their teeth as well. Some are just so sweet and let's not push it.

Now for the United States, my plan would pretty much be the same here except there are no more pilots. If that would have happened, we would have had to build more aircraft carriers. Those Big Boys had really found something they liked just like a treat for us, their smaller cousins. You know how crazy we go when it is treat time. A treat for a Big Boy was flying a plane off an aircraft carrier. If you don't like it, you go tell 'em. Be my guest! You should be the incarnate of Clyde Beatty, you can always win at cards, you can drink vodka out of a bucket, smoke cigars, run fifty miles an hour dead drunk, and I hope you get the picture. Believe me, their idea of a good time could be you.

In no time we had the United States under cat control as well. We had difficulties finding the leaders and what their dastardly plans would be. One leader had a great plan to put a woman's picture on either the ten or twenty dollar bill. She was fraught with confusion when asked to make a choice. Another leader said there were aliens all over the place. Another said, "God is gonna get us!" Another said, "Blah, blah, blah." Finally, ten leaders were found with the top leader setup having twenty four hour protection by Labrador retrievers. He had the "Go Ahead" signal tattooed on his armpit and needed a mirror to see it so he could tell the top Missile Men when to shoot or stop at the ready. We compromised the Labs with pork chops, cigars, and being invited to our card games. We even let 'em cheat some. They loved that best. All they had to do was lick the tattoo off the president's armpit for the trade. As it turned out it was some kind of herbal tattoo, and it made Big Joe, the top Lab who licked it off really bombed. The tat must have been cannabis based because Big Joe got awful hungry, gave me a call, then demanded more pork chops, and wanted to start cheating at cards immediately. If you ask me, I think Big Joe might be the real leader. 'Nuff to make a cat laugh!

# Casey Interviews Jesus

*I* have found that beside my tremendous mind, I also have the capabilities of going anywhere in time and seeing people we would all love to talk with. The top choice for many is Jesus of biblical writings, so off I go to interact with him in any manner I see fit to better find out what he "is really like."

It's a cold day outside of Jerusalem, and Jesus is just waking up. He has a big headache because the camels have wandered far from the hut.

"I have decided to be one of the camel herders and all around flunkies." Jesus says, "I have to go get the camels, we have to be in Jerusalem soon, and I don't feel very good from having too much wine, and where is Mary (as in Magdalene)?"

I said, "She is still in the loft. I think you fell out last night."

"Quit kidding me," Jesus said, "And cook up some breakfast."

"What do you want," I said.

Jesus said, "No more goat or turtle. Oh, to hell with it, just get me a glass of wine, and I will say a prayer."

I brought over a camel flask of wine, and Mary suddenly crawled out from under some straw. She said, "Well now, thank you very much. Jesus is kind of hung over this morning, and that is just a sheep's dream." (Sheep were thought to have good dreams in those days. Today we would say that is just the ticket.) "I told him to back off that flask last night, but he started to sing and pray," and she winked, "But he was so determined."

He said, "I am the son of God, and I have to be strong. Grrrrrrrrr…" Well, I joined him and said "Grrrr…." Mary laughed at us both.

Jesus jumped up and said, "Mary, hold thy tongue, oh young and healthy woman. The shepherd whom you are talking to may be a spy." He looked directly at me. In my disguise I had forgotten to change my eyes from cat to human. He looked into my cat eyes, and I looked into his blasted camel wine eyes He asked, "Are you a spy, oh shepherd of low caste? Tell me or by my holy power, I will cook you right now."

I said, "Heck no, Jesus, I am only a lonely shepherd wanting to help you with your mission. My name is James, and I am your servant."

"Ok," Jesus said, "I feel better now." (I took a peek into his mind and read all that had happened and will happen, and "suggested" to him that I was just what the doctor ordered. Gotta' lighten it up sometimes when you are talking to Jesus.) Jesus went on, "Yes, I can see you will be my faithful servant. Now, Mary please leave this stall, and let James and I make some plans." Mary squealed, and gave me the look of "Aha!"

Now we know, Mary is Satan in disguise, and she said beautifully and threateningly, "I will see you soon."

*"Well now,"* I thought, *"The devil has been living with Jesus, and now knows that Jesus was pulling the wool over his eyes as well. Mary Magdalene disguised here is the devil."*

I got the camels all ready and a sled for Mary. Her eyes were ablaze, but I calmed her down with a "suggestion" to her mind. Shut up and behave or you won't get to be president like Hillary Clinton. We got on the camels and goosed them as hard as possible to get to Jerusalem. In about two hours of sand and you name it, we arrived. Mary had stuff all over her, and her attitude was just as bad.-one mad she devil. Jesus knew all the best places to go for food, so we followed him. We went into some kind of a camel garage, got off, and were escorted inside. Big bongs were all over surrounded by food and wine and dancing girls.

Jesus told me, "Don't tell them that I am Jesus. Your name is James, and I will be Louie. Her name is not known. She is a slave. Jesus winked at her, and she, the devil, smiled like *wait until I get you back in the stall*. We all three got on the bong, and ate the food and the wine spread out before us on the tables. Until our thoughts were…and the bong and the bong and the wine and I yi yi yi! I don't know how Jesus does it. He was on his third bong and second flask of wine. I did not have a bit, but Mary, the devil, was completely blasted. She was spread out phooey with wine in one hand and a bong tube in the other. The devil was totally doped." I talked to the dancing girls, and they called him Jesus. They all knew his name, but acted like they didn't, and called him Louie as they giggled. One said, "And that ain't all." The other girls whooted and carried on, and I noticed they were sucking on the bong and drinking wine, as well. They were all plastered having a good time.

Jesus now sat up and said, "I want supper. This will be my last supper. Well, maybe my supper before the last supper." Humor was beginning to happen. Of course, we ate the roast camel, pig, sheep, and goats. The dancing girls had swiped barrels of wine from King David's cellar, so we could not go wrong. Jesus jumped up from time to time and said, "Oh, ye of this or that, and go to hell, and the fires of damnation, and on and on…" *Something like that…*

Mary grabbed him and said, "Calm down, you are just bumping your gums, and you will get in trouble if God finds out. I think I saw a shepherd over there taking notes."

"Which one," Jesus said, "Show him to me." Mary showed him to Jesus, and he looked like Walter Cronkite. Jesus pointed his middle right finger at him, and a lightning bolt came down and dusted Walter. (Dust to dust and all that stuff, you know.) Nobody missed a beat, but the message was clear. Leave Jesus alone. What happens here stays here. By now, it was pretty much impossible to have any type of a conversation with Jesus. He would say go and get more wine, or say take this or that, I was getting nowhere. Besides it had crossed my mind that someone might say I was an evil shepherd, and I would get the lightning bolt. All in all a fairly crummy look at Jesus and his life. Maybe he was having a bad day. But, we learned about Mary Magdalene, a biblical buffet, and that there was no marijuana laws.

I was very glad to get back home. I gave John a special meow, and he said, "Boy, you must be feeling terrible." He fixed water for me in the tub, and in I jumped in. John laughed so hard, and asked if I wanted deodorant when I got out. I was floating on my back in the water, and he chinchucked me a couple of times. I was so glad to be away from Jesus and the devil both. 'Nuff to make a cat laugh!

# The Fool on the Hill

$\mathcal{M}$y cat hackles were up. Something was going on close to me, and there, I see it now. It is a van parked down the street. I went immediately to check it out. It's easy for me. People think, "Oh there is another cat trying to catch a bird." How right they are. In this instance, it was a very big bird indeed. I just walked under the van and listened. Not only listened, but looked. The underside of the van was covered with many things one doesn't see under a truck. This one had state of the art technology for listening, seeing, sending and receiving messages and... it could do anything, and probably even had a "restroom" of some kind. It had its devices pointed directly to where John and I lived. It was monitoring and taking a continuous movie of everything we did. As the saying goes, "If you pull a tiger's tail, you better get ready to see its teeth." Here I come! In about two seconds I knew exactly what they were up to. It took me so long because another cat tried to get under the van, and I told him to leave discreetly, of course. Big problem was that they knew where we lived. Now, I knew where they lived, too. Something had to give. They were our enemies. They opened "fire" on us and could do so at will, not that they knew where we are. Ok, let them try this on for size.

The "group" who was doing this was not Tony and Joey from Little Giovanni's Italian restaurant. It was Vladimir and Petre. Guess what deli they came from? I had to stop them from what they were doing, and at the same time, make it kosher with the special black ops section of the United States Marine Corps. Make no doubt about it, if any foreign country invades our soil and attacks any part of the USA, they will be dealt with right away, and the rules of the alley apply. No rules. Or, just like the rules those of our enemies, no rules. They will try to obtain their objective in any way possible. I love it. They think they are tough, and I bet they have never been in a cat fight. (And, I don't mean the one with your old lady...oops! Just for fun, I wanted to turn these morons "loose" and make it all look like a big accident. I had already stored all the info in my "computer," I knew who they were, and who they worked for, and knew what they were doing. Now, for the fun!

I immediately told John what was going on and to call the "escort service" ahem. Four beautiful women in a Rolls Royce drove by, pulling up near the van, and then got out and did ditzy things to distract them and get their attention. They would drop their purse, break a heel, bend over a little, oh yes, and pick up things on the street. Then, get in and out of the car. One or another would then get out and have trouble lighting what looked like a "cigarette." Then, they would laugh loudly, and pass around to each other what would appear to be a champagne bottle. Look at their watches, and act annoyed saying things like, "Well, where are those people? They're late already." The Ruuskies, yeah, it's the Russians, still smoking hot about what we did with Raz Putin and company. The intellect of that country is Stone Age i.m.o. All they have to do is get along, but find it impossible as do so many others in the world. It's in their "levis"-their genetic makeup. They can't help themselves. Ask them and they will have a great excuse. But, an excuse is just that, and their excuses are so funny. For instance, "Why did you attack and try to take over Switzerland?"

The Russians say, "It vasn't us. Somebody dressed like us did it."

"Uh, ok, then why is it the men we captured, their tanks, and supplies, all came right from the Kremlin. Even their personal id's had Moscow addresses. They admitted it all to us."

The Russians will say, "Verrry klever crimenals. Ve are alvays trying to capture dem. Ve can't vait."

"We caught a Russian general who was there. He is pictured with Putin in many pictures and has been to the United Nations many times. He told us Putin said to "Go and get Svitzerland."

The Russian answers, "Vait until ve get a hold of him. Dhank you very much for the help."

"Uh, one more question, we have telephone conversations with Putin and many party members talking and given directions about taking over Switzerland. We also have movies of them talking together. Putin was seen, boldly giving us the finger when he discovered we were taking pictures and monitoring his conversation."

Russian retorts, "Clever evil actors, no doubt from ze vest, New York City is the capital. In case you vanted a very direct Russian answer, it is all simply a diabolical plot by the vest to discredit a great and traditional country, blah blah…."

One more and I promise this is the last question.

"Ya, ya, oh goodie," goes the Russian.

"When you walked in here, you had mud on your shoes which we found to be from the very area where the takeover of Switzerland was attempted. You are also one of the people we captured and set free after being interrogated. In fact, you are the general who was pictured with Putin and heads of state at the United Nations grand ball room. If that is true, it was certainly the Russians who planned and 'attempted" to take over Switzerland. You also told me, and I know this is "out of school," that if I could get you a couple of girls for you and your boys, you would be very thankful. Mix in a case of vodka, lots of ice, and room service."

"No glasses. Ve Russians drink right out of the bottle. Not like ze vesterners vasting money on glasses. Harrumph. Also, send up a good Italian tailor, a barber, a dentist to clean our filthy teeth and paint them white, or whatever you sneaky vesterners do, and a "special doctor" with many kinds of pills. Ahem, you are a man. You know vhat I mean. You said if I vould only do us these small favors, and oh yes, one year's lease on the top floor of the Valdorf Astoria, with room service, of course. Throw in a tour guide, and just for fun, make it be a chickey type who can speak Russian. Make it three chickies. Ya! Ya! I may have to ask for a few more "simple" things, but it is between us, man to man. Goddamnit! If you will do these things for us, we will do what you want, all for mother Russia, of course."

I continued, "And by the way, this has all been recorded visually and in sound. How can you possibly deny the Swiss blitz?"

The Ruskie says, "Just another vestern movie. You can make anything happen on the movies. All is nyet!"

Excuse kings-they still have royalty after all. Now they are being a royal pain to the U.S. Marine corps. Here come the teeth of the tiger. The boys in the van very quickly knew they must help. "Ya! Ya!" Jumped out, invited everyone in, and just like that, one thing led to another. I wanted it all to be as if it never happened like 'Mission impossible'.

The "girls" were really a select part of the special ops group and quickly compromised the creeps, and they may still be being interrogated. The van was picked up in a truck made especially for such maneuvers and zipped them away. No one will ever know, or long remember, or...where was I? Everyone was taken in, and the project was "secured." It was as if they disappeared.

What with the Russians, who knows? Maybe they believe some of their own baloney, and it carries over into other things. Baloney begets baloney. 'Nuff to make a cat laugh!

# Brigitte Bardot Still on the Go

*C*at golf is very popular in Paris. It all began when the most prestigious golf tournament in the world was being played in Scotland, England. The cats liked what they saw on television while their owners, like mine were watching the game. That is when I decided what I wanted to do. I told John that we should go and away we went. Thousands of cats, such as myself, almost like me, ahem, were now on our way to Paree. This would be almost as much fun as watching a bug crawl across a bougainvillea bush. We cats really love that! Thousands of cats converged upon Paris with one thing in mind-golf. We had to play cat golf, and we had to play right now. I quickly negotiated a 100 year contract with one of the greatest hotels in Paris. Well, that's where John comes in handy, but I wrote in the fine print. Meow. The hotel was sixty stories high with a gigantic roof and a pretty good place for a cat golf course, don't you think? The word got out as fast as you can think, and thousands of cats showed up on the roof. Some climbed up the sides.

I had the entire roof set up just like St. Andrews in Scotland and all the cats began to play at once. Of course, they were properly dressed. They looked like miniature golfers and instead of baseball caps they wore appropriately fitted Humphrey Bogart hats. They had caddies and carts as well. One entrepreneurial cat had built a cart made especially for cats. He had it souped up so it would go about 30 miles per hour and had a deli on it crammed full off caviar and, of course, French champagne. It also had a nap pad in case things got slow or woozy. He had thought of everything.

All the cats began to play cat golf at once. They played any hole they wanted, and some were seen to throw the ball at the hole if they were in a trap or whatever. Some just threw the ball period and never got out of the cart, just drank champagne, threw the ball, and never stopped. One cat used a sling shot, another used a baseball bat, and one ingenious cat, well aren't we all, ahem, had a type of gun he fired the ball out from. Keeping score was difficult and the cat reporters in the booth had a difficult time with it all. The entire city of Paris was completely agog with the cat tournament. They were so happy. People were singing in the streets. The Moulin Rouge was up and running briskly as ever, and the Left Bank was lit up 24 hours a day. The newspapers reported this was better than Dom Pérignon 1952, and the entire city was completely full of joy, happiness, and all that Paris had been and was expected to be. The cats were knockin' 'em out! Meow!

Many Parisians wanted to see the cat golf game in person. They booked rooms in the giant hotel and watched the tournament evolve. Cats going all over the roof at 30 miles per hour on their carts, drinking champagne, playing golf like pony polo, throwing the ball, or just carrying the ball in their carts and dropping it in the hole. Then, they just left the golf balls there since they had plenty more. One "golfer" had got some kind of a huge balloon in which he rode above the roof and grabbed the golf balls when they were shot or thrown or kicked in the air with no problem. The cats started taking shots at him, and eventually the cat with the golf ball gun scored a direct hit. Boom! Free golf balls available all over Paris. The kids loved it and made lifetime golfers of them.

Since some of the cats were quite young and had just been born on the roof of the Paree de Cato, as it had now been named, they needed a home where they could get their cat wheels under them. The children and people of Paris were only too glad to help the little kitty golfers with food and shelter until...well, until a long time. You know how kittens are, and I fondly remember how John took me in "on a dark and stormy night." I was lost, out in the cold and rain, my tiny cat eyes could hardly see, but I could smell. It was John all the way. He smelled like caviar and champagne. He put me in his pocket and that was my diet until I could get out and eat some potatoes or anything but caviar and booze for a while. It was too much of a good thing. The little kitty golfers would be cared for and groomed to be great golf players.

Meanwhile the tournament continued all day and night. It would go on for four days just like the ones that Arnold Palmer used to play in, only not around the clock. There were other exceptions-female golfers. They loved it too, but when they found out they needed announcers to broadcast the event live they decided to do that. They rode around in droves and talked constantly about what was going on. What the golfers were wearing, what they were eating, asking about their families, the carts, the weather, and simply just out and out cat gossip. People loved it. Soon many people were going about in Paris wearing the latest cat fashionable Humphrey Bogart hats and riding golf carts, bigger ones of course.

Since this tournament was such a smashing success and had brought the world's attention once again back to Paris, I decided to capitalize on it. I decided to build two more hotels that would not affect the beautiful French architecture or landscape in any way. One hotel was set up for real golfers like Arnold Palmer and such where human could play. It was so successful it surprised even me. All of Paris became so invigorated that the Cathedral of Notre Dame was hearing confessions night and day with lines going out into the Seine. More business generated was great for everyone in Paris. There were boats that had to be ready to hold the confessioners as they prepared to confess. Now Paris was completely alive all day and night. The sins of the terrible Nazi past would be completely expunged and their minds could be completely free. Or could they?

With such a huge endeavor I had foreseen certain situations might arise and the word went out to get the remaining Nazis. We cats had checked on those who did not go to confession. They were the Nazis. We knew because we had cats sitting in the confessional. It was a tough job and extra champagne was allotted to the confessional cats. One cat thought he had heard Brigitte Bardot's confession, and he is still receiving treatments.

With excellent information and the help of the police almost every Nazi was rounded up. Some had escaped by a cat's whisker to Rome and the Vatican, which we cats called the Vaticat. We controlled the Vaticat/Vatican completely. Almost every priest had a cat, and the pope was never without one. (I could make several bawdy jokes about the celibacy of priests and the synonym for cats but I won't. We cats are not only discreet but tasteful. Harrumph!) The few that have escaped to the Vaticat were under constant surveillance. We knew they would never be completely eradicated. We exchanged knowledge of their every move and action by letting a few of them be "free". Their pets were German Shepherds, and I mind melded with the German Shepherds, so that they ran away the first chance they got leaving them without their dog companions. It would make it so much easier to keep an eye on them.

Now that Paris was made completely anew and invigorated by my great idea of cat golf, it was time for us to go. Meow! Of course John got much of the praise for what had happened but he remained out and about mostly at the finer restaurants with me in his back-pack. It was only proper however, that he address the Parisian fathers on a job well done. It was short and to the point. He said in his best French, "Thank you for everything, but I don't miss De Gaulle. If you really want to know I met Brigitte Bardot and ooo la la! All they understood because of his terrible French was ooo la la! Being Frenchmen that is all they needed to hear or know.

Hmmm, I must have a talk with the confessional cat that is still under treatment. I heard he is riding around in a Bentley and throwing caviar and garlic out the window, getting real loose. John told me yesterday that he sold the car to a cat who told him some funny stories about Brigitte. You don't think? 'Nuff to make a cat laugh!

# Blondi

*I* have so many great abilities. One of them is that I like to go back in time and visit people who had a great mark on humanity in one way or another. Not all of these people were very pleasant. Some were completely evil like Hitler. How's that for starters? I placed myself in his great mountain resort where he would get away from "the maddening crowds." (And, be mad by himself, I would guess.) He had a German Shepherd whom I befriended immediately. Her name was Blondi. A beautiful dog but she told me she was so frightened of him that it was making her ill.

She said, "I am losing so much hair because I have no appetite. My bark sounds like a squeak, and I have the worst dreams imaginable. But, what's a dog to do? If I try to leave, I will be shot, and it is my duty to be loyal to my master. If I stay, I know I will at least be alive for a while. I have to make a decision before I become totally neurotic."

I told her, "I can help you leave here at any time, and you will be free, but will you give me some help before you go?"

Blondi said, "I feel so much better already. If he pets me many more times, I will just die. The sight and smell and sound of him scares me more than the wolves here in the forest. What do you want to know before you help me leave this souped up prison?"

I said, "I just want to know what his routine is. Where he entertains his guests? Where he does his watercolor paintings? (He had over two thousand of them.) I want to hear him talk. One more little thing, does he like cats?"

Blondi said, "He thinks cats are mysterious and can bring good luck. At present, there are none here. They brought some in to show the old nut, but it didn't work out. They hissed at me and that was the end of the cat experience."

I said, "Not to worry, it will all work out. You will be out of here, and I will see what the old nut, as you say is doing. Better not to let him even hear you think that." Poor Blondi shook at my attempt to lighten things up. Hitler was nothing to mess with.

"Wanna bet?" I thought. I first saw Hitler walking around on the stone balcony with some of his "friends." Eva Braun was there, his physician, Himmler, and three others. Blondi and I sat down not too far from where they were and I listened in. Before I eavesdropped, I took a look into their minds. Abject fear existed in everyone, except the old nut. Really not too old by today's standards, he was almost young. He "died" at 56. I don't have to tell you what was in his mind that was full of complete evil and horror.

He noticed Blondi and I sitting not too far apart and seemingly getting along. Adolph said, "How charming, Blondi has found a friend. What a beautiful cat! Cats are lucky. Bring the cat some of our best caviar and spring water! I feel lucky just looking at him." When Hitler spoke, people listened. Within two minutes my food and water was placed before me. Thought I better take a bite to please him. The fear he emitted was physically and mentally palpable, intimidating and threatening as well. Yep, Adolph, had it all covered. Hitler said it was time to eat and all agreed. He said we will eat out here on the balcony and all agreed. For some reason he laughed. The others laughed as well. Eva held his hand as he talked. She looked at him with confusion in her eyes. No kidding I thought.

Talk about all this money and nowhere to go. Ho hum. Soon Blondi would be free, but the others were going to still be trapped here with him.

After eating, guess who said let's play cards. Cards immediately appeared and contrary to what you hear, some kind of alcoholic liquid was placed on the table about a half gallon in a beautiful pitcher with big, sparkling glasses that were filled immediately by the waiter. (Yes, the waiter looked quite nervous, as well, and he knew if he spilled a drop he would be replaced. More pressure, I gathered, than pitching the seventh game of the World Series Games and seeing your wife with "another man" in the other team's dugout. I mean that is some big pressure.) Everyone picked up their glasses immediately, and their eyes showed a type of blessed relief. Their eyes told me that if they drank enough of this stuff they would forget this whole meeting. With more luck they might even forget where they were, who they were, and maybe end up in China. They wanted to get a buzz that would last forever. Each of them drank two glasses, another pitcher was brought out, and the glasses refilled. You know who said time to sit down and play cards. He asked Eva to deal. They would be playing some kind of German poker card game. Five cards down and then hope you lose. By now, all of them were smiling and looked like they had passed out, but still kept smiling and going through human motions. The game began. More liquid stuff was poured and I was almost getting drunk just from watching them drink.

Poor Blondi wanted out, and I said, "Just hang on for a short time, and you will be out of this hell house existence and be free at last. Eat all the food they bring us, so you will have lots of energy to run away from this mess." For the first time, probably since she had been in this place, she actually relaxed and acted like a dog does. She smiled at me and said, "Thank you so much! Do you think I can give him a big bite before I leave?" "Sure you can," I said, "But not too deep okay?" The card game and the chugging, 'er, drinking continued.

One by one each passed out, and fell out of their chairs onto the floor. One foolishly plopped his head on the table obstructing his view of the cards and was immediately removed. Gulp. All of them had passed out except for you guessed who. He smiled with complete delight! His eyes were aglow as he stood up and laughed with amazing strength and sound. He waved his arms around, even the one that was supposedly paralyzed. He jumped up on the card table, drank another glass of booze, and did some kind of a jig. Pumped his legs up and down, kicked the cards off the table, had another glass, (where was it all going?) looked out into the distance, and gave 'em hell. He yelled and screamed and pointed and stamped his feet. He smiled slyly, which by now, his eyes seemingly emitting a green light and farted! Big time! He looked down on the floor where his constant companion and physician laid imbibed with two quarts of strong booze passed out.

Hitler said to him, "By god Fritz, I told you that cat was good luck! I haven't farted like that since I was a humble asshole soldier. The good old days, farting and drinking all the time. Now, look where I am, drinking but no farting. But, you Fritz with your medical magic made me fart. Goddamn!"

He slammed down another glass of hooch. Some of it poured down his chest and ran out of his mouth. Kaboom! Another giant sounding fart exploded and blew the old boy off the table. He now crawled around on the floor giggling and laughing with delight. He then saw Blondi and I not too far off, and he was exhilarated. He started to crawl over to where we were. Giggling and hollering and laughing and having one blast out drunken farty wide awake unconscious good old shithouse time.

"Never had it so good," he said, "Come over here Blondi, and give me a lick!" Blondi, by now with the immediate promise of freedom, ran over immediately, and bit him viciously in the ass. Hitler howled with delight, whirled around, and tried to grab Blondi. She barked almost as loud as Hitler farted. Hitler said, "Ha ha, I knew I could fart louder than you can bark. I can do everything better than everybody."

Somehow, from somewhere, another glass of booze appeared, and he drank it right down. With steely eyes, still emitting a green light, and by now smoking a little, he yelled at Blondi, "One more time to see how good you think you are! If your bark is louder than my fart you win! This reminds me so much of fighting the Russians in WWI. We would all drink and fart and bite each other and have a helluva time. I miss the good old days! Goddamn!"

He was on his hands and knees, by now directly facing Blondi. She let out one helluva bark, and Hitler grinned slowly and slyly. He reached into his shirt pocket and took out three pills. He put them in another glass and stirred them around. (By just watching him, I almost felt drunk myself.) While stirring, he said with vigor and insanity, "These are the best fart pills. They are the strongest in the world, and you are supposed to take only one a week. Aha! I will take three at one time, and I will be the best farter ever, even better than Genghis Khan, the Pharoahs of Egypt, and especially that stupid President Roosevelt. I will win this barking/farting contest and prove that I am even greater than all in the animal world! Goddamn, never felt so good!"

He then chugged the mixture he had just whipped up and continued to stay in his crawling position. He shook his legs around, his butt was bleeding real good where Blondi had chomped on him, but he paid no attention. He liked it! In about thirty seconds, Adolph started to growl while smiling and crawling around on the veranda with surprising speed. All of a sudden, he stopped and got into the position you often see hunting dogs do while pointing out a pheasant. He had found the enemy, and he was going to let him have it. Being Hitler, he could do it all.

I said, "Blondi, let's get the hell out of here. There is about to be an evil wind that will blow no good."

In no time Blondi was free, and just before I came back, I heard five or six vicious, hellish, gut wrenching blasts. I took a brief glance and saw the old fart, 'er nut, being blasted around in circles over his fortress waving his arms and legs and screaming with delight!

Hitler yelled out while being blasted around in circles, "Whoever says I don't know how to have a good time will be shot, shot I tell you!" Thinking out loud, he muttered, "I hope I know how to land this thing!" Then, he continued to laugh hilariously at his attempt at humor. He needed nobody to share his happiness with because he had himself, and that was enough for him.

'Nuff to make a cat roar!

# A Whale of a Time

*T*rouble is brewing on the high seas. Unexplained lights from underneath the ocean have been seen frequently off the West coast, and that ain't all. Along with the bright lights come some type of planes that leave the water and zoom off so quick they become invisible. What is going on? People wanted to know! Well, I aim to find out. I am Casey, the most brilliant entity of all time, and make that into the future as well, a regular know it all. Should say irregular because I am a twenty pound beautiful cat. Almost a tiger, says John, the person whom I have lived with almost since birth. I was three days old when I crawled into his coat pocket while he was in a SPCA facility. I could read minds then, and "influence" them as well. John loved everything about me. I hardly had to "influence" him at all.

Besides, he needed help. He needed someone to tell him where to drive. I love to ride around in cars, and sometimes stand behind the steering wheel and drive. Even though I can't reach the foot feed pedals, I love to turn the wheel this way and that, and watch people look at us in horror as they see me driving. I know John is "helping" me a bit, so while I have my paws on the wheel, I can look at the other driver's reactions when they pass by. 'Nuff to make a cat laugh!

But, where was I? Oh yes, the ocean and the bright lights beneath the surface of the coast of California, planes shooting in and out of the water, and then becoming invisible. Heck of a dunk one would think at first glance, too much hooch, sea sickness, hallucinations, and wanting to be free maybe. Who hasn't had that roly poly feeling while being on a boat? Once that hits you, one wants to go directly to shore, and in many cases, to never return. Being green like a dollar bill is not fun. Ahoy there matey, and nuts to you. Just get me off this boat! I can go anywhere I want as well. So guess where I went? Aha, dear reader you are beginning to think like a cat. You know in advance what is going to happen. What you just felt when you knew I was going beneath the sea to check out the stories being told is on zillionth of what I know and can feel. There is a lot more actually, but I don't want to lose you. We have to see what is causing all those sea going activities.

I had John drive me to San Diego to where all the sightings were taking place. I could have gone there myself, but you already know how I like to drive, maybe, almost nearly my only frailty. I told him I was going to take a look, and I would give him a "buzz" when it was time to go home. I would probably need some caviar and a sip, as well, when I returned. Besides, I knew John liked to see me lighten up once in a while. It must be so intimidating living with me and all my greatness. Meow! I went to the exact spot where it was said to have happened, longitude and latitude, and all that. Yes, some smarty pants from National Geographic had seen it, and you know how smart they are. All of them trying to look like Jacque Cousteau and speaking their sentences backwards, like throw me over the fence my cow some hay. Sure, just let me do the talking, or we will never get our dinner. It all was well meaning, however. Harrumph!

First thing, I encountered on the bottom of the ocean was a pod of giant whales sleeping. Like all species they had their cops and lookouts, and one of the lookouts saw me coming towards them. (I was in total communication code by now. No messing around. Besides, I knew they could handle it. If you weighed twenty tons, nothing would worry you either.) His name was Jim. Very intelligent and serious, and he took his responsibilities as lookout while the others slept very seriously. He asked me, "Excuse me sir, I must ask you where you are going? We have a pod of whales sleeping right now, and well… they like to sleep safely." I said, "I mean absolutely no harm." (*like duhhhh... I guess I better take back calling Jim intelligent, but when somebody weights twenty tons...ahem.*) "I am just checking up on reports of lots of disturbances in this area, lights and ships, and all kinds of splashing around." Jim smiled, (Whatta' big smile… as big as a Cadillac) and said in his deep voice as quietly as he could, "Be glad to help. When the top whale wakes up, I will take you to him. Wait, hold on, here he comes now. Let me introduce you to him." Another twenty or so tonner came over quite delicately "actually" and smiled (I had to get used to all this smiling). We were introduced by Jim, "Casey," I had my name tag on, "meet Susie Q. Susie Q, please meet Casey." (More big smiling, such happy creatures. Getting used to it by now, but I was almost feeling like Noah must have felt.) We made appropriate 'glad to meet you' gestures and carried on.

I said, "Thank you for meeting me, lots of people up top are quite concerned about all the lights and things that are shooting out of the water and disappearing immediately." (Hoped she liked that term 'up top'. In fact, I hoped they liked everything I said or did. Speaking to a souped up box car at the bottom of the ocean can be difficult.)

Susie Q said, "Yes, we saw it too, but we whales are very peace loving, and since there is so much space down here it is pretty much live and let live."

I said, "Can you please tell me all you know about what I have asked you? So many humans are going bonkers about these happenings? I want to find out, if possible, exactly what is happening.

You know how humans are? (I smiled, and I wondered if my tiny Chinese cat smile intrigued her as much as her Cadillac smile flummoxed me?) Susie Q laughed and large bubbles dissipated around her. I took it for a laugh anyhow. Jim smiled discreetly, since he was on duty, and cops and such can't smile too much. Believe me… you haven't lived until you see a whale laugh. Stand up comedians would be in ocean eleven heaven to see and hear them laugh. Boom, boom, ha, ha is as close as I can come to describing it. She stood up? I mean was she sitting down or whatever already. Underwater, who knows?

"Good thing I have such great balance and awareness and... where was I?" she said, laughing while talking, (I mean this is what greatness is made of, so pay attention folks.) "Oh yes, those humans are a fright at times. Always going to and fro, trying to come under the water and do all kinds of strange things. So funny how we just leave them alone, but have to still keep a wary eye on them. Mostly, it is so hilarious. Why I remember the time off the coast of Bermuda…" and she started to laugh again. Jim even gave it an urp, little laugh acknowledgment.

Susie went on, "But, please forgive my manners. I must invite you in where we can properly talk and have some tea. Have to be careful out here. Some human may come down dressed up like a frog and try to put you in a cage. Don't worry, dear Casey, it will never happen while we are here." (Boy...was I certain of that.)

We went down into a place that was set up for whales. Everything was really big…ahem, guess it had to be. The tea cups for the whales were as big as a Buick. (Good thing I know my cars.) They had a special cup for me which was perfect. It looked like they could do anything and make anything they wanted. Fascinating! Wonderfully so! These whales were great! I knew right away that John would try to get one in a football suit and win all the super bowls forever and ever. What a running game! Or, any kind of game for that matter! But, I must get to the bottom of the reason that I came here to find. Explaining in mere words takes so long and is cumbersome, but I can't mind meld all of you.

I said, "Positively beautiful, Susie Q! This tea is just how I like it. Naughty you are! I am a cat you know, and I sense some "Irish" in this tea?"

Susie Q only smiled this time and said, "Oh yes, you seem like a worldly kind of cat and kind of cute too. I didn't think you would mind. All this," and she waved a flipper around, "must be a bit much even for a top cat like you?" We smiled knowingly at each other, me with my discreet Chinese cat smile, and her with a cute smile that went right around the block. Where is a Polaroid when you need one? By now, other whales woke up and came around and sat down, and ordered whatever whales order. I was going to say lots, but no, they were very discriminating and even dainty, completely mannerly in all their actions and words. I really loved those big whale laughs.

After tea, and if I can use the term small talk, Susie Q said, "Well, if you would like we can discuss what you want to know about. It won't take too long, and actually it is much more fun drinking tea and talking about how the "other half live". More laughter ensued, and I let out a pretty good meow. They were amazed! (No matter where I go I steal the show... Ha Ha Cha Cha!)

One medium sized whale named Doug said, "Wow, can you do that again. That was great! Never heard that one before!"

Suzie Q said, "Teenagers!" She winked at me, and it was like a shade being pulled down on a bay window, and then snapping open. It was great. (Pun intended.)

I said, "Why not?" I meowed several meows at different tones and ranges, and it was beginning to sound like a song. In fact, it was a song. My subconscious has snuck through. The song I was meowing was an Antonio Benedetti, Tony Bennett to you classic, 'If I Ruled the World'. To my complete surprise, a very large piano appeared, a microphone, and some little whale handed me a top hat, and a scarf. What could I do? I had to sing and put on a good show now for my audience, great as they were. All was set up perfectly for me, and by now, the entire "place" was full of the best football potential the world has ever known. I took the stage with my charismatic handsome style, smiled, sighed, sipped a drink of "tea" and said, "Thank you all for comin'." Laughter and much flipping by the whales carried on. I sang about five of my favorite tunes which were greatly received. I said, "Time for a commercial. I also want to tell you this is the best and "moistest" crowd I to which I have ever sung." The whale hubbub and drone level could not be forgotten. But, I still had to carry on with what I came here for in the first place, and I explained it all to them which they found hilarious even more. (*Hmmm, a singer and a comedian.*) Susie Q was laughing Cadillacs and Buicks. The rest of the whales were by now bouncing around on the floor, and I guess it was their form of dancing.

She said, "Let's go somewhere else, and I will tell you what you need to know." Susie Q said, "So simple really, you see. The light that you speak of is the glow in our bellies when we laugh. The objects you think you see coming out of the ocean is the air that explodes from our tummies if you will. In fact, you must see for yourself when we complete our laughter. You don't really see anything, but the water parting and great volumes of air whooshing out at mercurial speed. Of course, it also disappears if you want. Really, it was never there unless you consider air there." She went on, "Hmmmmm, actually there is no there there." "Oh, my god." she said, "I broke into Gertrude Stein, I so always wanted to do that. You make me so happy kitty cat. I know you now understand what really happens, but I pity you trying to explain it to the "boys above," and the one who are already beyond for even thinking such nutty stuff to begin with. Human are so, please forgive me, "anal" as you humans call it. Humans coined the term especially for their own race. I won't go on." *Wanna bet?* "But, if they don't quit trying to act and dress like frogs and come down here, and ..." she sighed, then laughed as a great light came from within her belly. After the huge laugh, a terrific blast of air shot out toward the surface at the speed of almost light. Yup, flash of lights problem solved. 'Nuff to make a cat laugh!

I heartily thanked them all, and said while holding up one paw, still wearing my top hat, "I shall return!" Boy, did they laugh at that one. Huge balls of light emitted from their greatness followed by blasts of air that rocketed to the surface and disappeared. Once again, the world will again be agog and wringing hands at aliens controlling the world from under the ocean.

I told John what all went on, but waited until we got home and were sitting on the roof. The entire gang was there-Wrigley, the very big quiet pipe smoking Lab, Seagull Joe the air taxi guy, my uncle Al and his teenage protégés. After telling everyone what happened, two of the protégées had to have their tails tied to the chimney, so they wouldn't fall off the roof from laughing. Wrigley puffed and woofed so hard that we could not see the lights of San Francisco. Al jumped on Seagull Joe for a taxi ride somewhere, and they flew off caw cawing and meowing into the night.

John chinchucked me, picked me up, and said, "My, what a busy kitty cat you are. Guess you won't be eating sardines for some time after that trip?" 'Nuff to make a cat laugh!

# Show of All Shows

*T*he best movie ever made in Hollywood will soon be made. After this movie, people will forever talk about it, rave about it, quote lines that were said in it, dress like the people in the movie, like when Clark Gable wore a shirt only with no back up? Grrrrrrr! They might even act like people in the movie, and smile like people in the movie. Most of all, people for many years will be going about their daily activities reliving portions of this great movie. Depending on what part you liked in the movie, you will act, talk, walk, smile, stutter, grunt, and you name it. Be creative! They could be man or animal. This movie will be so great you will never forget it, and it will consume your life completely for as long as you live. Now, here is how the movie got there, and what it is all about.

The ad went out all over the world and reached every household. Everyone knew that the greatest movie was about to be made, and the actor cast members must be found. Auditions were being held night and day. *("They" like to say 24/7, but that is so pedestrian and wannabe cool talk. Not here "Dahling".)* All you had to do was show up in Hollywood, take a screen test, and Bingo! If you had the "right stuff," you would be in the movie. You were immediately shown to a sumptuous giant hotel that would house the entire cast and take care of them for as long as it took to make "The Movie."

The screen test was "simple." You had to have "IT!" Eyes were so important, not only particular beautiful crashing eyes, but also maybe sneaky dirty nosey eyes. You had to have a particular kind of a body, maybe not like Michelangelo's David, but better is alright, and exactly like that was even better. You had to have a special aura about you that was communicated to all who saw you on screen. It had to say, "Boom! This is me. I am what I am on this screen and nobody else." (*Didn't mean you could not go to the best hotel in the world, which is where you stayed, and get loose, but you sure had to have a lot of zing on the celluloid.*) What you said and how you said it were of equal importance. Every word and nuance of pronunciation and diction were all of equal importance in "The Movie". Everything had to be perfect. No shit! (About time somebody took on perfection. After all, perfection is how you describe them. "The Movie" had perfection as well, and things were even better than before.) Harrumph! I am perfect, and it's about time some people catch up or mustard... Just give me a little smile, won't hurt.

Hollywood and its environs were inundated. Millions of people from all over the planet came to the movie capital of the world and brought along fantastic businesses while here waiting for an audition. They did whatever to make a living and in some cases, much more than "just" making a living. Hundreds of business sprung up, inventions were patented, and people were married. (Yup, even in Hollywood) Babies were here and there, and your imagination can fill in what else all those millions of people must have done to keep themselves living while waiting to get aboard "The Big Train." (It was also being called "The Big Train" as well as "The Movie." Nothing was being filmed outside of Grauman's Chinese Theatre yet, so everything was a go.) 'Night and Day', love that song as well, people were auditioned and tested. Beautiful men and women, and yes, to make sure all was above board, I auditioned as well. Now, I could tell you what they were thinking, but I won't. It is all good, and it makes for an excellent drone level throughout the entire Los Angeles area.

The screen test consisted of an actor getting on stage, and then being told what to do. They had to immediately perform what directions, dialogue, mood, look, attitude and hundreds of other necessities that an actor must have, and it had to be perfect. This was "The Movie-The Big Train," and it had to be the very absolute best, and then some. (As John Wayne would say, "Well, pardner, you signed up, so get goin'. Yeah!") Some people were signed on the spot and moved to one of the top floors of the newly built Grand Hotel which had rooms for two thousand. If the cast would be any bigger, they would simply build another hotel. Meanwhile, there were lots of places on the beach where the hopeful actors of being in "The Movie" or "The Big Train" could live. Pretty tough, huh? No one knew what the movie was to be about. They just knew if they had the "IT" factor, there would be a part for them, and maybe even have a starring role in the greatest of the greatest movies ever made, maybe forever. Suspense and nervousness was the news of every day. All this movie business ran around the clock. (Okay, if you want to sing 'Night and Day'.) Hollywood gossip had it that it would be a tremendous love story. It would have intrigue, fashion, jungles, deception, gold, world domination, humor, (I "suggested" humor to the script writers, ahem!) bon homie, psychopathic villains, sophistication, and the greatest music ever. There would be the most beautiful background music melding with the plot, so as to bring the viewers into the movie. If they closed their eyes, they would be a part of the movie as well, with interactive viewing techniques.

After one year, the entire cast was complete. They had to build two more great beautiful hotels with the next one being more luxurious and better than the last. (It took a lot to do it but then this is Hollywood, after all where they make anything possible.) Everyone was assembled on the Channel Islands. Altogether, there was a cast and crew of about four thousand. All were housed and guarded by patrol boats circling the islands in top security mode and on the set. No one knew they were there. (I told John a few cat tricks which he communicated to security, and they were amazed. Cats have been doing it for eons. We got the best place on the islands overlooking everything with a fantastic view! John laughed so hard about the cat tricks working that I had to get him a beer from the fridge to calm him down. He will do anything, well almost, to watch me try and get that fridge door open. I got scratches all over the place.)

The movie began. The hubbub all over the world was the only thing in the newspapers on every paper in the world. All the headlines and newspaper content were saying things like what is this and that, and why and blah, blah, blah. Everyone loved the news coverage and ate up every word. The entire world could not wait until the next day to read and hear about how "The Movie" or "The Big Train" was coming along.

Because of the security PT-109's type of boats commanded by John F. Kennedy which helped save our country from the morons, they were able to intercept hundreds of swimmers coming out of Santa Barbara and Ventura area trying to get on the islands. People and boats, barges and rafts, and one person used his giant Labrador dog to pull all him all that way. (Special treatment was given to that jerk, and the Lab was put up in the hotel on the top floor. John visited him, and they had some good woofs.) Windy weather with rain and lightening are common on the Channel Islands. The Channel Islands are considered open ocean areas, and it added to the excited fevered pitch of everyone working on "The Movie" or "The Big Train."

The movie direction, plot, and actors' skills were the highest caliber of all time. In addition, the greatest orchestras and singers were present to constantly, day and night, ok, 'night and day', add to and keep the atmosphere of the movie meshing perfectly. Momma Mia! I Yi Yi! Purrfecttt!

The wind, weather, darkness, music, scintillating dialog, clever rejoinders, actor performances, the moon and sun, (It was almost "shot" outside.) and the indefinable mixture of it all having the quality of being unable to describe or write it, made it all happen miraculously blended perfectly. It all occurred on its own with a crashing crescendo of lightening and sound combined at the very end of the movie. A giant wave came upon the shore with wind and fury, but subsided at the tripod of the camera filming the fantastic extravaganza. (Hmmm… what a coincidence, do you think?)

# Watch Out!

*J*ohn and I were going out for our usual walk. I was firmly and warmly in the backpack with my paws on John's shoulders looking around like cats do when they are in backpacks. Even though I was the most brilliant entity of everyone everywhere, I was still a cat. All of a sudden, John stopped abruptly and looked down intently. I noticed no alarm in my cat security system, so I looked down as well. Ok, it was just an ant hill with the usual scene, with ants going all around in lines everywhere with some kind of practiced order.

John had a very painful back injury, really bad, a slipped disc and such. He was told that smoking, ahem…"medical grass" would help the pain. He puffed on some every now and then. Right now, all he had left was too small to smoke. Really time to throw it away, but nope, not for old tightwad John. He rolled it up into a small ball, and put it right down into the ant hole. It was as big as ten ants and rolled right down, until it almost hit the queen's nest. Yikes! Meanwhile, John let out a John Wayne laugh and said, "Take that pahdner! Haw Haw!"

The queen was startled upon seeing this huge green ball roll into her bedroom and said, "What is that? Why did it get here? Where are the guards, and it sure smells funny? Hmmm…kind of tastes good though." The queen did not put up with any nonsense. Five attendants tried to move the big green ball, and in doing so, knocked some of it off into the queen's lap. She took a bigger bite, then another one. Then, she called for the ant leaders and told them to take a bite and test it out. Soon, all the ants that were in antenna communicating distance were told to take a bite. Then, something happened they weren't expecting. They became very invigorated. Their minds were "opened." *Ha! Ha! Maybe that's why John puffs that stuff. Hope he doesn't read this. Ha Ha! Just being catty, more Ha Ha's.* The ants began to walk around the sacred chamber very quickly almost making a noise as they hurried to and fro, and then the queen said, "I have an idea! Gadzooks!" (I have already used yikes and gadzooks, so now I have my cat back against the wall.) She said, "I have the greatest plan ever conceived by an ant."

"Yes, my queen," as all the now loaded attendants waved their legs and stuff in unison, "Pray tell, what is it?"

She said, "The ants are going to take over the Empire State Building. Get busy and contact more queens pronto, and we will make a plan that is bug proof!" Laughter was heard among the queen's top men. She said, "I understand, you are loaded and goofy, but one more foof foof, and that's that." The queen was getting hot, and the message was carried out as she commanded.

All the queens came to a "joint" decision to contact all the ants everywhere to go to New York and crawl all over the Empire State Building and make it their own overpowering it totally. *Wow! I'm only reporting this now, but stick with me. These ants are on to something, what just "might be the start of something big.* One of the attendants to the queen was an ant from Northern California where there was a lot of stuff, "grass" that he was familiar with. He told her all about it, and how it would help greatly in their journey. She agreed and ordered lots of it. The ant's name was Norman, and he said, "How much do you want, and where do want it sent? Then, there is, of course, the 'ahem' payment."

She said, "Norman, if you ever want to be in my bedroom again, get your skinny ass out of here, and give us all the grass we need. I think a boxcar load will do."

Norm, being cool to all types of negotiating talk, said, "I am your humble servant, and your wish is my command, my queen."

"That is much better," she said, and they both laughed like crazy. Boy, were they loaded.

All of the ants from everywhere headed to New York City. They were so happy, and most of them were loaded as they got the message that grass helps an ant do lots of things real quick. Really! Upon getting to New York, all the ants had to do was get to the Empire State Building and start crawling all over it, inside and out. By now, all the ants were loaded so they were double quick at whatever they did, and telling each other jokes, laughing and having a great time. In two days time, the entire New York Empire State Building was covered completely with ants inside and out, every floor, nook and cranny. Two feet thick on the outside and almost cram packed on the inside. Queens had to pass messages to tell them to slow down a little. Another boxcar of grass was on the way, and they didn't want to run out and lose any momentum before it arrived.

The entire world was alerted, the situation was made known, and they were shocked and very disturbed. (*Yes, dear reader, some countries were happy. Jeez, you think? No ants to bug them anymore.*) All the leaders in the country did not know what to do. How could we remove the ants from the Empire State Building? So many animal lovers and such came to the forefront and protested. Insect people chirped in, religious people, and you just name it. Well, it finally got the whole earth listening to the same thing at the same time, which was in itself, a miracle of sorts. An area of 200 yards was cordoned off around the ESB. (*Can't write all those words all the time. Even a cat has its limits. Harrumph!*) All the people who were in the building area were handsomely paid off, and promised their property back when all was brought under control again.

Every bit of the building was continually photographed and studied intensely. What could be done to get those zillions of ants off the ESB and return all to "normal"? I noticed in one photograph that three bum types had been overlooked, and that they had staggered into the building. How did they do it? After all, they were completely bombed, soaked with urine and crud, yet the ants paid no attention to them, and in they went. They were seen to be eating ham sandwiches and throwing wrappers out of the fourteen story windows. How could this happen? Scientists of great renown were brought in from everywhere and concluded that the funky smell of their bodies and clothes and their intoxication level were to such a degree as to make them invisible to the ants. Do you think?

The great mayor and his men made a tough decision. They would have to soak themselves in urine and crud and get bombed and see if they could get in. From there on, they figured it would be simple to remove the ants.

The mayor said, "Ok, let's get bombed and urinate and such on each other and see if we can get in.

"Yucky," said the top female to the mayor, "I won't do it!"

"Ok," the mayor said, "Who's next?"

All hands went up and she said, "Oh well, ok then. Since it's for a good cause, and I love the people." Everyone immediately urinated on her and she replied the favor. They then got smashed drinking booze as quickly as possible, and staggered through the gate to the front door to the ESB. Zingo! Zillions of ants were all over, but not the mayor or a lackey was touched. Their theory proved right. They brought along extra crates of booze and urine. It would not be good to run out of supplies in this situation. All agreed and stuck a few extra bottles of booze in their clothes and urinated on each other again. So horrible, but it was for the people. They had to research where the ants were holed up entirely and find out why they were taking over the ESB in the first place. These were the leaders of NYC, the greatest city of all time. By god, the world would take note. These ants had gone too far.

The Congress had known about this situation all along. When the mayor of NYC went on to the ESB himself and got blasted, it was time, some members of congress thought, to do the same thing. This was worldwide publicity at its best, and solving this problem could have great political advantages they thought together. All of congress showed up at the perimeter gate and said they wanted to get in there, and "lead the show." Sure, but one had better first get dipped in crud and get bombed before you do anything else. They all replied grudgingly.

I said to John, ""Way to go, you old cowboy you. Look at all the people you got in trouble. You got, well, the whole world into it. Now, all the countries are concerned and want to come and help us. All their leaders want to come here, and jump in crud too, get blasted, and go into the ESB, and lead people from there really good." Almost 'nuff to make a cat laugh but I have to save that for the end of the story. Right now, I am laughing already at how ridiculous human beings think about things.

John said, "Well, I tell yuh, little pahdner, you're getting all radical like. Ha! Haw! Ha! Haw! Haw!"

I cat batted his chauffeur hat off, he grabbed my tail, and I said, "Let's flip to see who pays for supper."

"Forget it," he said, "I'll pay. I never win when I gamble with you anyway. How about if I get dipped in urine like those folks there? Haw! Haw! Har!"

"See if I buy you another Bentley," I said, and we went into the Waldorf Astoria to have a bite.

Since I have my cat care pack on, there is never any consternation. Now, with all the ants taking over the ESB, the entire restaurant was booked by animal lovers from everywhere. We got the best table and could not wait until tomorrow morning to see what more would develop. The next day at daybreak from the top floor of the ESB, the entire congress of the United States and other leaders from all round the world were hanging over the railing where tourists look down on NYC. They were hooting and hollering and making calls saying they were going to save the ESB. Everything was in order they said.

Now, it needed reporters. You think? The reporters would have to submerge themselves in crud though too, and get bombed in order to get past the ants to get to the great leaders of the world. Yikes! Who would do that? Ba Ba and Oh My got the job. With gusto and smiles they jumped in the now big lake of crud and dirt, and they were already bombed before they jumped in, trying to keep their nerves settled to do this at all. They were scantily clothed as well, not wanting to wreck their expensive clothing for this job. They had brought a little airplane cart with them full of booze to last for a week. They waved and said this was for the people's sake, and they deserved to have it reported direct from the ESB.

Suddenly, a growling roar was heard! There were thousands of people all round the ESB trying to get closer, watching all the commotion day and night with television coverage on every station. Feet stamping to a great drone level, and the hubbub shook the ground. Guess who unexpectedly showed up? Vladimir Putin! To save ink, and to infer as to he really is, I will say Raz Putin. Oh, yeah, the czars are still around. This top cat knows. Raz quickly appeared at the perimeter entrance and jumped into the crud, totally submerged himself, jumped out, did a hand stand, and waved at the people. To everyone's shock and amazement, he was only wearing a jock strap, and was tastefully, but totally bombed on Stoli, and had to be to gain entrance to the ESB. He was followed by six minders who avoided the crud pool and were soberly doing their duty guarding Raz. The ants ate them up immediately. I think Raz liked it. He had the biggest cart of all, looked like about eighty quarts of booze, thinking that ought to do it. Raz's eyes looked like two pea holes in a snow bank, and I have been wondering when I could work that saying into this leadership conference report. Ahem...

Now that all the leaders of the world were jammed into the ESB, we had to have an on the spot report of what was going on. Both Ba Ba and Oh My came out on the ground floor and reported what they observed. They were nearly naked by now, and certainly big time smashed which they had to be or else the ants would eat them.

Ba Ba said all the leaders of the world were on the top floor and really getting it done. "Burp! Since Raz has come on board, belch, they are now going to build four more ESB all around this one with bigger crud pools, so everybody can have more room. Being squished on top on this thing all fouled up and stinking funny beyond belief is not good."

Oh My pushed Ba Ba out of the way and said, as Ba Ba now tripped and fell into a green puddle, "I seez everything comin' togedder, we are now one. Raz done it...with that jock strap and all, and...boom!"

Ba Ba jumped up and slammed into Oh My, and then they both went down into the green puddle. Three naked congressmen ran out and pulled them into the ESB real quick.

Meanwhile, the ants were in complete control. Nobody, but nobody, could get in or out unless you were plastered or had crud all over you. Big time business throughout the world was escalating. News of all the leaders of the world being bombed and peed on continually gave everybody enthusiasm and hope. All economies were doing fantastic, especially New York City. People were coming from all over the world to see the ants by the, you name it, controlling the ESB with all the leaders inside completely drunk and big time stinky smell. Naked too, now that Raz had showed up.

I had to know what was going on for sure, because you couldn't see very much with the building covered up in piles of ants. So, I "communicated" with the queen of all the ants. "What is going on in there?" I said, "Looks like the ants are ruling the world. Then again, you are the queen of queens, so can you tell me what is what?"

She laughed, and she said, "Oh, Casey, you are so funny. You got us ants all loaded like crazy, and now look at what we are doing. We have the leaders from all around the world running around naked and drunk on the top of the ESB. The entire economy and safety of the world has never been better, and... how much are you going to pay me for this. If I don't get what I want, I will call off the ants, and these goons will come out and continue to screw up the world."

I said succinctly, "Whatever you want, your majesty, of course."

She said, "You are so clever." She went on to say, "I also happen to know you are a very knowledgeable and powerful cat. All I would like to have is a place at your conference table of decisions and complete safety."

"Meow," I meowed in confirmation, and she laughed, and the deal was done.

The leaders of the entire world were still at the top of the ESB. By now, they had occupied the top ten stories, with all of them completely wasted and smelling like big stinkos. They were all fighting each other, competing trying to get on the top floor. Guess who was on the top floor? Oh course, good old Raz. He had talked to everybody, and beaten a few into kicking anybody down who tried to get on the top floor. It seemed to be a good situation to him being on the top floor of the ESB on top of all the world leaders, too. The top floor leaders were kicking down the bottom floor leaders, and they were happy. Completely blasted and they had to urinate on each other to keep up the stinko smell, or the ants would eat them. This could only work until the booze and stink lasted. I knew what was happening.

I told John, and he communicated to the marines to helicopter two months worth of crud and booze on all floors. The ants continued to cover the ESB, but never touched a hair on the heads of all the great leaders in the world as long as they were scorched and stinky. Beautiful! (No accounting for taste one must remember.) The world was in tremendous shape. Perfect! All the goony leaders were yelling and screaming naked and drunk and stinky high above New York for all to see. It was quite a show indeed! The economy of NYC triple dippled and other countries followed, doing things on their own that proved to work out even better. They built other ESB's, and covered them with ants. First of all, they contacted John, then he told me, and then I contacted the ants, and the world never had it so good. All the nutty leaders of the world trapped high in the sky with a command to stay drunk and stinky for all their lives, or to be part of an ant hill depository.

Ba Ba and Oh My never had it so good. Since Ba Ba was plastered, she could blather all over with her funky Ba Ba speech style, and Oh My would say "Oh my!" every time she fell down. A good time was had by all with their one big booze fest. The great leaders from all over the world saw the writing on the wall, except for one, Raz. He liked it. He jumped up on the bar, jock strap and that's all, and said, "Are you men or women? We must kill the enemy. Who wants to go first?"

A slobbering congressman from somewhere said, "Why don't you go first?" Raz promptly threw him over off the ESB. That was a sobering moment and more booze was called for immediately. The helicopters circled and continued to give more booze to the leaders while Raz and some followers kicked those below who tried to get on the top floor. It was like King of the Hill with piles of drunken stinky people fighting to get to the top.

A senator from Texas said, "Blah, poof, phooey, and uh huh." Raz threw him over the side real quick. People were starting to get the message. One tried to give Raz the old over the building push, and Raz sidestepped him and kicked his boo boo on over.

"Ho boy," Raz said, "Just like the old country."

Ba Ba said, "Oh, Raz, blab, burp, fa ba, ying ying, gittyup."

Raz said, "Long live the czars," was trying to grab hold of Ba Ba, and just started to throw her off the ESB when Oh My grabbed him by his jock strap, snapped it, and sprung him off into space. Saved from the top Russian and by a woman after all!

All were happy, and one great leader said, "By God, we got it done. Thanks to us, the world is now saved forever."

'Nuff to make a cat laugh!

# Whatta' Day in San Fran!

The boys and I were having one of our chimney meetings at one of the "power points" on the planet. It was all of the boys including Uncle Al, Seagull Joe, Wrigley, and me. Wrigley is our newest member. He is a very big and serious 120 pound Labrador. He "guards" the family of four next door. We went through our agenda checklist of topics to discuss.

X SPCA

X Costco

X Football for cats?

X Al & I go to Hawaii?

X Heaven for cats?

X What kind of heaven would you want?

Since I am the most intelligent living entity on the planet, having all the knowledge that was ever known and ever will be, (ho hum) I can also read, mind meld, and influence anything or person that has a mind. We, indeed, were on this point of the planet for a reason. I must also say that some people and their leaders do not have much for minds. If the "no minds" are also violent, crazy, and evil, they must be "dealt" with. All those in any way responsible for 9/11 are the best examples ever. Ok, no more political talk, but we must not forget, even we "kitties."

Where was I? Oh yes, we four "good old boys" decided we would like to go out for a day and see the town. "After all this is San Francisco," I said, "We might as well take John along. He might be more familiar with some of the human "stuff" than we are. Al and Joe laughed like crazy, and Wrigley silently nodded his very big Lab head. I told John what we were going to go, and it was all set to go.

First of all, we had to go to the best little disguise shop any- where. Hollywood Harold ran it like a clock, a Swiss clock, and he had it all. It used to be the best in Hollywood, but he got tired of making monster phooey. Harold dressed us in human costumes. Wrigley could almost pass for human as is on a very foggy day. Seagull Joe, Al, and I needed a little more work. Like Harold told us, "It's all in the attitude." Harold told us about the great actors saying, "Some could play and look like any part from a midget to Andre the Giant...any sex, voice, or attitude combined!"

John said, "How about Mister Ed, the horse."

Harold had an attitude himself, and said, "Sure, no problem, wise guys were easy, especially makeup for the back end of Mister Ed!" Harold was touchy, as some Hollywood folks can be, so we didn't laugh too much.

We were finally ready to go. Seagull Joe was dressed like a banker, and his bird's eye look was perfect. Wrigley was dressed as a retired cop, pipe and all. Al and I were dressed like up and com- ing CEO's. Harold was still simmering from John's wisenheimer remark and said to John, "Guess we can also dress you up to look like a respectful responsible member of society, but I know you can never "do the 'tude"-attitude." Harold could be quite clever and "catty" at times. I liked it. Harold and John agreed to meet soon in an Irish bar. Maybe work more on their snappy rejoinders and clever repartee. We called a taxi and jumped right in. I noticed Seagull Joe actually flew in.

I told Joe, "Character attitude-bankers don't fly!" Joe was too excited, and just gave me the "bird eye." We had to start the day off properly.

"Let's take a boat trip round the bay," we said, "and see and smell all the beautiful sights." (We were even though now polished actors, we still wanted to smell things. It was the natural animal instincts in us and couldn't be helped.) The boat trip was fantastic! Ships were there in the harbor, and we even saw one submarine coming in, all on deck were facing south saluting the city. (*Don't get "catty" now, and say, "Uh, how about the driver?" Those comments fall in the wisenheimer "cat"-a-gory. John will like you.*) A huge ocean liner was just docking in the bay as well. We saw about one hundred swimmers coming in from Alcatraz to the Dolphin Swim Club. I think I saw Wrigley smile and smell very hard. I knew he wanted to make that swim with them. John noticed Wrigley puffing hard on his retired cop pipe and guessed what he was thinking.

He said, "Wrigley, you must do that swim soon. Take the CEO's with you. Joe and his buddies can watch from the air or maybe float alongside you. When they fall off, then you can bring 'em to shore."

No doubt, a good time was being had by all. We even had a drink of San Fran's finest Irish coffee. Joe wanted to fly to the top of the ship, but I gave him the "cat eye." "Caw, caw!" was all he muttered. Upon landing, it was time for breakfast. Now Wrigley was smiling big.

We went to the Buena Vista, very close to where we docked. Those inside of this storied place were all in much hubbub and full of camaraderie. Because it was crowded, some people at a table made seats available for us, and we sat down. There were eight of us at the table altogether. (Really time for our acting ability to show through, especially Al. He is a very energetic, attractive "CEO," and well, you figure out the rest.) Our acting and attitude ability was working perfectly. Our three companions were attractive ladies, and they wanted to know the usual things about us, asking us typical banter. John "fielded" most of the conversation, but I could tell they were greatly taken by Wrigley and his sincere, thoughtful, sonorous look. I could see that it might be considered attractive to women. To me, however, being a cat, it was very dull. *"Why didn't Harold dress me as a retired cop?"* After breakfast, we wished everyone well, and hailed a taxi. We were going to Gino and Carl's, a man's bar. Well, some women go there, too. Hopefully, if women were there they would understand how swell CEO's and bankers were. Retired cops-humphh-they might decide to arrest you.

As we entered, and took a refresher drink, my cat alert senses were suddenly activated. Two big bully loud mouthed types were over by the jukebox being loud, stupid, and annoying the clientele. We knew the bartender, and John gave him a wink. I took a peek into the dullard's minds and "suggested" to them that an Alcatraz swim was just what they needed. Right now! They immediately ran out the door, got into their twenty foot double decker Falloblowo pickup, which was parked on the sidewalk, and drove it smack off a pier into the bay. Guess they were going to drive to "the Rock" on the bay floor. Probably with the windows open smoking unfiltered Pall Mall's. (Call for Philip Morris-Radiant and if you remember that good for you! I can't forget it.) Seagull Joe gave his buddies a call, and they pulled "the swimmers" to shore.

Marvin and Melvin, the pickup passion swimmers said, "The devil made me do it," Marvin said.

Melvin said, "Not so, my foot got stuck on the gas jammer."

Marvin said, "Nuts to you, it was the devil, I knowed it were."

Melvin said, "Not so!"

They began to biff it out on the bayshore. They soon ended up in the water again and were hauled in for some time in the clinker. (All's well that ends well.) Meanwhile, some young fish went joy riding on the bay floor. 'Nuff to make a cat laugh! We all celebrated by having a free round. Saving the world is strenuous. For some reason, Wrigley was smiling and puffing his pipe with gusto.

With John's connections, most of them good, we got permission to ride an elevator inside of the Golden Gate's tower to the very top. Wow! (Even, almost, for a cat!) It was a great way for us to tie up the morning! Thanks to our tremendous acting, attitude, characters abilities, we had a wonderful time. Melvin and Marvin were saved from themselves, and were now being counseled by the little Sisters of the Poor.

One little sister said to the boys, "Are you going to repent and per chance, ahem, monetarily help us poor little sisters so we can carry on our acts of human kindness? I'm sure it will speed up your departure from this dungeon."

Marvin said, "Ah wants ma' Falloblowo pickup back!"

Melvin chimed in and said, "Yeah, and who are you two little funny twerps aneehow? Har Har Har!" There was some muffled commotion, and the guard was called.

He said, "As Melvin and Marvin were "sleeping" on the floor, looks like these young men are not ready for redemption, 'er sisters?"

Sister Goodness replied, with great sanctity and measured tones, "I'm afraid the dear boys will need more "seasoning," good sir." Everyone went their ways while the dear boys continued to sleep.

The day was still young and to our delight, the warriors were having an NBA Playoff game that afternoon. We couldn't wait! We already had our disguises and would fit right in. We taxied over to the game just in time for the tipoff. The players' execution and conditioning were exhilarating! At times we may have put our character disguises aside. A couple times, I heard Wrigley let out a great big loud "WOOF!" Joe said he was going to the restroom, but I'm sure I saw him flying around at the top of the Coliseum. Al and I meowed discreetly, we thought. Some confused looks came our way, but I "suggested" them otherwise. The Warriors won, and we had to celebrate as ourselves. John knew we would, and we took a rented car towards home, for a wild sounding ride. Wrigley also puffed up a big cloud, and we could hardly see out the windows.

Al said to John, "Let me drive, I need the practice!" (Uh, ok.) He stood on the seat and firmly put his paws on the wheel while John took care of the foot pedals. (I think John, at times, while Al was meowing and turning his head to and fro, added some help!) We got across the Bay Bridge in record time.

By now, Al was bored. John asked, "Anybody else want to drive?"

Joe said, "I would rather fly!" and gave Al the "bird eye." Wrigley, woofed strongly, puffed on his pipe, and gave Al a serious look.

Al said, "Ok, already, I get it! I just don't think you have been around car racing very much. Why I remember the time...."

By now, we were at Louigi's Italian food fit for a king at the prices John likes. (Wink) By now, we had resumed our disguised identities. We were very hungry as well. After Al's driving we thought kiddingly, kind of, that we might never eat again. Atmosphere, food, and the cellar's best were all one could ask for here. Since Wrigley was a "retired police chief," he was allowed to smoke his pipe there. It was acknowledged by everyone there, and perhaps, you too dear reader, that the smell of excellent pipe tobacco can be quite pleasant at times. Not to be confused with lighting one up in a Fourth of July firecracker factory. Upon arriving home, we all agreed it was one of the best times we had in a long time.

Al said, "The food was great, especially the anchovies. I really know all you guys are jealous, and wish you could drive like me!" Truly 'nuff to make a cat laugh!

# Casey's Child...
# er, Kittenhood

*H*ow was your childhood? Mine was the best ever! Not only was I the most intelligent living thing in the whole cosmos, I also had free food and transportation anywhere at any time. Almost, I didn't want to wear John out. Once, we went to Paris and I had to drag him out of the Moulin Rouge, but other than that, he was reticent. Wherever John went I was in his pocket either sleeping or sticking my head out to see what was going on. We always had complete telepathic communication so I had input as to where we would go and what we would do. I absolutely loved it. Let me tell you just a few of our exciting adventures.

It was another dark and stormy night in San Francisco. We went for a walk along the embarcadero enjoying the sounds and smells of the bay and San Francisco. I was awake with my furry kitten head stuck out of John's coat pocket looking all around and taking in all the sights and sounds. It was the cat's meow! We decided to walk up Columbus Street and see what the night life was doing. St. Peter and Paul Church was on our way, so we decided to stop in, look at the candles, and smell the incense. As John sat down I noticed that on the other side of the church some people actually crawling and slinking under the seats making their way very slowly towards the altar. Huh? What was this? I told John what was going on, and then he immediately called Chief Inspector O'Malley of the San Francisco Police Department.

In less than ten minutes O'Malley appeared and we watched until all six of the "crawlers" entered the sacristy. We thought they were going to steal the chalices and other gold objects that big Catholic churches often use. All the crawlers were arrested for trespassing and attempted robbery, and taken downtown for booking and questioning. There was a big problem though since they only spoke Russian and they were being quite uncooperative as well. I, ahem, told John to have them let us in to the questioning room. It would only take a second, a zillionth of a second to be precise. I don't fool around. I found out they were not going to touch the chalices. The Russians wanted to go into the giant secret room beneath the church where they kept billions of dollars in golden church objects. It was half as big as a basketball court and stuffed to the roof with every type of golden object the Catholic Church had been using from all over the world for centuries. Call it the Little Vatican.

This famous church was built upon one of the power points of the world, as is the house where I live by the way. It was decided by the Catholic Church years ago that this would be a place where it would store and secure some of its' great wealth. The Russians knew about it somehow. How did they know? Simple, the infamous Father Rasputin of the late Russian Empire had passed his knowledge on down to his great, great, great grandson Vladimir Putin. Aha! The President of Russia, who is one of the richest men in the world in money and many evil secrets, decided to take the gold and further increase his wealth. He just did not know it would take boxcars to remove it all and ship it to Mother Russia. Chalk it up to bad intel gathering. Their mission failed temporarily and because the crawlers had diplomatic immunity, they were shipped back to Russia. They were led to believe that we only thought they were going to steal the gold in the sacristy. They knew there were riches below but had no idea how much. They would now go back to Putin-land, and then what could happen?

I have millions of furry followers all over the planet and there are thousands in the Kremlin. Putin even has a few cats living with him. They know everything. From now on they will report back to me every step and drink of vodka he takes. All will stay seemingly normal at the great church in San Francisco but the ever vigilant cat patrol will be on guard every second of every day. The bell tower is their favorite place. There was almost a fight as to who would get to guard from there, very complicated in the cat world. It was solved by extra caviar and my special hot toddy drink of coffee and Ireland's best. Heaven help anyone who ventured into the cat, 'er bell tower. There are about twenty five of my finest furry friends loaded with whiskey and caviar ready to pounce and bounce at any time. Let's face it...it's the cat's pajamas.

Putin would never know what was really going on or how much actual wealth was there unless he learned to speak cat or got too loaded on vodka and started to speak in cat tongues. Until things changed we would watch the devil we knew. New devils are lots of work.

It was so exciting and John said to me, "Great job, Casey. Let's have a bracer before we go back" as we headed over to our favorite restaurant. When we got there, they were telling jokes about John going to confession or was it Casey? (They had seen us go into the church.) Regardless, I was given the best caviar, and John had his usual hot toddy. Good pay for saving trillions of dollars from the most evil man on the planet. John walked home, and I fell asleep in his pocket...tough work for a kitten.

The house I, ahem, lived in was four stories high with two basements. The most bottom basement was top secret and had tunnels running out of it leading to a sturdy fashionable yacht by a marine outpost on the embarcadero. It also had an elevator going up through the middle of the house going to the top of the roof that ended in a huge false chimney. Around the chimney on the roof we had put tables and chairs so we could sit and talk, and watch the city, the bridges and the bay. This was also a major power point on the planet, and we treasured it greatly.

Our next door friend, Wrigley, a fashionably overweight Lab had discovered it with his sensitive and sometimes wet nose, and we invited him over. He proved to be an invaluable friend even though he smoked a pipe and would woof out in the middle of some important conversations. When he stood up he was almost as tall as John and at times, could be used for a decoy if we gave him a close shave, Humphrey Bogart hat, and a Savile Row suit that would conceal his "bulky" body. We told him about the church job, and he wished he could have been there. He seemed a bit hurt as he puffed his pipe to hide his sensitive eyes with great clouds of smoke. We assured him it was an on the spot job and had to be done right then. No time for planning or disguises. Wrigley woofed and like the great Lab he was said he completely understood. (I did not dare tell him about the bell tower.)

John would look at me sometimes and say, "You look like my grandmother around the eyes."

I said, "Sure, and does she have ears on the top of her head?"

He said, "She always wears a baseball cap, but when she laughs she puts her hand over her mouth, and once I think I saw some very sharp pointed teeth."

I said, "Does she meow much and eat tuna out of a can?"

He said, "Are you writing this down? I think if I ever do standup this might be what the doctor ordered." "But once," John went on,

(*I don't know why but he did*) "when I was a small, I heard granddad talking about seeing her tail."

'Nuff to make a cat laugh, and that dear reader is why I keep John around. I think cats have it all, especially me, but humor eludes us. We are so brilliant, beautiful, and blah blah. Funny… not so much… not knowingly leastwise.

As I continued to grow in my kittenhood, my head would stick out of his pocket all the time. He would later breakdown and buy me a backpack where I could stand up and look around or snooze. But for now, it was still comfortable with my head sticking out of his coat pocket. Yes, there were comments all taken with nary a meow, and I don't hiss. I loved to ride in the car on the front dash. Sometimes I tried to drive. My legs could not reach the foot pedals so John worked them. I would stand up on the seat and move my paws around on the wheel and look out the window just like John did. I had the most fun when a pickup load of dogs would go by, and I would wave and meow at them. Ha! Ha! That made me laugh too. I guess I must have a pretty good sense of humor to go along with the rest of my fabulous abilities. Once a dog jumped out, and I don't know where he went. I will never tell Wrigley about that. Then again I was only a kitten but Wrigley is so sensitive. It might send him off on a woofing tangent, smoking his pipe for sure.

Then, there was the time as a kitten I came upon some aliens. I had a talk with them not long before I saw them at the ocean's edge while we were going for a walk on the beach. I told them to be extremely low profile or else. I had to be extremely direct with them since they were not used to being told what to do. It was a mind reading session, and they said to me they would do whatever they wanted whenever they wanted.

I said, "Meow to you, too!" and erased a few of their minds in front of their friends and turned their space ships the size of Australia into a frog looking at their dopey friends like they were insects. They got the message. But there is always one goof in the group. The one who "forgot" the message popped up on the beach and was getting ready to put a few beachgoers into their spaceship for who knows what. I immediately sent the whole crew and their freaky looking machine back to alien headquarters in a glass marble.

The top alien said, "Ok Casey, we got the message and understand. We don't want to be Hiroshima." So, the aliens don't mess with me! Ahem!

Kittenhood comes and goes so quickly. I found out early on I was a great inventor. After meeting with our good neighbor Wrigley, I saw he had a lot of trouble negotiating his girth and pipe and tobacco to the top of the roof. I immediately invented a helicopter device that he could attach to himself and fly right up to the top of the roof in no time. He would use his tail for a rudder and wave his paws around to do the rest. He got pretty handy and decided to go for a spin one night when there was a full moon. He caused quite a stir. He managed to fly all over San Francisco and had silhouetted himself against the moon. A lot of people took "the pledge" after thinking they saw something like a sick Bogart wearing army boots (*I told him they did not match*) with its tail going back and forth, and a pair of stubby arms waving furiously. After taking his "ride" Wrigley came back to where we were on the roof and told us about his great adventure. We looked over the city as he was telling us what he just did. Cop cars, fire trucks, whistles, horns and lots of things were moving around and making noise.

"Woof, Woof," Wrigley said. He put his paws over his huge head, Bogart hat and all, and we knew he felt very bad.

John went over to Wrigley, patted him on the head, smiled and said, "Not to worry for a second, old fellow, you actually helped thousands of people see the light. They have thrown out whatever made them think they saw what they saw. The churches are now being flooded with people and the SPCA has been cleared. You, dear Wrigley, are a hero! However, first, you better get yourself checked out on helicopters if you plan to do that again."

'Nuff to make a kitten laugh!